I'm the Vampire, That's Why

"From the first sentence, Michele grabbed me and didn't let me go! A vampire mom? PTA meetings? A sulky teenager? Throw in a gorgeous, ridiculously hot hero and you've got the paranormal romance of the year. Get this one *now*." —MaryJanice Davidson

"Hot, hilarious, one helluva ride. . . . Michele Bardsley weaves a sexily delicious tale spun from the heart."
—L. A. Banks

"A fun, fun read!" —Rosemary Laurey

"Michele Bardsley has penned the funniest, quirkiest, coolest vampire tale you'll ever read." —Kate Douglas

"An amusing vampire romance . . . a terrific contemporary tale." —The Best Reviews

"Written with a dash of humor reminiscent of Katie MacAlister . . . amusing." —Monsters and Critics

"A savvy new take on the vampire romance . . . that will keep you laughing until the final pages."
—Paranormal Romance Writers

"A marvelous introduction to the world of vampires and werewolves . . . funny and filled with explosive sexual tension." —The Romance Reader's Connection

"Add the name Michele Bardsley to the ranks of talented paranormal authors who wield humor as a deft weapon." —*Romantic Times*

P9-CSB-588

Praise for the Novels
of Michele Bardsley

Wait Till Your Vampire Gets Home

"Has action aplenty and a free-spirited, wittily sarcastic heroine who will delight fans." —*Booklist*

"Witty. If you like your vampires with a dose of humor, I highly recommend Bardsley's Broken Heart series." —Romance Novel TV

"Bardsley has one of the most entertaining series on the market. The humor and wackiness keep hitting the sweet spot. Add Bardsley to your autobuy list!" —*Romantic Times* (top pick)

"Michele Bardsley's latest installment in the Broken Heart series is just as hard to put down as the ones before." —Bitten by Books

"Funny and entertaining. I can't wait for the next adventure!" —Manic Readers

"Michele Bardsley gives us another amazing addition to the Broken Heart series." —Night Owl Romance

"An enjoyable mix of humor and romance . . . fast-paced, steamy, and all-around entertaining." —Darque Reviews

"Fun and lighthearted. . . . This book will appeal to fans of MaryJanice Davidson, Katie MacAlister, and Kathy Love since it has the same mix of fun comedy, paranormal fantasy, and romance." —LoveVampires

Because Your Vampire Said So

"Lively, sexy, out of this world—as well as in it—fun! Michele Bardsley's vampire stories rock!" —Carly Phillips, *New York Times* bestselling author

continued . . .

"Five Ribbons! I laughed nonstop from beginning to end. . . . Michele Bardsley always creates these characters that leave readers feeling like they are our next-door neighbors. . . . I've been addicted to these books since the very first one was written, but I have to say, I think *Because Your Vampire Said So* is my favorite so far. . . . If I could, I'd give this story a higher rating. Five ribbons just doesn't seem to be enough for this wonderful story!"
—Romance Junkies

"Another Broken Heart denizen is here in this newest, hysterically funny first-person romp. The combination of sexy humor, sarcastic wit, and paranormal trauma is unmistakably Bardsley. Grab the popcorn and settle in for a seriously good time!" —*Romantic Times*

"Vampire romance readers will enjoy the return to Broken Heart, Oklahoma. . . . Michele Bardsley provides a fun paranormal romance with an interesting undead pairing." —The Best Reviews

Don't Talk Back to Your Vampire

"Cutting-edge humor and a raw, seductive hero make *Don't Talk Back to Your Vampire* a yummylicious treat!"
—Dakota Cassidy, author of *The Accidental Werewolf*

"A fabulous combination of vampire lore, parental angst, romance, and mystery. I loved this book!"
—Jackie Kessler, author of *The Road to Hell*

"All I can say is *wow*! I was totally immersed in this story, to the point that I tuned everything and everybody out the . . . entire evening. Now, that's what I call a good book. Michele can't write the next one fast enough for me!" —The Best Reviews

"A winning follow-up to *I'm the Vampire, That's Why*, filled with humor, supernatural romance, and truly evil villains." —*Booklist*

Over My Dead Body

Michele Bardsley

A SIGNET ECLIPSE BOOK

SIGNET ECLIPSE
Published by New American Library, a division of
Penguin Group (USA) Inc., 375 Hudson Street,
New York, New York 10014, USA
Penguin Group (Canada), 90 Eglinton Avenue East, Suite 700, Toronto,
Ontario M4P 2Y3, Canada (a division of Pearson Penguin Canada Inc.)
Penguin Books Ltd., 80 Strand, London WC2R 0RL, England
Penguin Ireland, 25 St. Stephen's Green, Dublin 2,
Ireland (a division of Penguin Books, Ltd.)
Penguin Group (Australia), 250 Camberwell Road, Camberwell, Victoria 3124,
Australia (a division of Pearson Australia Group Pty. Ltd.)
Penguin Books India Pvt. Ltd., 11 Community Centre, Panchsheel Park,
New Delhi - 110 017, India
Penguin Group (NZ), 67 Apollo Drive, Rosedale, North Shore 0632,
New Zealand (a division of Pearson New Zealand Ltd.)
Penguin Books (South Africa) (Pty.) Ltd., 24 Sturdee Avenue,
Rosebank, Johannesburg 2196, South Africa

Penguin Books Ltd., Registered Offices:
80 Strand, London WC2R 0RL, England

First published by Signet Eclipse, an imprint of New American Library,
A division of Penguin Group (USA) Inc.

First Printing, May 2009
10 9 8 7 6 5 4 3 2 1

To Elaine Smythe,
who lives on forever in the hearts of those who love
her and in the pages of this book.

To Terri Smythe—
Terri's Angels love, love, love you.

ACKNOWLEDGMENTS

My children freaking rock.

My daughter, Kati, is fabulous. She's smart, wicked funny, talented, and has a big ol' bleeding heart. She's got an attitude, too, and she's mouthy. I adore her. I can only take credit for bringing her into the world and making sure she survived until adulthood—all the rest is her.

My son, Reid, is brilliant. He's only eleven, but he has a killer sense of humor and the kindest heart. He tells cool stories and has awesome ideas. He wants to change the world. And you know something? He will.

To my children: I love you forever.

I adore Renée, Terri, Dakota, Jaynie, Juanita, and Lori (Chapman, just so we're clear, you-know-who-you-are doubters). I am so very blessed to have you as friends. I would even give you chocolate instead of keeping it for myself—that's how much y'all mean to me.

Jose, you have good taste in tattoos (and you, too,

Beth, 'cause I know you're reading this). And hey, no more sugar and carbs, dude. I'm sorry, but going to the hospital is BAD. Cut that shit out already!

I gotta give props to Jackie Kessler, who wrote *Hell's Belles*, which is such an awesome book. I fell in love with the way she told that story and every story since. The woman has mad skills—www.jackiekessler.com.

I worship at the altar of Mark Henry. The man can flat-out write. I'm horribly jealous of his talent. If you have not checked out Amanda Feral's fabulous and fashionable adventures, you are sooooo missing out. Go forth and buy—www.markhenry.us.

Toni McGee Causey writes very (very, very, very) funny novels about Bobbie Faye, the terror of Louisiana. I adore her and her creator, the übertalented Toni—www.bobbiefaye.com.

To all these writers I owe a world of thanks for inspiring me and for writing such kick-ass books for me to read.

I owe a debt of gratitude to those people who read this novel and offered comments: Renée, the plot master and handholder; Dakota, the deadline ho and fabulous line editor; Terri, the voice in my head yelling at me to "write the fucking book, already"; and Butch Treese, the ultimate fan who knows my books better than I do. Thank you, thank you, thank you!

No acknowledgment would be complete without gushing about my literary agent, Stephanie Kip Rostan, her rawkin' assistant, Monika Verma, and all the wonderful people at Levine Greenberg Literary Agency.

I also gotta give high fives to my ever-patient editor, Kara Cesare, and the staff and crew at New American

Library. Nobody deserves Godiva more than you guys.

I gotta say this to Miss Dakota and her man, Rob: That kind of bright and shiny love couldn't have happened to two nicer friends. Here's a chocolate martini for the rest of us who hope every day to find the same.

I would also like to mention Brenda Anderson. I just wanted to say to Brenda Anderson that you are a valued member of the fan group. Brenda Anderson, we don't care that your brain juice is a quart low. Ours is, too, and we don't even have an injury to account for why we do the stupid shit we do. And dear, dear Brenda Anderson, the one who lives in Pittsburgh and didn't say hello until Friday at RT 2008 and then never came back to the conference so I could properly torment you, you wanted to see your name in print. Here you go: Brenda Anderson, Brenda Anderson, Brenda Anderson, Brenda Anderson, Brenda Anderson, and for good measure, Brenda Anderson.

And last (but never, ever least), I want to say how much I adore the members of my Yahoo! Group: http://groups.yahoo.com/group/MicheleBardsley/join.

Obviously you have stupendous taste in paranormal fiction. Even though I lurk too much and I forget to send out prizes and I post erratically and I torture you with random sentences from my WIPs, I really and truly lurve you all. Mostly because you're as crazy as I am. Don't bother denying it.

"That which is Below corresponds to that which is Above, and that which is Above corresponds to that which is Below, to accomplish the miracles of the One Thing."
—The Emerald Tablet of Hermes Trismegistus

"Be ye angry, and sin not: let not the sun go down upon your wrath: Neither give place to the devil."
—Ephesians 4:26–27

"Well, I think I learned a valuable lesson: Always take down your Christmas decorations after New Year's, or you might get filleted by a hooker from God."
—Dean Winchester, *Supernatural*, "Houses of the Holy"

Chapter 1

Killing Braddock Hayes changed my life—such as it was—forever. Committing murder should change a person, at least a person who still has a conscience, and I sure as hell had mine.

My name's Simone Sweet. My personality obviously doesn't match my name. How could someone who was truly sweet rip open the carotid artery in a man's neck and enjoy the thick, bloody flow of his life onto her lips?

I'm a vampire, and folks may believe that vampires walk around and kill indiscriminately. All right, some do. But not me. Not the ones I lived with in Broken Heart, Oklahoma. We had rules.

The same rules I'd tossed out the proverbial window the minute I sank my fangs into Brady's neck and drank all of his essence.

I knelt before my sacrifice, penitent yet darkly thrilled by what I'd just done. My gaze drifted up past the pine trees. The moon was out. It shone through the feathery branches like the bright eye of the goddess, the one the lycanthropes worshipped. She had surely witnessed my act and was passing judgment on me. Could a deity that wasn't mine punish me?

The shitty part was . . . I'd killed someone before. Before I even knew vampires and werewolves were real. Before I knew that the world in which humans lived was an illusion they created. Paranormal creatures have been with us for a very long time. It's not so much that they're good at hiding. It's more that humans are better at ignoring what they don't understand, and denying anything that doesn't make sense in their reality.

Yes, I'd killed someone when I was human. He deserved it. I have to believe that he deserved it. But as I looked down at the corpse of Braddock Hayes, a man who'd done nothing but try to help me and my family, I couldn't lie to myself anymore.

Nobody deserved to be killed. Not even killers.

I stood up, shaking, my body full of blood and that strange, addictive ecstasy. That was the danger of draining a human. Vampires liked it. We enjoyed blood nearly as much as women enjoyed shoe sales or free Godiva samples. That forbidden joy was why vampires who either belonged to the Consortium or followed the rules of the Ancients took only one pint every evening from willing donors.

Blood smelled like rust.

It almost looked like rust, especially when it was drying on clothes and clotting on skin. Staining my outsides, the way my sins stained my soul. It wasn't the same as before . . . when I killed Jacob. Oh, there was blood then, too. But not like this.

I cocked my head, listening to the sounds of paws *thwump*ing on the marshy ground and crashing through the underbrush. Lycanthropes had exceptional senses. That edge made them superb guardians of the undead.

I was still staring at the moon when a black wolf skidded into the clearing. Damian, the leader of the guardians. He sniffed Brady, his big furred face swinging toward me. He barked at me, his jade eyes glittering in accusation.

Then he lifted his snout into the air and howled.

Patrick O'Halloran and his father, Ruadan, sailed into view and landed between me and Brady. They could fly not because they were vampires, but because they were part *sidhe*, or fairy. They both looked like a young Pierce Brosnan with raven black hair and stormy silver eyes.

They would judge me.

Maybe the paranormal world wasn't so different from the human world, after all.

Patrick crouched near Brady, but there was nothing he could do. I'd made sure of it.

I returned my gaze to the sky. A circle formed around the moon; its red glow stained the white orb just like the blood I'd moments ago spilled. It was almost time. I had to wait only a little while longer.

"Why, Simone?" Patrick asked quietly. "Why did you kill him?"

Strangely enough, I had killed Brady and Jacob for the same reason.

Freedom.

Damian put the cuffs on me. Patrick explained that the ornate silver was imbued with fairy magic. I wouldn't be able to get out of them.

Duh.

Brady was dead. And with Gran and Glory . . . I shook off the heinous thoughts. I'd already lost everything important to me. I was hollow inside, but at the same time, the power within was an uncurling viper, readying to strike. Brady's blood throbbed inside me, giving me more strength than I'd ever had before.

"Damian, return to the festival and guard the queen," said Ruadan. "Take her to the hospital, Patrick. Dr. Merrick wants to see her."

"I'm standing here," I pointed out. "You don't have to talk about me in third person."

Ruadan and Patrick ignored me.

My gaze fell on the body of Brady. Ruadan magicked up a sheet to cover Brady. I was grateful for that kindness.

"Simone," said Patrick. His voice was soft with empathy. How could he be nice to me after what I did? "We need to go now."

"To Dr. Merrick."

He nodded. I could see in his gaze that he thought I was nuts. Being crazy was an acceptable excuse for all that I'd done. But here's the thing: I wasn't insane.

Patrick wrapped his arms around me, presumably to do the ol' gold-sparkly trick and get me to the hospital. None of them knew it, but I was the least of their worries.

I couldn't stop looking at the man I'd killed, or rather at the sheet that outlined his form. *Oh, Brady.* My insides quivered, and I felt the heaviness of sorrow. I pushed it back.

No, I couldn't afford grief.

Not yet.

Chapter 2

Six days earlier
Saturday, June 15

"That's a very fine ass," whispered Her Royal Highness Patricia Marchand. "A definite ten."

More like an eleven. My gaze had been roving the object of our mutual assessment for the last five minutes, which was how Queen Patsy caught me. But after taking a gander at the jeans-clad buttocks of Braddock Hayes, she seemed to understand why my gaze was superglued to the view.

"Simone Sweet," said Patsy under her breath, "you have a naughty streak."

I only smiled. I might be dead, but my eyes still worked—not to mention various other parts. Granted, certain parts hadn't been in use longer than others, but that was okay by me. Vampires had to be finicky about that sort of stuff, anyway. Having sex meant saying "I do" for a hundred years.

No, thank you.

Patsy and I returned to watching the scenery. She was married to a very hot man named Gabriel, and, in fact, probably shouldn't be ogling Brady. Not that I was gonna tell her to stop.

Even though it had been dark for at least an hour, it was still ten degrees hotter than hell. Winter had stretched on and on, clawing greedily into April. Spring had lasted all of ten seconds. The heat had rolled in, sucking all the joy out of the smallest breeze. Now it was the second week of June and we'd been afflicted by the roasting heat that usually tormented us in August. Since I was a vampire, I wasn't sweating buckets. I didn't have to breathe in the liquefied air, but I could still feel it rattling in my useless lungs.

Brady, however, was very much human and prone to sweating. He stopped wrangling with the equipment and stood up, whipping off his T-shirt. I'd been eyeballing him for a while now. He had moved to Broken Heart in February; he was a former member of the Paranormal Research and Investigation Services. Our resident dragon, Libby, and her parents, who had founded PRIS, lived here, too.

Brady and I had kind of become friends. I used the term loosely because, really, I didn't have friends. Oh, I knew people in town, and most of 'em were friendly enough. I was just real careful not to get too close to anyone.

Come to think of it, Brady was probably the one here who knew the most about me and my family— and that wasn't a whole lot.

My gaze returned to the man who was doing such a good job of occupying my thoughts.

"Oh, my God," Patsy and I breathed together. We

looked at each other, then at the glistening muscles of a half-naked Brady. I'd seen this view before, but I never tired of it. Brady was a hard worker, and smarter than everyone here—even Doc Michaels. But he wasn't the sort to shoot the shit.

He had a linebacker build—big, broad, muscled. His tanned skin was scarred with slashes and pock-marked with holes. Knives and bullets, I was sure—though I'd never asked. According to the rumor mill, he was a man who'd literally survived the slings and arrows of life, a life I could only guess at. But I knew a thing or two about surviving, and maybe that's why I admired Brady. And maybe, too, it was why he sorta scared me. I had a few scars myself, inside and out. Even though he'd never given me a reason to fear him—well, I had the kind of terrified feeling in me that never went away.

We stepped back as Brady maneuvered the fifty-sixth pole into place. One hundred and thirteen of the five-foot-tall, six-inch-wide metallic poles would be in-stalled around Broken Heart's perimeter. Calculations for where they needed to go had taken nearly as long to complete as making the darned things. I should know, since I was the one who built the outer casings. All the whirligigs on the inside had been created by Brady and Doc Michaels. I didn't understand the tech-nology, but I knew how to work with anything made of metal, and I could fix just about any mechanical device.

Part of my job was helping to work the bugs out of the individual components; every single pole would have to play nice with the others to get the Invisi-shield up and running. Once it was operational, it would be the same as if Broken Heart had disappeared from Oklahoma's map.

"I've done my official freaking duty. My feet are killing me," said Patsy, rubbing her very pregnant belly. "I'm gonna be a cliché and go home to eat ice cream and pickles."

I laughed. Patsy was nearly eight months along with triplets. Having babies was a perk of being vampire and werewolf—you were kinda alive. She and Gabriel were the only *loup de sang* in the whole wide world—at least until their children were born.

Up until June of last year, Patsy had been Broken Heart's only beautician, and I'd been the town's only mechanic. My role hadn't changed much, but Patsy had become queen of not only the undead, but also the furry. Well, she wasn't quite official on that score. Even though the original seven Ancients had turned over their undead Families to Patsy's rule (not all willingly, mind you), the lycanthropes were a more traditional bunch. Broken Heart had been chosen to host the annual Moon Goddess festival, where Patsy would receive the official blessing of the priestesses. Then she'd have the additional headache of bossing around werewolves.

"Hey, there's my ride," said Patsy.

A white Mercedes glided over the field, stopping when it was next to Patsy. In the driver's seat was Gabriel. His moon-white hair was drawn into a long ponytail, framing his handsome face. He had the most amazing gold eyes, eyes that were only for Patsy, as she maneuvered herself into the car.

"How are the shocks?" I asked, leaning in as Patsy strapped on her seat belt.

"It rides smooth as silk," said Gabriel. "Even off the

road. It was amazing work, Simone." He grinned. "Too bad it's not dragon-proof."

In February, their last Mercedes had been blown up by a pissed-off dragon. Now we had one living in Broken Heart—Libby. She was married to a vampire named Ralph, who was daddy to the cutest twin toddlers. Libby and Ralph were gonna have the first dragon born in five hundred years. Needless to say, they'd been busy fireproofing their new house and everything in it.

I patted the side of the car and chuckled. "I'm working on it, Gabriel. One miracle at a time."

My gaze was drawn to Patsy's belly—three miracles in there, and almost ready to come out, too. I looked at Patsy and grinned. I was thrilled for her. She deserved some happiness.

"If the shield works we won't need to worry about fireballs blowing shit up," said Patsy. "You take care, hon."

"You, too." I shut the door, and off they went.

I watched the Mercedes wheel around and head toward the dirt road. Even though I wasn't exactly part of the town, at least not the way most folks were, I really did like the people here. But I'd also learned the danger of getting too close to others—and I couldn't shake the habit of keeping myself to myself.

"Hello, my friends," shouted a German-accented voice. The man jogging toward us was Reiner Blutwolf. He was an old friend of our resident lycanthrope security detail, three gorgeous triplets whom I really didn't have much to do with. Truth be told, they were even scarier than Brady—especially Damian. That guy almost never smiled. The closest he ever came was when he was around the jovial Reiner, who oozed charm.

I was probably the only one in Broken Heart who didn't buy his act.

He always had candy bars tucked into the top pocket of his work shirts. I'd never known a lycanthrope with that kind of sweet tooth.

"Hello, Simone," he said, flashing a blindingly white smile. What did he brush his teeth with? Bleach? Maybe he chewed on Greenies or something. Oh, now . . . that was mean.

I grinned broadly. Nobody could out-jolly me. I had perfected the art of hiding behind bright smiles and perky attitudes. I could make Pollyanna look like the Grinch. "Hello, Reiner. You doin' all right?"

"I am now that I've seen your smile."

Oh, puh-lease. His bright blue eyes were on mine, and I looked away. I suppose some might call him handsome. To me, he looked like a less pretty version of Brad Pitt. Finally, I nodded my thanks for his lame-ass compliment, then pretended I wanted to get a better look at the pole Brady was wrestling into place. With my vampire strength, I could help easily enough, but so could the three other vamps standing around and watching him struggle.

"Would you like some help, Brady?" Reiner rounded the other side of the pole, stepping into my personal space. I didn't appreciate the subtle intimidation, and I scooted away.

Ugh. Reiner always picked me out of the crowd first, unless Damian was around. He reminded me of Roogie Roo, the old terrier owned by my friend Lyle. I was allergic to dogs and Roogie Roo knew it, which is why he loved me. I couldn't resist letting that silly dog sit on my lap, even though I'd spend a full day sneezing and wheezing. In the same way, Reiner seemed to know I wasn't keen on him, so he tried extra hard to get my approval. Hah. I'd be damned if I let him onto my lap.

I brushed against Brady and stopped, startled that I'd gotten so close. His sweat-slicked arm slid along mine, and if I'd had a heart it would've skipped a few beats. I felt safer by him than I did Reiner, which was not a comforting thought. I glanced up at Brady, whose chocolate brown gaze was on mine. His eyes narrowed; then he stepped between me and Reiner, clapping the man on the shoulder.

"I have a date," he said. "Maybe you and the bloodsuckers can finish up this one. I'll be back in a couple of hours to help with the others."

"I didn't realize you and Simone were . . . together," said Reiner.

I expected Brady to protest that I wasn't his date, but he merely smiled, picking up his shirt to wipe off his face. "Well, now you do."

I looked at the ground so my shocked expression wouldn't give away Brady's little white lie. I'd much rather Reiner believed I was dating Brady—maybe he'd back off a little. Why was he so set on impressing me, anyway? I was just a single mom who made her living working at a garage. I was nobody—and I liked it that way.

"C'mon, sweetheart," said Brady, tugging my hand into his. He threw the shirt over his shoulder and walked me to his truck. If I had the ability to blush, my cheeks would've been on fire. As it was, I couldn't look at anyone we passed by. A few weeks before, Brady just up and offered to take me to the build sites and home again. I really liked his Ford Dually, which was red as blood and rode like a wet dream. I'd caved, and now everyone would think it was because we were an item. Gah.

Brady opened the passenger's-side door and helped me into the seat. Then he rounded the truck and got in. He pulled a clean T-shirt out of the glove box and tugged it on. Then he started the engine, flipped the air-conditioning on high, and backed the truck toward the road.

Most of the time we rode home in companionable silence, listening to country-and-western songs. We were both suckers for Hank Williams Sr. and Patsy Cline. But he didn't turn on the CD player, leaving only the silence to thicken between us.

"What was that all about?" I blurted.

"What was what?"

"Announcing to Reiner—not to mention the rest of Broken Heart—that we're dating."

"Why? You got a boyfriend who might protest?"

He knew I didn't, but that wasn't the point. I ached to ask him if he wanted to date me, but I couldn't form the question. Who was I kidding? Say what you will about Brady, but he was the protective type. I'm sure my reaction to Reiner made Brady put on his white-knight armor. How could he be interested in me? Nobody noticed me, not unless they needed something fixed.

"Look, Brady. I don't think we should tell people we're dating when we're not."

"Good point," said Brady. "How about I take you out tomorrow night?"

I turned to stare at him. My mouth opened, but no words came out. The truck hit a rut and we both bounced up. My head nearly grazed the roof. I grabbed hold of the door and Brady chuckled.

"Relax. It's not like I can kill you."

An angry retort died on my lips. Everyone knew I didn't do anger. I was the most forgiving, sweet, kind soul you'd ever meet in this life or the next. At least that's what I let people believe. Even before I'd been Turned into a vampire, I was second chance personified. Not a day went by that I didn't remember, or try to honor, those sacrifices that had freed me from my old life.

The truck picked up speed, and at the next juncture turned right toward my house, which was only a mile away. My little three-bedroom home was on the old McCree farm, just yards away from Broken Heart Creek.

Somehow or another, Brady had gotten into the habit of arriving at the house at nine p.m. to play Candyland with my six-year-old, Glory. She was my miracle baby, in so many ways, but she wasn't sociable. She hadn't said a word for the past three years, and no doctor or therapist could figure out why, much less get her to speak. I finally stopped paying MDs and shrinks to tell me what I already knew. My daughter would talk when she was good and ready—if she decided to talk at all.

When we arrived, Glory had the board set up and the pieces ready to go. I had never been invited to a game, but I didn't mind. Glory had taken a real shine to Brady, and I couldn't deny my daughter the pleasure of his company. Brady was the only one who could make her laugh, and I'd pay any price to keep hearing that sweet sound.

I walked into the kitchen, sniffing the leftover scents

of bacon, buttery eggs, and toast slathered with home-made strawberry jam. Sometimes being a vampire just sucked. I missed eating something fierce.

Grandma Elaine was at the sink doing the breakfast dishes.

"Hi there, baby," said my grandmother, not bothering to turn around.

I grinned. Vampire stealth didn't fool Grandma Elaine. Nothing did. I rubbed her shoulders. "You go on and sit. I'll finish up."

"All right. I'll have another cup of coffee."

Several years ago, Grandma had been in an auto accident that killed her husband and blinded her. She was the epitome of strength and carrying on, a fine example of not letting bad things get in the way of good living.

She knew her own kitchen like the back of her hand and soon had a steaming cup of coffee—oh, was that a hint of cinnamon in her freshly ground Sumatra beans? Mm-mmm. I missed coffee.

"She ate real good," said Grandma Elaine, as she sat at the table. "She's been waiting on Brady practically since she got up."

"She say anything?"

"You know the answer to that."

I couldn't help but ask. I longed for Glory to use her voice, but I knew nothing I did would make her. I'd tried everything, and then I'd tried it all again.

"Quit worrying about that child," said Grandma. "She's all right."

I finished up the dishes and slid into a chair across the table. "I know she is." I paused. "Did she go down to the creek today?"

"No, but she will. It's her habit. It don't hurt nothing, Simone."

Glory would lead her great-grandmother to the creek and spend an hour or two staring at the muddy water and moving her lips, like she was talking to someone. Grandma might be blind, but she wasn't stupid or careless. If she trusted that Glory was gonna be okay, then I had to believe it.

"I noticed the gardening tools on the porch," I said. "You still trying to get something to grow around here?"

"Ain't nothing wrong with planting seeds and hoping for the best." She chuckled. "Besides, I'm more stubborn than that old ground. I won't give up."

She never did. My grandmother loved to garden. And even though she couldn't see the results of her efforts anymore, she still loved it. Unfortunately, nothing liked to grow on this land—at least not anything near the house or the old barn falling apart out back. I didn't like that barn. Something bad happened there—and don't ask me how I know. I got the heebie-jeebies in that place even before I became a vampire.

Like I said, we lived on the old McCree farm; the McCrees were one of the first five families to settle Broken Heart. The story went that Mary McCree discovered her husband, Sean, had an affair, and in her anguish, she threw herself into the creek and drowned. If the little hometown tale was true, I felt bad for Mary. I knew what it was like to feel that kind of anger, but I'd also paid the price for my fury. People in pain do stupid, stupid things.

Anyway, Broken Heart had a sad history of drawing people in bad relationships. Nearly all of us who were left, at least those who hadn't been paid off and shipped out, had relationship tragedies. Ever since the Consortium rolled into town and bought everything, lock, stock, and barrel, it seemed the curse of Broken Heart had been broken.

Or maybe it just changed form. Sometimes, people like me who didn't have bad luck would have no luck at all.

With Candyland safe and sound once again, Glory went off with Grandma Elaine to do her schoolwork. She wasn't yet ready for attending Broken Heart's school, so we homeschooled her. Glory loved to read, hated math, and liked to do science experiments.

I walked Brady to the porch, like I'd done every night before.

"It's nice, what you do," I said. "Glory's happy when she's with you."

"She's a good kid." He hesitated. "What about you, Simone? You happy when I'm around?"

Chapter 3

Brady leaned on the porch post, staring at me. His question lingered in the air between us. I hadn't thought about my happiness in a long time. I'd been in survival mode for so long that I couldn't wrap my brain around happiness. Three years ago, I was miserable. One year ago, I was killed and made into a vampire.

Maybe it was time to consider the idea of being happy.

So long as I didn't get used to it. I was well aware that expectations bred disappointment.

"Simone?"

"Sure." I nodded. "Yeah. I like having you around."

"Well, that's a start."

I looked away from Brady's tender gaze and toward the night sky. In this part of Oklahoma, the stars twinkled like jewels studded in black velvet. Crickets chirped, wind rustled the long grass, and in harmony with it all, the creek burbled.

Brady didn't say anything else, and I didn't want to ruin the moment. I stepped down onto the rutted path, hoping he'd take a hint and follow me over to his truck. This was the first time he'd stayed so long; he usually chose to say his good-byes and go back to the build sites. I stayed home with Glory until it was time to open the garage.

"You never said yes." He was right behind me, and I felt his touch along my arm. My skin prickled.

"To what?" I turned, my undead heart trying to do a jittery mambo.

"To our date."

"You don't have to go to all that trouble," I said. "It's silly to go out with each other just to prove we're not liars."

He chuckled. "I don't give a shit what people think about me." He leaned down, his hands light on my shoulders. His eyes were dark, hungry. It'd been a long time since a man looked at me liked that. Both fear and excitement snared me.

"Are you as sweet as you pretend?" His warm lips ghosted along mine. I couldn't move, but even this gentle caress was enough to make me remember how sweet a kiss could be. Oh, how I wanted to embrace him and take the gift he offered. I let my lips mimic his, but I kept my hands fisted. I couldn't let go, and I couldn't let him in.

Brady lifted his head, his brown eyes filled with questions. "I've wanted to do that since the day I met you," he said in a raspy voice. He leaned down and did it again, in the same soft, patient way.

My knees wobbled.

"Okay," I said. "Okay."

His lips hitched into a sexy grin, and he stepped

back. Had I the ability, I would've sucked up some air. But vampires didn't really need constant use of their organs, and my lungs refused to operate.

"Until we meet again," he said, Roy Rogers style. He tipped an imaginary cowboy hat and turned, sauntering to his truck.

Oh, my God. I was going on a date with Braddock Hayes.

I opened the garage at ten thirty p.m., just like I did every night except on Sundays. Sundays were for family, and when I was human, it was also for church. Becoming a bloodsucker didn't make me any less of a believer in God, but it did make it difficult to attend a place of worship. Broken Heart was slowly turning into a town that catered to the paranormal. However, I doubted we'd get us an undead preacher any time soon.

Main Street was empty, as usual. I pulled my truck around the back, cut the engine, and hopped out. I didn't get a lot of business. Most paranormal beings didn't have a big need for automobiles, much less auto repair, but I still managed to keep busy. Not to brag, but I could fix just about anything. I was too stubborn to let anything mechanical get the better of me, so I never gave up. The owners sometimes did, though. That's why I had a few projects in my garage that I tinkered on whenever I got the chance.

I always thought it was a shame that I got Turned by a Master from the Family Velthur. I didn't mean to seem ungrateful. It was just that the Family Zela can manipulate any kind of metal, and I did a lot of metal work. The Family Velthur's power was the manipulation of liquid, mostly water. Don't get me wrong; sometimes it came in real handy.

I'm probably not explaining this right. Y'see, every vampire was from one of the seven Families. All vampires got what Doc Michaels called the basic package: strength, speed, übersenses, and mind mojo. Then each vampire Family manifested a specific power. Family Ruadan flew, Family Durga wrangled demons, Family Amahté communicated with the dead, Family Lia controlled fire, Family Koschei had mondo mind powers, Family Velthur mojo-ed all liquid forms, and Family Zela manipulated metals.

The garage was located off Main Street, not too far from the Old Sass Café. I had a three-bay garage, a small office that always smelled like oil, and a back lot filled with car debris. My storage shed was out there, too. I loved that perfume of grease and gas. I associated that smell with the first time I walked into Joe Montresso's garage and he gave me a job. I didn't know jack shit about anything, much less engines and such. But he taught me everything. And I built a career on that kindness. I built a whole life around it.

Since I was officially open for business in ten minutes, I left the glass door unlocked. I rounded the waist-high counter. Below the counter was my work space. It was too tiny to call a desk. An office chair wouldn't fit back here, so I just used a bar stool donated from the Old Sass Café. As usual, piles of paperwork filled every available spot; my inbox/outbox and file folders were empty. Don't talk to me about organization. I was one of those people who could find what I was looking for in the mess I made, but never in a neatly filed folder or color-coded binder.

I tossed my keys on the receipts for jobs done and

flipped on my ancient computer. I could've gotten a new one—I could've gotten a new everything. But I didn't take the Consortium's deal. I owned my plot of land and my business; just like my grandmother owned her land and her house. We agreed to stay, and they agreed to stop harassing us about selling.

Last year, Broken Heart had been a small town on the verge of extinction. People were moving and businesses were closing.

Then the vampires came.

Okay, it was like this: Lorcan O'Halloran had the Taint, which was a nasty disease that rotted the insides of vampires until they went crazy. Eventually, they died. Some just walked into the sunshine rather than suffer. The Consortium, however, bled Lorcan dry and filled him with royal lycan blood. He turned into a hungry, crazed were-vamp. The radical cure saved him, but not before he'd killed eleven of us single parents.

Don't ask me how ol' Lorcan managed to do that— it seemed a crazy coincidence that he noshed on the unmarried. Scarier still was that all of us Turned. Usually, only one in ten humans survived. The Consortium and Ancients had all kinds of rules about Turning, but I never paid much attention. I would *never* Turn a soul. I'd committed enough sin in this lifetime, thank you.

Anyway, I was scrubbing oil stains off the driveway. I'd stayed really late at the shop, hoping to work off my frustrations with life in general. One second I was scraping the concrete with a stiff brush, trying to think of the words to "Summer Nights," and the next I was yanked up by my ponytail. The smelly, furry beast bent me backward like a dancer dipping his partner, and savaged my neck.

I woke up on a steel table in a white room, fang-deep in a nice-looking man who said his name was Velthur. Yeah, *that* Velthur. The vampire who started my Family four thousand years ago was the one who Turned me. No other Turn-blood had been given that privilege. I wonder sometimes if that's why my power seemed a little stronger than most of the other Turn-bloods.

I heard the men's dress shoes clicking on the side-walk about fifteen seconds before the door swung open. The hair on the back of my neck prickled. Even before I looked up, I knew who it was.

"Hi, Reiner. Long time, no see."

He grinned at my little joke, his eyes dipping to my chest. Why did men always check out the boobs? Even when they've seen 'em a hundred times before. Figuratively speaking. I wore a red tank top under my denim overalls. I owned a lot of tank tops and overalls, and several pairs of sneakers. It was my uniform. I didn't have much cause to own dresses and heels. I was short, but I had a helluva bust.

I cleared my throat. Reiner took the hint and dragged his gaze back to my face. "You are very lovely, *Liebling*."

"Thanks." I guess. I tucked my hands under the counter and clenched them. "You need something fixed?"

"Just my heart," he said. He walked to the side of the counter and leaned against it. "You've broken it."

He didn't know it, but I was immune to his kind of slimy charm. I looked up at him, all confused innocence. "I sure don't know what you mean, Reiner. Did I do something to hurt your feelings?"

"You're dating Brady." He put a palm against the center of his chest and sighed. "I never had a chance."

He looked a little wolfish, which, of course, was in his nature. All the same, I didn't enjoy the look in his eyes. If the jerk didn't get off my counter, I was going to break more than his heart. Try all ten of his fingers. I swallowed my anger and stood up. I picked up my keys and stuck them in my pocket.

Aiming a sunny smile at him, I said, "I gotta get to work."

I rounded the counter with every intention of pushing past him and leaving. Unfortunately, there was only one way in and out of the office. I had to go out, turn left, and open another door to get into the garage.

He turned to face me, effectively trapping me between him and the desk. I was five foot five, and Reiner was a good foot taller than me. If he was trying to show me he was bigger and stronger, then mission accomplished. I wanted badly to take a couple steps backward, but I wouldn't give him the satisfaction.

"What do you want?" I asked, keeping my tone friendly. I heard the tremor in my words, though. I just hoped he hadn't.

"I would like you to assist with a project."

Reiner asking for my help was so unexpected that my fear abated. I eyed him. "What kind of project?"

"It's a gift for Queen Patricia," he said. "Something I wish to give her at the Moon Goddess festival." He grinned like a little boy who'd found where his Christmas presents were hidden. "You're the perfect woman for the job."

Reiner leaned closer, his grin widening. His gaze

dipped to my mouth. I didn't like this, not at all. I couldn't decide if he was being threatening or flirtatious.

Then he lifted his hand.

Jesus. Terror spiked my belly and desperation bleached my courage. I couldn't stop the shiver, couldn't stop the half step back. The open palm slap had been my husband's favorite. It stung like hell, brought tears to my eyes, and left a satisfying red welt on my cheek. The welt faded, but the humiliation never did.

"Are you all right, *Liebling*?" The hand he'd raised went to his ear, which he scratched.

For an odd moment, I wanted to blurt, "You got fleas?" I held my tongue, though. It wasn't wise to insult werewolves. Besides, if he did have a flea condition, it was none of my business. I was all about minding my own freaking business. And so should everyone else, goddamn it.

My gaze flickered to the hand Reiner dropped to his side. He had long fingers and nails glossy from a manicure. Big hands, like Jacob. Nausea roiled, and I swallowed the knot forming in my throat. I hadn't had a flashback like that in a long time. Jacob no longer had control over me, over what was mine.

The two candy bars in the top pocket of his shirt crackled as he shifted position, his eyes more curious than menacing. He saw the direction of my gaze and took out one of the candy bars. Baby Ruth.

"Would you like one? They are very good."

I shook my head. I didn't want any treats from him. I just wanted him to go away. I studied the checkered linoleum as my thoughts whirled. Had Reiner dropped by because he wanted my help with this mys-

when he was around the jovial Reiner, who oozed charm.

I was probably the only one in Broken Heart who didn't buy his act.

He always had candy bars tucked into the top pocket of his work shirts. I'd never known a lycanthrope with that kind of sweet tooth.

"Hello, Simone," he said, flashing a blindingly white smile. What did he brush his teeth with? Bleach? Maybe he chewed on Greenies or something. Oh, now . . . that was mean.

I grinned broadly. Nobody could out-jolly me. I had perfected the art of hiding behind bright smiles and perky attitudes. I could make Pollyanna look like the Grinch. "Hello, Reiner. You doin' all right?"

"I am now that I've seen your smile."

Oh, puh-lease. His bright blue eyes were on mine, and I looked away. I suppose some might call him handsome. To me, he looked like a less pretty version of Brad Pitt. Finally, I nodded my thanks for his lameass compliment, then pretended I wanted to get a better look at the pole Brady was wrestling into place. With my vampire strength, I could help easily enough, but so could the three other vamps standing around and watching him struggle.

"Would you like some help, Brady?" Reiner rounded the other side of the pole, stepping into my personal space. I didn't appreciate the subtle intimidation, and I scooted away.

Ugh. Reiner always picked me out of the crowd first, unless Damian was around. He reminded me of Roogie Roo, the old terrier owned by my friend Lyle. I was allergic to dogs and Roogie Roo knew it, which is why he loved me. I couldn't resist letting that silly dog

road. It was amazing work, Simone." He grinned. "Too bad it's not dragon-proof."

In February, their last Mercedes had been blown up by a pissed-off dragon. Now we had one living in Broken Heart—Libby. She was married to a vampire named Ralph, who was daddy to the cutest twin toddlers. Libby and Ralph were gonna have the first dragon born in five hundred years. Needless to say, they'd been busy fireproofing their new house and everything in it.

I patted the side of the car and chuckled. "I'm working on it, Gabriel. One miracle at a time."

My gaze was drawn to Patsy's belly—three miracles in there, and almost ready to come out, too. I looked at Patsy and grinned. I was thrilled for her. She deserved some happiness.

"If the shield works we won't need to worry about fireballs blowing shit up," said Patsy. "You take care, hon."

"You, too." I shut the door, and off they went.

I watched the Mercedes wheel around and head toward the dirt road. Even though I wasn't exactly part of the town, at least not the way most folks were, I really did like the people here. But I'd also learned the danger of getting too close to others—and I couldn't shake the habit of keeping myself to myself.

"Hello, my friends," shouted a German-accented voice. The man jogging toward us was Reiner Blutwolf. He was an old friend of our resident lycanthrope security detail, three gorgeous triplets whom I really didn't have much to do with. Truth be told, they were even scarier than Brady—especially Damian. That guy almost never smiled. The closest he ever came was

terious project? Or because he wanted to throw down with Brady? Either way, I wished Brady was here.

Ah, hell. I'd like to think I was an independent woman, one who didn't need to be rescued. I knew I could save myself—I already had. Sometimes a girl just wanted a white knight to show up, lift her onto his horse, and race away from the danger. Yeah. Even a girl like me, who gave up on white knights long ago.

I was overreacting, but I couldn't quell the anxiety pouring through me. Reiner hadn't really done anything to harm me—or even to suggest he'd harm me. Yet he was still blocking me, and I really wanted to get to the door.

"Simone."

For a second, I couldn't believe my ears. That deep voice belonged to Brady.

Reiner's eyes widened in surprise and he looked over his shoulder. I was surprised, too. How had Brady managed to get into the office without me or the lycan noticing?

I sidled around Reiner. Brady stood just inside the door, looking like the last piece of chocolate cake on the buffet. He snaked an arm around my waist, and my knees nearly buckled.

"Hi, honey," he purred.

"Hey, there." My voice was quivering and so was I. Brady noticed, too. His mild expression didn't change, but I felt the tension in his muscles.

"Reiner," he said jovially, "you're not trying to flirt with my girl, are you?"

Reiner shoved his hands into his pockets and laughed. "Trying, but failing, I'm afraid."

He sauntered to the door, forcing Brady and me to move farther into the office. Reiner pushed open the

door and paused, looking at me. His gaze told me all
kinds of things I didn't want to know—such as that he
liked a challenge. Then he nodded to Brady, and left.

I tried to pry myself out of Brady's arms, but he
swung me fully into his embrace and stared at me. I
could see the concern in his gaze, but I was barreling
past rational straight into freaked out.

"Don't!" The confusion and fear jackhammering
through me thanks to Reiner transferred easily to
Brady. "Let me go!"

"I'm not him." He released me and then cupped my
chin, looking deeply into my eyes. "What did he do?"

"Nothing." The denial was automatic. How easily
old behaviors surfaced in moments of fear and fury.
I'd worked hard to not be the Old Simone. The one
who wept and begged and cowered and caved.

The crazy thing was that I wanted to stay in Brady's
arms. I felt safe there—like nothing bad would happen
to me if I held on to him. Maybe that scared me more
than the fact that he was just as big, strong, and intimidating as Reiner.

"Really, Brady," I managed. "He asked if I'd work
with him on some kind of doohickey for Patsy. He
didn't do anything to me."

"Bullshit. You're trembling."

"Maybe I'm all a-flutter because of you," I snapped.
I jerked my chin out of his fingers and stomped
around him.

Brady followed me out of the office and into the
garage. I was more annoyed at myself than at him. I
should have better control. It ranked that I felt off-
kilter. Stupid men.

I didn't have actual paying work today, so I figured
I'd just tinker on one of my toys until somebody

needed me. Two of the bays had oil-changing pits. Both were grated, so I walked across them toward my work space, which took up most of the third bay. Brady's thick-soled boots clunked behind me.

I gritted my teeth and whirled around.

And smacked into Brady's broad, muscled, *ooh-la-la* chest.

He grabbed me by the elbows, which stopped me from falling backward. My palms pressed against his pectorals. His heart pounded fiercely underneath my hands.

I looked up at him. "Your heart is beating too fast."

"Maybe I'm all a-flutter because of you."

I dropped my hands and scuttled away, feeling awkward. "You probably ran all the way here just to prove you could."

"Spock provided the speed."

Spock was his Kawasaki Vulcan 900 Classic, which I'd admired the first time I'd seen Brady racing around on it. It was cherry red and gleaming silver. An orgasm on two wheels.

Jacob had loved motorcycles, too. He owned three, and I was never allowed to touch, much less ride, one. Maybe all military men craved risk, in any form. Brady sure did. And so had Jacob. Damn it all. I didn't want to count the ways that Brady was like my dead husband.

I walked to my worktable and studied the gadgets. I couldn't focus on anything in particular because my thoughts were scrambled. "Is there a reason you dropped by, Brady?"

"Yes."

I looked over my shoulder. He jerked his gaze from my ass and grinned. I glared at him. "Well?"

"Your buttocks are to the female form what Da Vinci was to the world of art," he said.

Had I the ability to blush, my face would've gone brick red. Sure, I thought that Brady's ass was a work of art, too, but I wasn't going to *tell* him. "Wow. That was so lame."

"It was more gentlemanly than what I was actually thinking."

"And that's supposed to make me feel better because . . ."

Brady took my hand, and I reluctantly turned to face him. "Every time I get around you, my tongue feels thick and my brain turns to mush. I like you, Simone. A lot."

I stared at him. I would've never guessed that Brady's gruff exterior hid a romantic soul. My mouth had gone dry, so I licked my lips. The action drew Brady's attention. His eyes went dark and I saw his Adam's apple bob as he swallowed.

"I like you, too," I said. My voice had gone husky.

He grinned, and my nonexistent heart went pitter-pat. I liked Brady, I really did. But I had a bad feeling about this whole thing. Maybe a tiny part of me believed I didn't deserve another relationship. I didn't deserve love. And hell, it wasn't like Brady and I could be together forever. He was human. And I was vampire.

So whatever happened with Brady was just for fun. Hmm. Maybe, for a little, itty-bitty while, I could let myself have some fun.

"What's the real reason you came to see me, Brady?"

"We need your help with one of the posts. It's being stubborn."

"Why didn't you just call me?"

He jerked his head to the left, and I looked out the bay window. The outside lights shone down on the Vulcan like it was heaven's chariot. "I thought maybe you'd want a ride on Spock."

I glanced at him. Had Brady seen my longing when I'd been within reach of that sexy bike? Or was he just trying to impress me with his manly prowess? My belly squeezed in excitement. Oh, who cared! I wanted that ride more than my next breath (you know what I mean). And getting to put my arms around Brady was an awesome bonus.

"Yeah," I said, grinning. "Hell, yeah."

Chapter 4

From the field journal of Cpl. Braddock Linden Hayes
08 APR 98

The tattoo makes my skin itch. It feels strange, not at all like the other tattoo I got when I was seventeen. They removed that one—but not the memory of getting it, or why I put two intertwined hearts on my wrist. Shayla's been gone for five years. I shouldn't miss the tattoo, but I do. Just like I miss her.

Jesus. I hope like hell no one ever reads this damned thing. Shayla always said I was sentimental. Sentimental isn't allowed here. I'm glad for the structure, for the exhaustive training, for the way they beat the feelings right out of you.

The new tattoo is small, a series of black concentric circles with a dot in the middle. We all got one. We're the only five men chosen for this program. They want us to believe that the tattoo is the mark of the elite, but that's bullshit. I know a tracer when I see one. They want to make sure they can track their pet projects.

I guess I should stop writing my title as Corporal, though my men have yet to get out of the habit of addressing me as such. We don't have rank and none of us are attached to any military branch. We're invisible. Off the grid. That works for me. I don't have anyone—not since Shayla had the audacity to die. I don't think I've forgiven her yet. Who knows where I might be right now if she was alive. Damn sure not in the Nevada desert sweating my ass off.

Tonight, we begin the last of our training program. I don't know what else we can be taught—we've already learned hand-to-hand combat, weaponry, first aid, vehicular control (a.k.a. stunt driving), and survival techniques. You could drop us anywhere in the world and we'd know how to kick ass, which weed to rub in a wound and which one to cook, and how to repurpose a Volvo. "Repurpose" is the new word for "steal." Hah.

Fuck it. If getting marked like a stray dog, erasing my existence from the data banks of the world, and learning weird shit means we can take out the terrorizing bastards no one else can touch, then I'm all in. Shayla would hate that I joined the army and that I volunteered for this program. But I think she would also be proud of me. She said I was her hero.

I'm damn well trying to be.

Chapter 5

We sped along the empty road right through town. I didn't see a single person on the sidewalks or streets. Most folks were either in their homes or hanging out at the Consortium compound where the library and school were located.

The Old Sass Café was about the only place that got any regular business, and even it was empty of customers. After Ralph married Libby, he quit as the short-order cook and manager. He decided that raising a were-dragon might require more than the usual parenting skills. He was currently training as a dragon handler.

Phoebe Tate, who used to be the café's only waitress, had taken over as cook and manager. Marybeth was the new waitress. She was a Turn-blood, too—the daughter of Linda Beauchamp Michaels. Lorcan was her Master. He actually Turned Marybeth on purpose, at the behest of Linda. Look, it's a long story, okay? The point is that the Old Sass Café was under new management and the only viable business—other than mine—still operating on Main Street. The hope was that Broken Heart would become a real town again, populated by supernatural beings. I heard that there were a few paranormal towns in Europe, but none in the United States. 'Cept for us. And we weren't much to fuss about.

My arms were happily clenching Brady's muscled waist, my cheek pressed against his back. I heard his heart rate increase as he kicked up the speed another notch. He was enjoying the adrenaline spike, and so was I.

Heat slapped at us, punishing us for finding any sort of breeze in the sullen night air. I closed my eyes and pretended like I could breathe in the faint scents of honeysuckle and fresh-cut grass. The only thing missing was a big dose of sunshine. I loved to feel the sun warm my face. It's true. I liked baking my skin. When I was a teenager, I'd put on my bikini and slather on the baby oil. I didn't care about the sweat or the heat or the bugs, so long as I got to bask in the sun's rays.

Trading off the ability to tan, to breathe, and to eat probably wasn't much to give up for all that vamp mojo. Getting Turned was better than getting dead—*of course* it was. I just missed being a human. I wondered how long it would take to feel like a total vampire—or if I ever would.

Too soon, the ride was over. Brady took the bike over the field and stopped a few feet away from the damaged post. I hugged his waist a smidge longer than necessary. He held Spock, and I scrambled off. I removed the helmet, the one Brady had insisted on, and left it on the bike. Damian, Doc Michaels, and a few vamps from the build team stood around the post.

Doc was studying a component, flipping the piece over and over. Damian squatted next to the post and studied the side. He frowned as his fingers traveled from the top to the bottom.

"Hey, y'all," I said. "What's going on?"

"Sabotage," said Doc. He handed me the fragment. Whoa. The electronic parts were fried.

Damian shot Doc a look of frustration; then he stood up and faced me. "Maybe you have another theory?"

I knelt next to the post. It was cracked and both sides of the fissure were scorched. "Did you check the nearby posts?" I asked. "Are they the same?"

Damian shook his head. "Just this one." He glanced at Doc. "The damage does appear . . . strange."

Yeah. Like something had zapped it. I leaned down and peered at the bottom, then followed the jagged line to the top. The damage originated there. I displayed the piece Doc had given me. "Was this on or off?"

"Off," said Damian. "About two feet away."

The piece had once been part of the hinged lid. I looked inside the chamber; überelectronics should've glowed green. The rest of the components were also charred. Whatever had happened, it toasted the whole thing.

The Invisi-shield was designed to operate even if some of the posts went down. Brady said it could function at 75 percent capacity, but only for a few hours. The plan was to fortify each post with additional techno-security and Wiccan protection spells. But every single post had to work to get the system up and running. None of the extra protection measures could be put into place until they were all operational.

I looked inside the damaged cylinder again. I didn't really know what I was looking for—inspiration, I guess. Then I saw a speck of light at the bottom. I heard a faint buzzing noise.

Vamp vision was great, but I couldn't make out what was causing the yellowish light or the faint sounds. "Let's get it out of the ground and get it to the shop. We'll have to put a new post here." Although all the poles were ready to install, and yes, I'd made some extras, I still needed to figure out what had killed this one. We needed to make sure it wouldn't happen again.

I stood up and walked to Brady, who had stayed by the bike. His gaze made my pulse stutter (and hell, I'm dead). He took my hand and kissed my knuckles.

"Brady," I said, both pleased and embarrassed. "What are you doing?"

"Keeping a rein on my self-control," he said. "Do you know how sexy you looked . . . um, examining that post?"

"If you make a joke about me examining *your* post, I'm going to punch you."

He grinned. "I would never say such a thing." He leaned close and his lips grazed my earlobe. "Unfortunately, I'm a guy, so I can't help but think it."

I laughed. God, he was incorrigible. He let go of my hand. Then he turned and picked up my helmet, handing it to me. "Hey, Damian, can you make sure the post gets to Simone's workshop?"

"Yeah," said Damian. "You coming back?"

"If you were with the most beautiful girl in the world," said Brady. "Would *you* come back?"

"Brady!" What had gotten into the man? He never really smiled, rarely joked, and wasn't the talkative type. Now he was flirting with me, bragging about me to his friends, and acting all . . . happy. It was really freaking me out. In a good way. No, a bad way. Okay, a bad-good way.

Crap.

I put on the helmet and climbed onto the bike, wrapping my arms around Brady. He revved Spock (showoff), and the Vulcan roared as we took off. I yelped, then laughed and held on for my undead life as we sped across the field and back onto the road toward town.

Brady parked on the driveway, but he stayed on the bike as I wiggled off. I removed the helmet and shook out my hair. Then I extended it toward him. He lifted his visor.

"Keep it," he said. "For next time."

I clutched the helmet and stopped short of yelling, "Woo-hoo!" Instead, I smiled and said, "Okay."

"We're still on for tomorrow night?" he asked.

"It's Sunday," I said.

He tilted his head.

"I spend all day with the fam. Gran cooks a big dinner and then we play Yahtzee. I try to work on little jobs around the house. Gran usually has a long to-do list for me." I nibbled on my lower lip, feeling nervous. "So . . . um, can you come around nine?"

"Sounds like the perfect date."

"Good." What the hell was I doing? *Having fun.* Yeah. Fun. Anxiety skittered through me. I liked Brady a little too much to attempt casual and light-hearted. Besides, I'd never been the just-have-fun kind of girl. The only man I'd ever slept with was my husband. And before Jacob, I had rarely dated.

Brady slapped the visor down, then gave me a little salute. The Vulcan's engine revved, and that sexy roar vibrated right through me. Woo-hoo! I watched him take off, admiring both him and the bike. After he zoomed out of sight, I turned around and headed into the garage.

I couldn't believe I'd agreed to date Brady. I felt discombobulated. Okay. Wait. No need to feel that way. I pressed a hand against my chest and tried to suck in a steadying breath. Ouch.

Okay, so I couldn't steady my nerves. I'd learned my lesson about trusting too easily. I wouldn't make the same mistakes again. All I had to do was guard my heart.

While I waited for Damian to deliver the damaged pole, I tinkered on an old toaster. I thought the heating element was the problem, but it still didn't operate after I replaced the Nichrome wire coils. There had to be another reason the electrical circuit wasn't working. Hmm. Maybe something with the bread carriage or the spring—

"Simone?"

"Ahhh!" I jumped a foot (literally!) at the sound of a female's hesitant voice. I whirled around, wide-eyed. Sheesh! Had my vampire senses turned off? This was the second time in the same day I hadn't heard someone approach.

Darlene Clark stood behind me.

"Sorry, hon. I didn't mean to startle you."

She smiled at me, but since her fangs were showing, I wasn't exactly comforted. She was my height, though she tended to wear ankle busters that made her three inches taller. She had blue eyes, curly black hair, and even before she was a vampire, skin like cream. I'd never seen her in anything but dresses—and none of those were Wal-Mart specials. Darlene was a blood-sucking Snow White.

"Can I help you with something, Darlene?"

"It's my water," she said. She looked embarrassed. "The pipes are busted in the kitchen."

"Again?" I grabbed a wet wipe from the tub I kept on the worktable and cleaned my hands. In December, Darlene's kitchen pipes had frozen over and then burst. Her home was one of the oldest in town, right along with the LeRoy house, which had been relocated to the compound, the Silverstone mansion (the queen's digs), and the McCree farm. I helped plug the leak, fix the pipes, and then clean up the mess. Like I said before, the ol' water woo-woo came in handy now and again.

"I fitted you with new copper pipes. What in the world could've happened?"

Darlene nibbled her lip. "I don't really know."

Everyone in Broken Heart had the Oklahoma drawl, but Darlene's was thicker than most. Mine had been diluted by living in Nevada, but every now and then it crept into my words.

"All right," I said. "I'll meet you over there."

"Oh. Well, I have the car. You could just hop in." She smiled again, but her gaze skittered away.

Unease wiggled through me. "Why didn't you just call?"

"I guess I wasn't thinking straight. Marissa's playing with Jenny over at Jessica's house. I wanted to get it fixed before she got home."

Marissa had just turned seven; she was a year older than Glory. Her hair was a darker blond and her face more oval-shaped, but they looked a lot alike. Marissa must've taken after her father, whom Darlene had divorced a couple years ago, because I couldn't see anything of the mother in the little girl. Except maybe the propensity for fancy dresses and shiny accessories.

"I'm sorry, Simone." Her hands fluttered around her face. "I just get so scatterbrained."

"Looks like you skipped eating, too." I eyed her fangs. I always met my donor before I headed in to work. His name was Rick. He was twenty, working his way through med school, and was so matter-of-fact about the process, I didn't feel so . . . *icky* about the whole thing. I don't care how sexy the movies make it. Sinking my canines into the neck of some willing victim gave me the heebie-jeebies. But that's what vampires had to do to survive—and to tell you the truth, I'd done worse to ensure I'd live another day.

Darlene ran her tongue over her teeth. Her gaze fastened on my neck, and I flinched. Unease jack-rabbited right into freaky-deaky. I grabbed a wrench off the table, and her gaze lit up.

"Oh, good! You've decided to come with me."

No, I've decided to bash your skull in if you point those fangs in my direction. Darlene always was one brick short of a full load. Becoming a vampire hadn't given her any extra IQ points.

Darlene wandered toward my worktable. I scooted away, but kept the wrench in my hand. I was really popular today. I glanced at Darlene, who was studying the scattered tools with a disturbing intensity. Despite having daughters only a year apart, we lived now the way we had as humans—saying hi now and then, unless something needed fixing. Neither one of us had ever tried to arrange a play date. Most folks knew

Glory didn't talk, and she didn't really like socializing with anyone.

Come to think of it, neither did I.

Okay. All right. *Maybe* I was overreacting to the tension. Or maybe there was no tension. And yet, my inner alarm was clanging. I'd learned to listen to my instincts—and damn it, they were screeching like a cat in the grip of an affectionate toddler.

"Darlene?"

Her vacuous blue gaze met mine. She was pushing on one of her fangs and staring at me.

"Maybe you should go eat," I suggested again. "And I'll be at your house in, say, twenty minutes?"

"But the water . . ." She drifted off midsentence, her gaze meandering. As the seconds passed, she seemed to drown in her own thoughts. Then she finally said, "I suppose if you can't get there any faster, it'll do. I mean, I may need a whole new kitchen in twenty minutes."

I couldn't believe my ears. I swallowed the thorny knot of anger climbing up my throat. "On second thought, I suggest you call a plumber," I said sweetly. "I think the Consortium has one or two on staff."

She blinked. "What?"

"Call. A. Plumber."

Her mouth dropped open and her eyes lost their vacant look. "My goodness, Simone! There's no need to snap at me. Just call me when you're ready to pop by, okay?"

She spun around and left the garage, her high heels clicking disdain across the concrete floor. I had worked really hard not to lose my temper around folks. But I was beginning to wonder why I should be peaches and cream all the time, especially to people like Darlene, who didn't seem to know I existed unless she needed my skills.

I faced my worktable and tossed the wrench onto it. Anger beat a tempo at the base of my skull. I don't know why I felt mad. No reason to be, not really. Darlene's visit and dealing with the so-called sabotaged pole had just put me off-kilter. And . . . well, maybe my growing feelings for Brady figured somewhere into the mix, too.

My cell phone rang. I plucked it from the holster and flipped it open. "Hello?"

"Simone, it's Reiner. I'm bringing the damaged post to you. I thought I might throw a stone at two pigeons while I was there."

I puzzled over the odd sentence. *Oh.* I couldn't stop the chuckle. "You mean kill two birds with one stone?"

"Ah. Yes." He paused. "I have the design for the queen's gift, the one I hope you can help me complete."

Even though seeing Reiner again ranked between stepping on a rusty nail and licking an electric fence, I had to admit that I was curious about this project. I don't know why he thought I could help. Guess I was gonna find out.

"What do you think?" asked Reiner.

We'd been studying his carefully sketched plans for the last ten minutes. The object, at least on paper, was twelve inches high with a base six inches wide. Angled on the left was the statue of a robed figure holding a gnarled wooden staff; on her right side was a big black wolf. Suspended above them was a crystal orb. Reiner explained the statue was the Moon Goddess and her lover, Tark. The orb was a stylized moon. I glanced at him. "You want the woman to raise her staff and when she does, the orb will glow blue?"

He nodded. "I based the design on some of the ancient icons, which are still on display in the temple. There used to be many temples, just like there used to be many lycans and Roma. Now, there is only one temple—and not so many of us."

I knew that the lycanthropes were a dying race. At least, they had been until Patsy and Gabriel's union gave them hope. Of course, the *loup de sang* drank blood like vampires—and not all lycans appreciated that, er, quirk.

"You know, when we lived in our little village, I served my princes. I was their loyal bodyguard, their friend. I was also their best tracker." He smiled softly. "Better, even, than Damian." His tone was reminiscent, and underneath it, something I'd could only describe as yearning. "Do you know the story, Simone?"

"What story?"

"Sixty years ago, in the mountains of the Schwarzwald—the Black Forest—Roma and lycans lived together peacefully. Damian had married and was soon to be a father. After years of watching our women mourn and our children die, we had hope."

He snapped his fingers and the sound echoed in the stillness. "Then it was gone. Destroyed by the Ancient vampire Koschei and his Wraiths. Those who survived went elsewhere. Even the princes exiled themselves." Reiner's despair was so thick it coated every word. He traced the lines on the paper. "Their father was the last royal alpha of pure blood. Their mother was an American. She was the daughter of a royal and a commoner. In the very early days of our kind, such a match would've never been allowed. The royals are different genetically."

I nodded. I knew that because the Consortium had explained it at the same time they'd explained why they'd been unable to replicate the cure for the Taint. Right now, the only way to rid a vampire of the disease was to transfuse him with royal lycan blood. As far as I knew, only two vampires had received the treatment: Lorcan and Faustus.

"Is it true that werewolves were once guardians of vampires?"

"Lycanthropes have been around much longer than vampires. It is true that some vampires glamoured lycans as guards much the same way they glamoured humans as drones. Of course, the Consortium does not condone either practice. Patrick and Lorcan befriended us. They helped us when no one else would. And that is why Damian, Drake, and Darrius offer their skills and their loyalty."

"What about you?" I asked. The question startled both of us. I usually wasn't so nosy, especially not about someone I wasn't sure I liked.

"I joined the Consortium because I appreciated its vision, its goals. But I cannot help but think my people were meant for some larger purpose—and that we have lost our way. We are direct descendents from the Moon Goddess. Her blood runs in all our veins." He rolled up the paper and wrapped a rubber band around it. "I do not know why She allows our children to die or why She has blessed Gabriel and his vampire bride with fertility."

I knew right then he'd lost a child. The catch in his voice and the sorrow in his eyes told me so. Maybe when his village was attacked, or maybe just in the course of trying to raise a lycanthrope baby. . . . Who knew?

I never thought I'd ever feel anything but disgust for Reiner. I didn't want to admit that the man was capable of feeling as wounded as me. For a long time, I thought I had the market cornered on pain. After I'd escaped Jacob, I'd beaten my soul bloody with the spiked stick of regret. It was hard to let go of my guilt. Then I learned not so much to let go, but to bury it. What I'd done was still there, shiny and sharp just below the surface. Waiting for me to dig, waiting for me to cut myself and bleed out.

"I'm sorry." I meant the words, though I fought the urge to lay a consoling hand on his shoulder. We might both have painful pasts, but that didn't mean I trusted him. "Y'all have suffered so much, Reiner."

"You have no idea." His gaze flicked to mine. "Or maybe you do."

Chapter 6

"I see the shadows in your eyes, Simone. You think your smile can hide them, but no, nothing can ever hide that pain—not from someone who understands it."

"Let's not pretend we understand anything about each other," I said. "You've got your woes, and I've got mine."

"We are not so different."

"Yeah," I said softly. "We are."

Reiner inclined his head, an acknowledgment or a denial—I didn't know which.

"You will help me make the statue work?" he asked.

I wasn't sure agreeing to spend any more time in his presence was a wise thing to do. But I liked his idea, and I knew I could figure out how to get that staff to rise—clockwork parts, maybe—and that moon to glow blue. "A week isn't a lot of time. The festival's on Saturday."

"I have the parts already crafted. It is only a matter of putting them together and getting them to work."

"Okay," I said. "Come by on Monday around eleven p.m. and we'll get started."

Reiner grinned. "I look forward to working with you, Simone."

I wish I could've said the same about him. Instead, I just stuck my hands into my pockets and gave him my best Pollyanna smile. He looked at me an instant longer than necessary; then he left the garage, whistling.

I felt the tension drain from my shoulders. It was probably stupid to work with a man who caused such contentious feelings. I couldn't point to one single thing he'd actually done to make me not like him. It's just that my instincts were a-buzzin' again—and I intended to proceed with caution.

I looked at the cracked post sitting on my worktable. I really wanted to get started on it, especially since half the night was already gone. I wasn't sure Darlene still expected me, and if she was, too bad. I got out my cell phone, dialed the Consortium's headquarters, and asked for the plumber on call.

"That's Dunmore," said Arin. He was a nice older lycan who knew just about everything and had it all organized, color-coded, and filed. "He just moved into town a couple weeks ago all the way from England. He's a lycan."

"As long as he can fix water leaks, I don't care if he's the pope."

Arin laughed, said good-bye, and transferred me. The phone rang a couple of times, and then a brash English voice offered, "Dunmore's the name, plumbin's the game."

"I'm Simone. I run the garage on Main Street."

"I know you. You need me to come round and fix your pipes, love?"

"Uh, no. But Darlene Clark sure does. Did she call you?"

"No. Give me the address. I'll go on over and see what I can do."

I told him how to get to Darlene's house, and then hit END. One problem solved; a million to go.

I leaned over the table and patted the shiny black pole. "It's just you and me, buddy. And it's time for the autopsy."

I traced the jagged burn. I had no idea what had caused the damage. It was as if it had been zapped. Lightning? That made no sense. Magic. I knew the Family Ruadan had some ability to create orbs and other objects from fairy magic. But I'd never seen anyone, not even an Ancient, just . . . *kapow* something. I peered down the broken top. The light I'd seen on my first examination was still there, but much fainter. So was the buzzing noise.

I didn't want to split it open or cut it in half. It might be possible to save the internal electronics, either to build another Invisi-shield pole or some other kind of electro-whatsit. I couldn't stick my hand down all the way to the bottom and pry out whatever was lodged there.

Crap.

I grabbed a mini flashlight (I had several) and pointed it down into the post. The tiny glow and its buzzing stopped. I turned off the light—and they returned. Weird. As much as I didn't want to mess up the delicate internal electronics, I was itching to know what the hell was going on.

Usually, I'd get out my plasma cutter, but Velthur had taught me a trick or three. I could use my Family power to create a water "laser" that was faster and more accurate (and okay, more fun). I kept a bucket of water near the worktable, and in no time I'd created a thin ribbon of water that sliced the post like a hot knife through a cold stick of butter (Mmm . . . butter . . . on fresh baked bread with a dollop of jam).

The post dropped into two pieces. I propped the bottom half up and peered into it. The light at the base was easier to see and the buzzing easier to hear. I couldn't quite figure out *what* was flickering. It wasn't the electronics. They glowed blue, and this light was goldish.

Then I noticed a thin red string stuck on the far side. I plucked it from where it had snagged and followed the material down. My forefinger pressed something pointy.

"Ow!" I yanked my hand out, and up came the string. The tiny cut on my finger healed instantly. My attention returned to the thread. Dangling at its end was a big, black thorn. I looked at it in amazement. "What the hell are you?"

"Pixie trap," said a tiny voice. "Thank Brigid you figured it out. And I thought humans were dumb."

I looked down. The gold light was perched on the edge of the work table. I could just make out a humanoid shape—and only because I had vamp vision. To human eyes, it probably looked like sunshine glinting off a spinning coin. "Um . . . hello?"

"Now, don't go makin' me change me mind about humans." The voice was so small, I couldn't determine if it was male or female. The light rose from the table and hovered in front of my nose. "You saved me life," it announced, "and so I am yours until I can return the favor in kind."

"What?"

It sighed. "I'm *sidhe*, okay? And you saved me. I'm bound to you until I save your life. That's how it works."

"How what works?"

"The baking of delicious cakes and fruit pies," said the fairy in disgust. "Magic, you idiot. And here I thought bein' beholden to a human wouldn't be so bad—not like the giant. Always steppin' on me, and once the bastard accidentally swallowed me. We're immortal, for the love of Brigid! I don't die just because I have to sit for a day or two inside a giant's gullet. Only one way out, y'know. They don't have pixie therapy. I have to *live* with the trauma of being shit out the pimply ass of—"

"I get it," I interrupted. "So, are you *sidhe* or a pixie?"

"Same difference. *Sidhe* aren't just one kind. There's lots. Is this where we live?" It buzzed around, then returned to hover by my nose again. "By all the saints! You love dirt like the giant loved his brick cake. *Tsk, tsk.* I may be bound to you, but I refuse to live in squalor. Even the giant made me a nice nest, with lots of shiny things, and brought me honey every day. You do have honey, don't you?"

I wanted to ask *Do you ever shut up?* But instead I mumbled, "You got a name?"

"Spriggan."

Knowing its name wasn't helpful in determining gender, but really, did it matter? I had no intention of keeping it around. First, it was annoying. Second, it was giving me a headache. And third, it was annoying.

"Okay, Spriggan. You're free. I hereby relinquish you of all obligations to me. Go on. Shoo."

"I don't do *shoo*." It rose about an inch, directly in my line of sight. I crossed my eyes trying to stay focused on it. "You are never to shoo me again. Magic can't be bossed around. You can't change the rules. What would the world be like if there weren't *rules*?"

"Free of pixies?" I ventured.

"A comedian, are you? Gah! I should've never rescued the giant. If'n I hadn't rescued him, then I'd still have my nest and my shinies and my honey."

"And the possibility of another ride on the Colon Express."

I heard the tiny indrawn breath of indignation. "Goin' to be a sassy one, I see. Tell you what. You go on and get into life-threatening danger and I'll rescue you. Then we'll be free of each other."

"Is that really the only way to get rid of you?"

"O' course not. I just keep secret all the *easy* ways to end my bleedin' curse." He (er, she?) sighed. "I'm a pixie. Part of bein' a pixie is repayin' a kindness. It's not a choice, mind you. It's just the way it works. I've accepted it, and so should you. Now, where are you going to build my nest?"

"On a rocket ship to the moon," I said. I waved it away. "Just go flit around somewhere else so I can think."

"You can think?" it said. Then it spun away, giggling. I bet the giant had eaten the damned thing on purpose.

I probably should've called Damian or Doc Michaels to let them know sabotage wasn't the cause of the pole's malfunction. Instead, I dialed Zerina.

Zerina was a foul-mouthed, badass fairy, or *sidhe*,

who had tried to open her own sort of beauty shop. She didn't get much business because she followed her own creative muse when it came to hairstyles. If you saw someone walking around wearing a scarf over their head, then they'd probably gotten a Zee do.

She was not the vampire kind of *sidhe*. Maybe she would know more about my little problem—like how to make it disappear.

She picked up on the first ring. "Bloody hell! What do you want?"

"Hello to you, too." Was the natural disposition of fairies to be cranky and insulting? "I need your help."

"I agree. You need a makeover, and fast. You still wearin' those overalls and trucker's caps?" Her British accent was thick with censure.

I refused to be judged by a woman who looked like a magician's drunken assistant on her normal days. "I don't want a makeover. I want you to get rid of a pixie."

"I'm not a pest removal service." She paused. "Did you say pixie? Here, in Broken Heart?"

"No, in France, because I thought, What the hell? I like the Eiffel Tower and croissants and French accents. Of course it's in Broken Heart!"

"No need to get your knickers in a knot," she muttered, although she sounded more bemused than irritated. "It said it was a pixie, then?"

"Yeah. Well, it also said it was a *sidhe*."

"Blimey. I'll be right there."

"Look, I just wanted advice—"

The phone went dead. Argh! I snapped the cell phone shut. My skin prickled, and out of the corner of my eye I saw a spurt of pink sparkles. I spun around and watched Zerina pop into view. She looked like she was in her early twenties, with a neon pink haircut, pageboy style. Her eyes were pink, too. Today, she wore a neon pink bustier, black miniskirt, and zippered black calf boots with pink skulls on the sides.

"What's its name?" Her gaze was glued to the twirling and zipping and flickering gold dot.

"Spriggan."

She looked at me and grinned. "They're all called spriggan. It's what the Celts named the little buggers. Gold means it's a male. Females are silver." She glanced at me. "I haven't seen a pixie for almost a hundred years. Used to be you couldn't walk through a field without kicking up a cloud of 'em. They like nature. Really good at makin' things grow. Sorta like bees on steroids. Only they use their magic."

Aw, man. I didn't want a Pixie 101 class. Still, I found my curiosity peaked. "He said pixies were immortal. If they can't die, then what happened to all of them?"

"All *sidhe* are immortal," said Zerina. "Nobody knows why the pixies vanished. They just did. Why did this one pop up here? And why now?"

I didn't know the answers to either of those questions, and wasn't sure they mattered, anyway. I'd seen so much weird shit in Broken Heart in the last year that it was really hard to surprise me. After watching a dragon swoop out of the sky and destroy a Mercedes, pixies weren't all that impressive.

I showed Zerina the red string with its dangling black thorn.

She frowned. "Where did you find that?"

"Inside one of the Invisi-shield posts. Spriggan was stuck inside, at the very bottom. He said it was a pixie trap."

"Part of one." She looked up. "Oy! Get your sparkly ass down here." She took the string and dangled it in front of Spriggan. The little blur darted backward. "How'd you get to Broken Heart?" demanded Zerina. "And do tell, oh ye of tiny brain, how'd you get trapped?"

The gold dot zoomed to Zerina. "You can't just boss me around, you know. I'm not bound to you, only *her*—the one who saved me. And even *then*, I'm not required to put up with bad behavior. I refuse!" He paused, presumably to take a breath for another verbal berating, and then he cried, "Brigid save me! The outcast!"

Chapter 7

Spriggan zipped to me. Outrage bristled from him; his gold light blinked furiously. "Remove her from my presence immediately."

Zerina and I weren't exactly pals, but right now, I liked her better than Spriggan. "Everyone's welcome here," I said. "What's your problem?"

"She is an abomination!"

"Well, in this town she's in charge of the beauty shop, and if you don't pipe down, I'll let her do your hair."

He issued a tiny "Hmph!" Then he shot to the ceiling, the epitome of pissed-off fairy. I heard his teeny mutterings and rolled my eyes. I looked at Zerina. "You wanna tell me how to make another pixie trap?"

"That's your question?" She laughed. "I don't know what to make of you, Simone Sweet. He tells you I'm an abomination and you don't even blink. Aren't you curious about his accusation?"

"I make my own judgments," I said, "and no as-sumptions about folks. Besides, words are just words."

"You're wrong. Words are power. That's why he won't tell you his name. If you know it, he'll have to do all that you say—because if you did save him, then he's your shiny little slave until he repays that kind-ness." Her pink gaze assessed me. Then she nodded, as if she'd made some sort of decision. "Sit down. I'll tell you a story."

I had a sofa tucked into the corner. I led her to the beat-up old thing, then curled into one corner of it. She sat on the other side and crossed her legs. Her leather boots rubbed together as she adjusted her position. She didn't look at me. Instead, her gaze was on the ag-itated pixie.

"I'm more than four hundred years old. That's very young for my kind. Most fairies have been around for-ever. The gods created them, just the same as they cre-ated oxygen and amoebas and mountain ranges."

I knew the story of Ruadan, the first vampire. Even before he was Turned, he was *sidhe*. More than four thousand years ago, he'd died on a battlefield and his mother, the goddess Brigid, begged her own mother, Morrigu, for the life of her eldest son. I'd met Brigid once. And even though I knew she ex-isted, I couldn't quite shake my own belief system. I'd been raised a Christian, although there's not much room in Christianity for vampirism. Not in a good, demon-free way.

"But Ruadan . . ." I muttered.

"Yeah. His dad, Bres, was half-human. His human blood made him weak. He died trying to take over Eire. That stupid war killed him and his sons. If Brigid hadn't made a bargain with her mother, Morrigu, who is older than time and scary as hell, he wouldn't be walking around. Neither would any other vampire." She waved her hand dismissively. "The *sidhe* are many. And they've bred with humans and other creatures. Pixies, however, aren't born. They're magic incarnate. A gift from the gods to the Earth. Until they disappeared."

"Maybe it's like the honeybees," I said. "They're disappearing, too. It's called colony collapse disorder. The adult worker bees just . . . fly away. And you know the weird thing? Predators like the wax moth don't go into the CCD hives and take the honey. I think it should bother us. The bees disappearing like that."

Zerina's pink eyebrows nearly touched her hairline. "You must watch the Discovery Channel a lot." She smiled to show she was joking. I smiled back, but truth was, I watched the Discovery Channel all the time. "But yes," she said, nodding, "maybe it is like that. Maybe the pixies removed themselves from the world."

I pointed to my new friend. "Except him." Spriggan had zipped to the far end of the garage, presumably to stay as far from Zerina as possible. "He said he was bound to a giant."

Zerina's expression was pure shock. "There aren't any giants. Not anymore."

Wasn't that what happened to species over the course of time? They either died out or evolved to fit the changing world. Then again, paranormal creatures didn't really fall into the same categories as the rest of Earth's creatures.

"As I was sayin'," continued Zerina, "pixies were made by the gods. It's one of the reasons the little bastards are so arrogant. Blessed with noble purpose by their makers, and all that rot." She snorted. "But me? I was made by humans."

My mouth dropped open. I snapped it shut, but I couldn't stop staring at Zerina. She wasn't a real fairy? She sure acted like one. "How is that even possible?"

"Alchemy." She stretched her arms over her head and yawned. I knew better than to believe she was bored. I had never heard this story. I bet no one in Broken Heart knew it, except maybe Gabriel. Zerina had been part of the group who'd arrived with him last November. They'd all been outcasts, for one reason or another. Now they weren't.

At least, I'd thought that was the case. It never occurred to me that Zerina might still feel out of place. Not that she tried very hard to fit in or make friends.

She didn't seem interested in saying more. Or maybe she just needed to be prompted. "So you mean like the sorcerer's stone kind of stuff?"

"Yeah, but not in a Harry Potter sort of way." Zerina's expression bled amusement. "Alchemy was more a medieval thing, but most men interested in the mystic mumbo jumbo followed Hermes Trismegistus. You know, the *Emerald Tablet*?"

I shook my head.

"I don't want to bore you with the history," she said. "The sect that created me built their beliefs around the elementals, creatures of fire, water, earth, and air. They called air elementals sylph.

"As far as I know, I'm the only one. And I'm certainly the only one ever created by a hermitic order of humans who got the formula right. I think they were just as shocked to see me as I was to see them."

I stared at her. Here was a woman, an otherworldly creature, fashioned by mystics—or rather, plain ol' human beings using mystical knowledge. I was in awe. "Is that why Spriggan calls you an outcast?"

"I've been called worse," she said. "No, he's upset for a good reason, I suppose." She blew out a breath. "The humans . . . well, they used pixies to make me."

It took me a minute to process Zerina's words. "You said pixies were immortal," I pointed out. "They can't be killed. Right?"

"The law of conservation of energy."

I looked at her blankly. Hey, I may understand mechanics, but that didn't mean I was a physics genius.

"Energy cannot be created or destroyed," recited Zerina. "It can only change form."

Realization dawned and I felt my stomach squeeze in horror. "Oh, my God. They transmuted the pixies into . . . you?"

"Got it in one."

"Oh." I began to see why Spriggan was so repulsed by Zerina. What if she was made up of the essences of his friends and family?

"If you think about it," she mused, "no one can be killed, not really. We all just . . . change form."

My thoughts were inexplicably drawn to the death of my husband. I shuddered to think what his essence changed into—nothing good, I was sure. Evil perpetuated evil.

"You need to call in the Mod Squad," said Zerina as she popped to her feet. "They're gonna want to know about your pixie problem."

"Yeah," I said. Gah. Nothing like presenting another issue to a pregnant, crabby, lycanthrope-vampire queen to make a girl's oh-so-fun day even better. "You got any hints about the care and feeding of pixies?"

"Hide your jewelry, because they like shiny objects, especially anything silver or gold. They eat honey and like to sip on morning dew drops."

"Are you serious?"

"Unfortunately," she responded. "Pixies are fantastic gardeners, if you like that sort of thing. Also, if you show them any kindness, they have to repay it. And that little spot of joy is all yours till he saves your life. Pixie traps are nasty magic. He was probably dying when you plucked him from the post."

"Terrific."

"No good deed goes unpunished." Zerina chuckled. "Even though he's bound to you, you can only really boss him around if you know his true name. And he owes you a wish."

"What? Like a genie?"

"No. Like a fairy. Well, like a pixie. Magic has rules," she said, reiterating what Spriggan had already told me. "And pixies are pure magic. Sunshine of the gods. And pains in the asses for the rest of creation. All the same, he owes you a wish. You caught him."

"How many do I get?"

"One per customer," said Zerina.

I nodded. "Right. Because magic has rules."

"And I have a sense of self-preservation," she said. "The last time I saw Patsy, she was threatening to rip off the tail of the next lycanthrope who asked if she needed any help. Especially any who suggested a wheelbarrow might be in order for transporting her."

I laughed, then slapped my hand over my mouth, slightly ashamed. "Whoever said that to Patsy must be suicidal."

"Drake always was a risk taker." She grinned, then

waved to me. She disappeared into a poof of pink sparkles.

I unhooked my cell phone and started dialing.

I just loooooooved meetings with bureaucratic big-wigs. No, really. Ten people staring at me, then at the pixie, then at the damaged post, then at me (shampoo, rinse, repeat) . . . woo-hoo. Fun on a bun. Patsy, Gab-riel, Damian, Doc Michaels, Jessica, Patrick, Eva, Lorcan, Brady, and our just-visiting-from-Russia Consortium Chairman Ivan Taganov stood in my garage. I mentioned the ping-pong staring part, right?

The only nice thing about the whole shindig: Brady stood so close to me that I felt the heat emanating from his body. I also heard the strong beat of his heart. He smelled earthy, the tang of sweat mixing with his scrumptious male scent. And beneath it all, *with* it all, the ferruginous succulence of his blood.

"Simone?" asked Patsy.

I shook off my thoughts (since when had I started thinking of Brady as a snack?) and turned toward Patsy.

"Let me get this all straight." She rubbed her belly, looking really tired for an immortal being with über-power. "You found a pixie. You rescued him, and he said he's yours until he saves your life. Then you called Zerina—God help us—and her big contribution was to tell you he's a dude."

"And he's the only one anyone's seen in a hundred years," added Gabriel.

I held up the red string. "*And* he was in a pixie trap."

Everyone's gaze turned to the string. I hadn't felt it pertinent to mention the whole made-from-pixies confession. Gabriel probably knew, anyway, but it was Zerina's story to tell.

"I've done a lot of research about the *sidhe*. If I remember correctly, pixies can't lie. And they must answer direct questions," said Eva. She was Broken Heart's former librarian and now schoolteacher. She was also married to Lorcan—yep, the very vampire whose craven hunger killed us all. I didn't hold it against him. At least he hadn't meant to nosh on us. He had the excuse of being out of his damned head.

"I don't know," I said. "Zerina was direct and he didn't answer her."

"Because he doesn't have to. He's only beholden to the one he owes. You."

I was silent as I considered Eva's words. I told the crew everything, skipping only Zerina's story about her origin. So they knew what the little gold dot had done from the second he popped into view. Well, except for his reaction to Zerina. That would lead to questions I didn't feel comfortable answering.

"I asked what his name was and he said Spriggan," I pointed out.

"Which is *one* of his names," mused Eva, smiling. "You must ask him his true name."

Zerina had said that I would have control over him then. Did I want control of the little booger? I guess I didn't have a choice. He was mine until God knew when. Ack!

"What about the wish?" asked Ivan, his Russian accent thick. His glacier blue eyes were on Spriggan, who'd retreated to the opposite corner of the garage. He couldn't leave because of his debt to me (oh, brother!), but he obviously didn't want to be the object of everyone's attention, either.

I studied Ivan covertly. He was a big man, nearly as tall as Brady, but much more muscular. He had black hair and was the only vampire I'd ever met with a goatee. I didn't realize I'd sidled closer to Brady until I felt his fingers curl around mine.

I guess Ivan's size and manner intimidated me more than I wanted to admit.

"Brigid is the one we should talk to," said Ivan. "She will know how to use the wish."

"Which belongs to Simone," said Jessica. "Besides, Brigid had some family business to attend to. She can't help us with this one."

Ivan's gaze flicked to the brunet. Jessica was mated to Patrick, and they unofficially ran Broken Heart. Or had, until Patricia had been named queen and took over the duties. The Consortium still had its hand in things around town, though. But they usually consulted and deferred to Patsy's wishes.

Speaking of wishes . . .

Jessica countered Ivan's fierce glare with one of her own. She fingered the gold half swords on her hips, looking as though she wanted to lop off his head. The swords had been created by Brigid herself from fairy gold. They were indestructible. And Jessica was really good at flinging them around.

"One damned thing at a time," said Patsy. "Simone, find out the little guy's name. Then we should get more cooperation. We gotta know why anyone would build a pixie trap when there aren't any pixies. And how the hell did he end up in one of the Invisi-shield posts?"

"Spriggan," I called. "Come here."

He floated toward us, obviously reluctant, and finally hovered before me. His glow dimmed—a sign of his petulance, no doubt.

"What's your true name?" I asked.

He sighed. "I am Flet."

"Who set the trap?" asked Patsy. "How'd you get here?"

Flet said nothing. I wanted to tug on his tiny ears. "Answer her," I said.

"Whatever you say, my liege," he said, his teeny voice dripping sarcasm. "I don't know who set the trap. Most people who set traps don't warn their prey ahead of time. Seems to defeat the purpose, don't you know."

"Flet," I warned. "Don't rant."

"Sure, an' take all the joy from me," he groused. "The circle wasn't closed, so I got out, but the blackthorn's poison slowed me down. I tried to magic my way into the post. You see how well that worked out."

"What do you mean, the circle wasn't closed?"

"When you invoke magic, you have to close the circle. The thread was the circle and the ends weren't touching."

"So, either someone's incompetent or they wanted you to escape." This observation came from Brady. He locked eyes with Damian, who nodded. Apparently, the lycan had been thinking along the same lines.

"How did you get here, in Broken Heart?" I asked, repeating Patsy's second question.

"Not sure. I saved the giant and then I woke up starving. There was honey, and I went for it, straight into the damned trap."

"Did he say giant?" asked Eva.

I nodded. "Zerina said there weren't any more."

" 'Tis true," said Patrick. "The last time anyone saw

one alive and walking around was more than four hundred years ago."

Hmm. Zerina had been created about that same time. Flet had known she was the outcast, but seemed not to know that the pixies and giants were no longer around. "Flet, where did you live before you came here?"

"Dorchester," said Flet. "Though me and mine have lived forever. We were part of the world before it was the world. We settled among the Dumnonii and lived peacefully in their kingdom for thousands of years."

"The Dumnonii were a Celtic tribe that occupied part of what's now Dorset," said Eva. "There's a very famous giant there, near a town called Cerne Abbas."

"Yes!" said Flet excitedly. "That is where last I lived. The giant rescued me from a spider's web and I became his for a time."

"Wait," said Patsy. She moved the hand rubbing her belly to her forehead. She closed her eyes and sucked in a breath. "There's a giant wandering around England?"

Eva laughed. "No. The Cerne Abbas giant is a chalk outline on the hillside. Many pagans claim it's been on the hillside since the second century, maybe even earlier, as a fertility symbol. It's more likely the giant was carved into the hillside four hundred years ago, perhaps representing Oliver Cromwell as Hercules. The giant carries a club and it's . . . er, naked."

"Jesus H. Christ," muttered Patsy. "I'm so not in the goddamned mood for naked anything." She patted her husband's shoulder. "No offense, babe."

"None taken," he said, drawing her into his arms.

She leaned her head on his shoulder and said, "I'm

cranky, hungry, and dragging ass here, folks. Let's get down to brass tacks already."

Four hundred years ago, the last of the giants had disappeared—and one had appeared as a drawing on an English hillside. Around that same time, Zerina had been an alchemical wet dream realized. Three centuries later, all the pixies were gone. . . . All but one. How did it all link together? Maybe it didn't. Shoot. It wasn't like I was Sherlock Holmes. Still . . . I narrowed my gaze. Flet flickered backward a few inches.

Then I asked softly, "What was the giant's wish?"

Chapter 8

From the field journal of Cpl. Braddock Linden Hayes
08 MAY 98

After almost four months of exhaustive preparation and instruction, we reported at five a.m. to begin the last phase of our training. Four more weeks of busting our balls, and we would finally be deployed to execute our purpose.

The General marched us to the field outside the barracks. Some poor bastard was blindfolded and chained to a metal post. The General explained that this guy, who looked like he'd wandered away from his IT department, was a vampire.

We laughed.

The General ignored our snickers. He said that vampires were real. In fact, he told us that most of the creatures of our childhood nightmares were not only real, but also considered paraterrorists. We had been training not as an elite counterterrorism assassination alliance, but as the first covert paraterrorism extermination team. (Yeah. We were ETAC PETs.)

We didn't laugh, not then, but we didn't believe him, either. I was starting to wonder if the last phase was all about the psych-out. What makes more sense? That they were fucking with our minds or that the schmuck who struggled against his chains was a vampire?

The sun started to rise.

And the guy started to smoke. And scream. And beg for his life. We stood at attention and watched as the sun fried his ass. He exploded into ash.

Nobody said anything for a long time. Then the General led us to Building 41. From day one, it had been made clear that B41 was off-limits. Anyone who attempted to enter the facility without clearance would be shot.

We were taken into a laboratory. Five of us and five upright metal tables. Shit. No way would anyone back out. We'd signed away our lives—so we fit ourselves into the slots and let the lab coats strap us in.

Nanobytes. That's what they called the tiny robotic critters they injected into us. The injections burned. It was like they were shooting acid into our veins. The one in the temple hurt the most. I didn't scream, but holy God, I wanted to.

The General said this was only the first round. Different nanobytes for different jobs, but there's a required seventy-two hours between injections. We walked back to the barracks, and I felt like I'd woken up from a three-day drunk in Tijuana.

It's too late to change my mind. And it's damned sure too late to regret. But I think we are in deep shit. Right up to our fucking necks.

Chapter 9

Everyone stopped talking to one another and stared at me. I couldn't be bothered with them. My gaze was on the pixie.

"He wanted immortality," said the pixie smugly. "He wanted everyone to know that he was a great hunter and virile man. So I gave him all that he asked for."

"Only he didn't phrase the wish quite right, did he?" asked Brady, catching on immediately.

Flet's ego had been engaged, and he answered Brady's question without my prompting. "He wouldn't make a wish until I'd saved him. An' I must grant a wish to the one who captures me."

"We get it," I said. "Magic has rules."

"And where would we be without rules?" Flet's glow flickered in irritation. "Chaos! Only one of our kind has magic without rules, and she governs chaos."

"How do you govern *chaos*?" blustered Ivan. "Pah! This little fool lies to us!"

"Morrigu is the Queen of Chaos," offered Lorcan, "which you well know, Ivan." He looked at me. "Go on, Simone."

I glared at Flet. "If you keep nattering on, I'll give you to Zerina," I warned. "Tell us about the giant's wish."

"I was!" He huffed indignantly. "Dunn was good at hiding, good at hunting, and good at staying alive all on his own. But the villagers wanted to be rid of him, so they poisoned their own sheep and he ate one. I saved him from death, and was free. But I still had to grant his wish.

"'I want to be immortal, Flet,' says he, 'and I want everyone to know that I am a great hunter—of game and of women.'" Flet's attempt to boom in a giant's voice wasn't all that effective. Still, the pride vibrating in his tone probably matched the giant's well enough.

"Oh, my God," said Eva.

"Yeah." I said, nodding. "The Cerne Abbas giant was once real."

"Was Dunn the last giant?" asked Eva. Her gaze was on Patrick.

He shrugged. "Possibly. We didn't return to Ireland until the late 1800s. Dad said he once met Fionn mac Cumhaill, who was a giant even among giants. Mostly, they kept to themselves and stayed out of the way of humans."

"No more giants?" asked Flet in a bemused voice. "The world is better off, then." This, from the little snot who'd tried to convince me his life had been grand as a giant's pet.

"And no more pixies," I said. "Did you get that part, too?"

Flet snorted. "Pixies were part of the world before it was the world."

"You said that already."

"Bears repeating, I say. Pixies are alive and well, and don't you forget it."

I dropped the subject. It dawned on me that Flet had repaid the giant's slights, real or imagined, in a clever and cruel way. No way did I want to be on the bad side of a pixie. Or a permanent fixture on an Oklahoma hillside.

Since Flet could neither tell us how he'd gotten from England to Oklahoma nor where he'd been for the last four centuries, Patsy ended the meeting.

"We've replaced the broken post, and it works fine. The Invisi-shield should be operational in time for the festival." Patsy's jaw cracked as she yawned.

I felt the pull of dawn, too. The closer it got to sunrise, the more tired I felt. That was the way of vampires. We had no choice about when we went to sleep or when we woke up. Although the older vampires got, the more strength and power they accrued. Some, like Patrick and Lorcan, could even tolerate weak sunlight.

"I think there's something going on and we need to stay alert," Patsy continued, "especially since we have guests coming in to town for the big shindig. Unfortunately for Simone, she's stuck with Flet. Sorry, hon. I can requisition a fly swatter, if you like."

"Hey!" protested Flet.

I laughed. "No. I'm sure he'll behave."

"Well, let's go home, people. The sun will rise soon, and I have a bucket of hot wings with my name on it."

I saw Jessica's look of longing and caught her gaze. "Yeah," I said. "It'd be nice to eat again, wouldn't it?"

As everyone else departed, Brady and I walked with Jessica and Patrick (and Flet) out of the garage.

"Sometimes I'll just lick a Godiva truffle," she said, her voice filled with yearning. "It makes me sick to my stomach, but God, it's worth it."

"You'll get used to our ways, *mo chroi*," said Patrick. "It's been only a year since your Turning. I don't even remember what food tastes like."

"I don't imagine the food you were used to eating was exactly good to begin with," said Brady.

Patrick laughed. "'Tis true. All the same, I have no cravings. At least you can still ask your donors to ingest gastric delights."

"Chocolate-tinged blood isn't as good," declared Jessica. She grinned. "That sounded really whiny, but I don't care. It's been almost a year, and I still want to stuff my face with champagne truffles. Do you know that Godiva makes a pumpkin pie truffle for Thanksgiving?" She groaned, and pressed her hand against her stomach.

"If only eating the food didn't make us throw up," I said.

"Plus, where would it go?" asked Brady.

"The insides don't really work anymore. The heart pumps when we feed, but most of the other organs aren't necessary," said Patrick. "If a vampire managed to keep the food down, it would just . . . rot."

"Gross. We know how it works, buddy." Jessica smacked Patrick on the shoulder. "If only that Invisishield had magic powers, too. Any vampire who stepped within our borders could suddenly eat with no consequence."

"Oh, man! I wish that could happen," I said, thinking of the big dinner my grandmother would cook tomorrow. All I'd be able to do was smell it and salivate (figuratively, of course). "I wish we could all eat again. And that it would just disappear. We'd get to enjoy it, you know? Then it would magic away."

For a moment, Jessica and I contemplated the very idea of enjoying real food again. Then Brady squeezed my hand and I jolted out of my revelry.

"We better scoot," said Jessica. She looked from me to Brady, her eyes sparkling. I don't know what she was thinking, but knowing Jess, it was something embarrassing. Like Brady and me . . . doing things together. Once again, I found myself experiencing a blush that wasn't real. I couldn't blush, but my cheeks really wanted to. Whatever we did, it was no one's business 'cept ours. Small towns, paranormal or not, didn't allow for much privacy. Yet I'd still managed to keep my secrets just fine.

"G'night Simone. Brady." Jessica's grin widened. Patrick nodded to us, the same knowing twinkle in his silver eyes, and then he wrapped his arms around his wife. They faded out of sight in a shower of gold sparkles.

"That's a neat trick," said Brady.

"The perks of being *sidhe* and vampire." I let go of Brady's hand long enough to turn and lock the garage and then the office. Then I dropped my keys into my pocket. Brady led me past his Vulcan (sexy, sexy now), walking around the back side of the building to my little truck. Flet was in a much better mood than I thought possible, especially after getting bullied by us mere humans. He flitted this way and that, exploring the area without a care in the world.

"So, we're still on for tomorrow?" asked Brady.

"Of course." We loitered near the truck. Even

though I needed to get home, I was reluctant to start the trip. Brady's eyes were on me.

Nerves plucked my stomach like a harpist pulling on gilded strings. Wait. This was Oklahoma. Think Johnny Cash strumming the opening chords to "Walk the Line." That was me. My stomach wobbling. My heart trying to thump (and failing). My knees knocking. Hoo, boy.

"Time to say good-bye, I guess," I murmured.

"I had something different in mind," whispered Brady.

"Like what?"

"Hmm." He stepped closer, his gaze never leaving mine. I might not have a heartbeat, but I could hear his. *Thudthudthud.* How could Brady possibly be nervous about approaching me? It gave me such an odd thrill to know that I affected him as much as he affected me. I had never considered my own feminine power. I had been with only one man my whole adult life. Jacob. And I'd never felt . . . well, giddy with him.

Brady invoked emotions that I'd thought forgotten. I understood lust, though I don't think I'd ever experienced it. Wanting Jacob was the same as wanting security. I needed to be taken care of, directed, and loved. At least, I thought he loved me. Honestly, I didn't know anything about love—not the kind of love I saw between couples like Jessica and Patrick. A real, healthy relationship—that was something I didn't know how to cultivate at all.

Well, well, well. Hadn't I decided Brady was gonna be fun? God. I couldn't just have a fling, and I knew it. I didn't want to back out, but I wasn't sure I could go forward, either. Stuck between a rock and a hard place—or rather a bruised heart and a handsome man. Same difference, really.

"Where do you go, Simone?"

"What?" I blinked and found Brady leaning against the truck, mere inches from me.

"You do that a lot." He tapped my temple. "You just . . . wander away."

"I have a past," I blurted. Shit. Why'd I say that? Well, then. In for a penny, in for a pound. "I go there, even though I don't want to. I'd rather forget it all."

"We all have pasts. We all have regrets, too."

"I know." I dared to reach out and touch his shoulder. Warm. Firm. Muscled. My fingers drifted down his arm and back up again. I placed my palm against his neck, felt the rapid pulse that beat there. For me.

My fingertips skirted his jaw. His skin felt rough, the shadow of a beard protesting my light touch. Brady's nostrils flared and his eyes darkened. He didn't make a move, though. He let me touch him. His heartbeat revved again; his muscles tensed. Patience was not his virtue. Brady was a warrior. He was a man who went after what he wanted—the hunter, the conqueror, the hero. And yet he stood there, every part of him bristling with the need to take the lead, and let me do as I wished.

Excitement spiked in my stomach.

Or was that terror?

Something primal and hot kicked up inside me. Had I said I hadn't felt lust? Brady sure inspired a lot of it. I want to wrap myself around him and just . . . nibble. Lick. Taste. The thought of piercing his throat with my fangs made hunger twist inside me. I could smell his blood; hear its rhythm as it pulsed through his veins. Brady was my aphrodisiac. For some reason, when I thought of feeding on him, it didn't squick me out. In fact, it kinda turned me on.

I let my gaze rove the corded muscles of his neck. Sweat trickled, probably because of Oklahoma's insane humidity and heat. Summer was a bitch. My nostrils flared. I'd never thought of sweat as sexy, but the musk of it, the dance of it on his flesh was intriguing.

My mouth went dry and I licked my lips. Brady's gaze was drawn to the motion. He lifted his hand to cup my chin. Slowly, he drew his thumb across my lower lip. I barely resisted the need to suck on that digit. Again, I had the strangest urge to sink a fang into his flesh.

I wanted to drink from him. I wanted to taste his essence on my tongue, absorb it into my body. I wanted to strip him bare and worship him.

Whew. Day-amn. I needed to get a hold of myself. I dropped my hand at the same time I withdrew my face from Brady's gentle snare. I intended to step back, to break whatever spell wove its magic on us.

Brady refused to be rebuffed. He reached out again and took my hand, tugging me until I was flush against him. Had I the ability to breathe, my lungs might've given out right then. Emotions tangled: excitement and fear, desire and reluctance, need and caution.

My palms flattened on his oh-so-muscled chest. God, he was warm. I hadn't realized how much I missed my own heartbeat, my own breath, until I stood here, toe-to-toe with Brady, and felt the life pulsating within him.

I thought about what he said about the past and regrets. He wasn't a man without his own secrets.

"What do you regret, Brady?" I asked softly.

"Not kissing you," he answered. Now, that was an excellent response, but it also completely avoided the question. I needed to learn that technique.

But Brady had other things to teach me.

"Step on my feet, short stuff," he said. He was at least six inches taller than I was, and standing on his thick-soled boots gave me a nice boost.

He wrapped his arms around my waist and gathered me close. That's when I felt his erection. It pressed against my belly, thick and urgent. My thoughts skittered. Not that we could have sex—I mean, not all the way, because as much as I liked Brady, marriage was out of the question. I couldn't bind myself to a human, and no way could I Turn him.

"You're doing it again," he murmured. "You don't have to worry about the past."

Yeah, I did. In a big way.

"I was thinking more about the future." I licked my lips again. "Where could this . . . whatever *this* is . . . possibly lead, Brady? Maybe it's not the right thing. You and me."

I cleared my throat, trying to swallow the damned knot clogging it. Leave it to me to be all practical in a romantic moment. I stared up at him, but he didn't seem deterred.

"Kiss me," he demanded softly. "Then you can tell me to fuck off."

His lips skimmed mine. The tender assault caught me off guard. I clutched his shoulders, my knees going mushy. No worries about falling; Brady's arms were snug around me.

My vampire body was bereft of the usual human responses to arousal. No breathlessness. No spike in blood pressure. No frenetic pounding of the heart. All the same, my body hummed in expectation. Despite my lack of body temperature, I still felt heat stab my belly.

Another brush of his lips.

The heat traveled south, pooling in a part of my body that hadn't seen action in a long time.

Whoa.

The third time Brady's lips met mine, they stayed there. Soft pressure. Then moving away. A breath. His. And then again, the capturing of my mouth, this time longer.

I clung to him, not a true participant in the endeavor. It wasn't that I didn't know how to kiss. It was that I was swept away by him.

Had I thought he wasn't patient? How stupid. The man had plenty of patience.

"Simone," he whispered. My name sounded like a prayer. Then he went in for another mouth-to-mouth assault (*ohwowohwowohwow*). His lips opened slightly, an invitation for me to do the same. I gladly RSVPed, and then his tongue swept inside and joined mine. He tasted like peppermint. And faintly of coffee. (I missed coffee so much, darn it!) His tongue dueled with mine (because love is a battlefield). He was tender but relentless, and oh, so good at this kissing thing.

He thrilled me all the way to my toes. I felt like I was having my own personal earthquake.

He drew away, a centimeter or two, took a breath, went in again. Every nerve ending in my body tingled. My nipples hardened and poked into Brady's broad chest.

He noticed.

Brady groaned, drawing away yet again, his breathing harsh, his lips wet and swollen, his eyes glazed. I imagined I looked the same way. I sure felt like I'd been set on fire from the inside out.

His heartbeat was frantic, his muscles tensed. And I think his erection had gotten bigger. Hoo, boy. Even if we could have sex, I wasn't sure I could ride that monster.

Yowzer.

"We better stop," I said. "I need a cold shower as it is."

He grinned, man pride etched all over his face. "Me, too." He loosened his hold enough for me to step off his boots. He didn't let go of my waist.

"What's it gonna be, Simone?" he asked. "Will you give us a chance?"

Chapter 10

Sunday, June 16

From the moment I awoke, Brady's questions circled my thoughts. *What's it gonna be, Simone? Will you give us a chance?*

I'd said yes. Was it a lie? A hope? An actual beginning? I didn't know. But I felt lighthearted. And dare I say . . . happy? Yeah. Happy.

Even though daylight savings time meant that the sun didn't set until eight or so, I usually popped awake by seven p.m. My vampire self recognized night as night even though the sun didn't do us the courtesy of going away for another hour. I couldn't go outside until it did. And we'd made sure all the windows were covered with thick curtains. Gran lived in the dark, anyway, and Glory didn't seem to mind the adjustments we'd had to make. She understood I was different now. I wish I'd been able to accept all the changes as easily as she seemed to have.

When I entered the kitchen, Flet was sitting on Glory's shoulder and watching her scratch a brown crayon across a page in her SpongeBob Squarepants coloring book. Glory was very precise, using only the colors that matched the characters on the cartoon itself and always staying within the lines.

To my surprise, Flet had taken instantly to Glory and she to him. He didn't seem to care that she didn't talk; in fact, he probably enjoyed having the full run of the conversation.

A bear-shaped honey bottle and plate drizzled with its sticky goodness sat on the table. Flet shot over to the plate, shoved a handful into his mouth, then zoom, back onto Glory's shoulder.

I leaned down and kissed my daughter's head. "G'morning, sweetheart."

She looked up at me and smiled.

"Hello, Flet," I said.

" 'Tis evening, you know," he said in response. "You vampires sleep far too much. And pixies are day creatures. I can't live a life in the dark. I need the sun, for the love of Brigid!"

Glory looked at her new friend and put a finger to her lips. Flet shut up. Well, I'll be damned.

They returned their attention to coloring. I joined Gran at the stove. She'd already started dinner preparations. Rick would be here soon, so I could get my pint. I'd enticed him into the Sunday arrangement by loading up some GladWare with Gran's cooking.

Man, oh, man, I wanted to swipe a finger through those mashed potatoes. The roast beef was in the oven, stuffed into a plastic bag with onions, carrots, celery, and spices. The smell of cooking meat drove me crazy.

It seemed cruel that being a vampire took away your ability to eat, but not your desire for food.

Being blind hadn't slowed Gran down, not even in the kitchen. She'd figured out everything she needed to know to put together meals, and off she went. I wrapped my arms around her shoulders and kissed her cheek.

"That smells so good." If I had the ability to drool, I'd be doing it right now.

"I just hate that you don't get to eat no more," said Gran.

"Yeah. What's immortality when you can't suck down a slice of apple pie and homemade ice cream?"

"I wish you could eat, honey. I really do."

I looked at my grandmother, who was cutting up tomatoes with impressive skill. I realized that Flet owed me a wish. And with it, I could give Gran back her sight.

"If you could see again, would you want to?" I asked. God, that sounded stupid. Of course she'd want to see again.

"If a miracle restored my vision," said Gran in her patient, all-in-God's-time way, "I would rejoice."

How about a fairy wish given by a grateful grand-daughter? Although Gran would probably say that was the instrument by which God's will was done.

"Flet," I called.

I heard his tiny sigh; then he slowly floated to me. "Yes, my liege?"

"That never gets tired," I snapped. "Cut it out, all right? I want to make my wish."

"You already did." He turned and headed toward Glory. I reached out and snatched him by a tiny arm. He yelped.

"I did not make a wish, you little f—" My gaze shot to Glory, who was staring at me with quirked eyebrows. "*Fairy*," I finished through gritted teeth.

Flet's tiny expression looked ashamed. Oh, crap. Not good. "Spill it," I demanded. "Now."

He pointed and made a circle with his forefinger. A mirror the size of a cantaloupe appeared. Its gold rim shone as if just polished. The glass rippled and then I saw me and Jessica. We stood outside the garage with Patrick and Brady. I recognized the setup from last night.

"*If only that Invisi-shield had magic powers, too,*" said Jessica. "*Any vampire who stepped within our borders could suddenly eat with no consequence.*"

"*Oh, man! I wish that could happen,*" I replied. "*I wish we could all eat again. And that it would just disappear. We'd get to enjoy it, you know? Then it would magic away.*"

The mirror disappeared. I poked my face down into Flet's. I don't know why I could see him better today than I could yesterday. Maybe he was allowing it, or maybe I was just getting better at focusing on him. Either way, now I could see that he had short blond hair, eyes the color of earth, gossamer wings spun from gold, and he wasn't wearing any clothes. Terrific.

"Before we get into this, I want you to put on some clothes."

Flet looked as though I'd asked him to dip himself in acid.

"Pants. Shorts. Something to cover up your ding-a-ling if you're gonna hang out with my daughter. *Capisce?*"

He wiggled his fingers and a pair of brown shorts appeared on his tiny self.

"Better. Now . . . we're talking loophole, right?" I asked. "I said 'wish,' and you took it upon yourself to grant it, knowing that it wasn't official."

" 'Tis true," he admitted.

"As much as I miss eating, I would've much preferred that you restored Gran's vision. That wish could've been used to help someone with a real problem, Flet."

His mouth set into a mutinous line. He didn't like being upbraided, but too damn bad. He was my pixie, I was stuck with him, and he wasn't going to act like a petulant toddler.

"Can I trade the wish?" I asked.

He shook his head. "The rules of magic and of pixies cannot be broken. One wish. Once granted, 'tis done forever."

He glanced at Gran, who continued with her dinner preparations. She didn't seem to mind that the little bastard had cost her the opportunity to regain her sight.

"All vampires can eat human food so long as they are within the borders of Broken Heart, as defined by the Invisi-shield. As you wished, once swallowed, the food will be magicked away."

If he'd hoped to cool my ire by reaffirming the wish I hadn't wished intentionally . . . He. Had. Not. He flinched, his eyes going wide when I shook his little leg. His whole body flapped back and forth.

"Hey, now," he protested. I stopped, mostly because Glory was still watching me anxiously, her tiny bow lips pulled into a frown. Argh! I didn't want to be accused of shaken pixie syndrome.

"I lost my wish to your pettiness." I said. "You owe me."

"Only until I save your life."

"Oh, no. This isn't about repaying a kindness. It's about compensation for doing wrong. You got me?"

Flet stared at me, tiny arms crossed. There he was, cute (but so was Ted Bundy) and magical (in a bad way) and immortal (thus forever annoying), and I waited for him to blast me with his fairy crankiness. Instead, he said, "I am sorry, Simone. Though I cannot give you another wish, I shall find another way to make up for my . . . wrongdoing."

Even though he'd choked on that last word, he sounded sincere. Somewhat mollified, I let his leg go. "Thank you, Flet."

He nodded, then flew back to Glory. She used her pinky to pat him on the head. His glow brightened, and once again, they both focused on coloring.

"I'm sorry, Gran," I said.

"Don't worry about it, child. God's will is being done. If it is His plan that I see again, then it'll happen."

I really didn't want to get into another God discussion. I'd gone from true believer to reluctant skeptic. How could there be God, the God of my upbringing and religion, and also creatures not mentioned in the Bible? I'd met a Celtic goddess, and now I sorta owned a pixie who was supposedly made by the gods (as in, more than one).

"Stop worrying," said Gran. "You'll find your way again. And when you do, you'll find God, too."

Yippee.

Gran held up a spoon and I looked at the creamy mashed potatoes piled on it. They were still hot, and steam rose from the starchy goodness. I could smell the butter; she must've use two sticks of the stuff.

Gran laughed. "Go on, Simone."

When I had first Turned, I'd been unable to resist trying food every now and again. I yarked it all up and felt miserable even after the purge. After a while, I accepted the limitation of my vampirehood.

"Whether you intended to or not, you got your wish." Gran waggled the spoon. "I'm not gonna hold this all day."

I stuck the whole thing in my mouth. Oh. My. God. How could I have ever taken for granted the creamy deliciousness of simple mashed potatoes? It tasted like nirvana. I licked the spoon clean.

Gustatory repercussions were usually swift, and I waited for the cramping and nausea. As pissed off as I was at Flet, I had to admit eating again was way cool. I stalled making a mental list of favorites I'd stuff my face with. I wanted to make sure the wish was just as Flet said.

"How you doin' there?" Gran asked, her voice laced with humor.

"I'm fine. No, I'm great." I grinned and did a little jig. "I can eat again!"

After I sucked down a whole bowl of mashed potatoes, I whipped out the cell phone. The first person I called was Jessica. I explained how the wish was made and that I'd eaten without a single gastrointestinal consequence.

"You've been smelling gasoline again, haven't you?" Jessica asked. "I told you that it would rot your brain."

"We've seen a zillion weird things in the last year, Jess. Out of all the crap you've witnessed, *this* is what's unbelievable?"

She paused. "Good point."

"Tell her about the potluck." Gran had gotten out more ingredients and started making more food.

"Gran's inviting everyone over for a potluck," I said. "Bring your favorite dish, your kids, and your appetite."

"Shit. You're not kidding." She laughed. "All right. I swear to God, Simone, if this is a joke, I'll skewer you myself."

"I wouldn't joke about gorging on Godiva chocolate."

"Oh, my God. I'm so eating a truffle. Right now. Bye." She hung up.

Chuckling, I scrolled down the address book and started dialing.

By the time I'd finished calling everyone, I was starving. Not for food, but for blood. The ability to eat was an illusion. A pixie magic trick. It didn't nullify our natures or satisfy our appetites.

It was approaching nine o'clock. Rick was late, and Brady would be arriving soon—as well as just about everyone else in town. I really wanted to have the whole slurping-of-blood thing out of the way before everyone got here.

While I'd been making phone calls, Gran and Glory kept busy pulling out the extra set of dishes and clearing off counter space. When I was human, we'd never invited anyone over. I'd been too afraid to reveal too much about myself or my family. I had trust issues. Big time.

Even though I wasn't entirely sure about having an impromptu potluck, I couldn't deny the joy it was bringing Gran. She'd sacrificed a lot for me and Glory. Seeing her genuinely happy made me happy, too.

"Knock, knock," called Brady's voice from the living room.

"Come on in," I called, smoothing my dress. Glory clapped her hands, then ran out of the kitchen, presumably to let her favorite friend into the house. She must've forgotten that Flet was on her shoulder, and he squeaked in protest as she took off. Then he shook his tiny self and zipped after her.

As was our habit, we always left the main doors open. The screen doors kept the bugs out and let the Oklahoma night air inside. I kept the air-conditioning on high, and didn't mind paying a little extra for the pleasure of having the best of both worlds.

There was something magical about nighttime in Oklahoma. No, really. I wanted a little of the magic (without withering away in the damned heat). The night was as black as Starbucks' double espresso, the stars floating in it like shiny dots of cream. The breeze brought with it the smells of my adopted state: sweet honeysuckle, verdant earth, the sting of pine.

I heard Glory squeal in laughter, and Brady chuckle. Then his boots clomped on the wood floor as he neared the kitchen.

I stopped short of asking Gran how I looked—and not because she was blind. It was more a matter of revealing that I cared what Brady thought about my appearance. It made me uncomfortable to think I wanted to please him.

I'd decided to wear a pink summer dress. It stopped above the knee, and its thin straps tied around my neck. I wasn't a high heels kind of girl, but I had a pair of sparkly pink flip-flops. After my shower, I'd given myself a rare pedicure (pale pink, of course). Hey, I'm a girl. I'd left my hair down and brushed the strands until they shone. I'd even put on some light makeup.

Brady appeared in the doorway, Glory clinging to his back, her small face alight with joy. Flet hovered about Glory, not looking particularly thrilled that his charge was so enamored with Brady.

Brady's gaze took in everything, from my long hair to my pale pink toes. His expression was worth every bit of time I'd taken with my appearance. He mouthed the word "Wow!" and his eyes went all dark and hot.

My stomach knotted. Oh, baby. I did a little curtsy, smiling up at him.

"Hello, Brady," said Gran. "Didja hear the good news?"

I hadn't called him because I figured I could tell him everything in person.

"Not yet," said Brady. "You look gorgeous as usual, Elaine."

She turned and waggled a spatula, her wrinkled face going red. "Smooth talker. Glory, girl, leave the man alone, and come help me with the biscuits."

Glory scuttled off his back and skipped to her grandmother. In her hand, she clutched a daisy. Carefully, she put her flower aside and dragged the step stool to the sink, where she washed her hands. Then she used her foot to push the stool next to her grandmother and stood on it, leaning down to peer into the mixing bowl.

Brady had given my daughter a flower. My heart squeezed. The man was so thoughtful. Something I would've never believed when I met him in February.

"I have something for you." Brady left the kitchen briefly and returned with two bunches of flowers. One he handed to my grandmother, and the other to me.

"They're beautiful," I said. Warm fuzzies pummeled me until I felt all toasty and cottony. I got vases out from underneath the sink then filled them with water.

"Thank you, Brady," said Gran as she inhaled the fragrant bunch of wildflowers. "They smell wonderful."

I arranged the plants on the table, which drew Brady's attention to the number of settings. His eyebrows winged upward. "You expecting more company?"

"Yeah," I said.

Flet had been drawn to the flowers. He flew over them again and again and gold dust fell onto them. They brightened, straightening up in the vases. Whoa.

With Glory and Gran busy making biscuits, and Flet distracted by the flowers, I figured it was a good time to duck out. I took Brady's hand and led him out the back door. On one end of the huge enclosed porch were Gran's lemon trees, and on the other, a large swing that I had built and tethered myself.

We sat down, and I told him about how Flet had granted the wish, thus allowing vampires to eat again, while at the same time taking away my ability to make another wish. All because he was annoyed with me.

Brady shook his head. "Hotheaded little bastard."

"Well, he did seem genuinely sorry about what he'd done."

"Being sorry doesn't fix the situation."

"There is no fixing the situation. There's only looking at the bright side of what's been done."

Brady smiled. "You are an optimist."

Hah. If he only knew.

We sat hip to hip. The warmth of Brady's thigh

filtered through my dress and scuttled up my leg. His arm was draped around my shoulders.

Crickets chirped. The breeze rustled the wind chimes dangling around the perimeter of the porch. Gran had a real thing about wind chimes; she couldn't see, so she wanted to enjoy every sense she had left.

"You look so beautiful," Brady said.

Pleased by his compliment, I looked up at him. He licked his lips, his eyes dark with the same longing I'd seen earlier.

"What? I'm not equally fabulous in my overalls and tennis shoes?"

"Oh, hell no. I'm not getting caught in that girl trap." His fingers drifted across my cheek. "Every time I see you, I'm struck breathless by how pretty you are."

"Good answer," I said.

He kissed me gently, ever Mr. Patience. Seeing as how he'd walloped me last night with that mouth of his, I figured I'd try a little payback. Nervous but determined, I moved my lips down his jaw.

He shuddered.

Wow. Since I was being all Miss Brave, I put my legs over his. Brady called me on that bet, then anted up by pulling me onto his lap. Now I was cradled under his jaw, my shoulder pressed into the crook of his arm, and my palm flattened on his chest. His heart revved, and if that wasn't evidence enough of his arousal, the jeans-clad erection snuggled against my thigh sure enough was.

"Simone," he whispered into my hair.

I kissed his jaw, slid my tongue along its curve, and then went down, lower, to taste his neck. He smelled delicious. Beneath my lips his carotid artery pulsed.

Life. *Blood*. Mmm. I was so hungry. As much as I didn't want to admit it, no amount of mashed potatoes in the world could ever satisfy me. Not like the exquisite delight that was a human's blood.

This moment right here, the moment when my fangs descended, the moment my inner beast rose and sniffed, licked, *wanted* . . . yeah, this was when I felt most like a vampire.

"Simone," murmured Brady. His hand tangled in my hair.

I was the seductress. The predator. Pleasure rushed through me. Under the hand I had pressed against his chest, his heart beat frantically for me. I abandoned that—it reminded me of his humanity—and grasped the other side of his neck. He willingly angled it to the side.

I kissed the tender spot where the artery pulsed in invitation. Then I flicked my tongue across it.

Brady moaned.

I did, too. Hunger gnawed at me. And Brady seemed willing enough. And though I'd only ever drunk from two people (Master Velthur and my donor, Rick), I wanted to literally taste this man. This wonderful, sexy, delicious man.

I clutched him, my nails raking the skin as I sank my fangs into Brady's succulent neck.

Chapter 11

From the field journal of Cpl. Braddock Linden Hayes
17 JUNE 98

Finished our first mission tonight. It's goddamned stupid to write down any of the details—"plausible deniability" is our liaison's favorite fucking phrase. But the good thing about working in such a tech-heavy unit is that no one worries about paper and pen. If it's not digital, they don't give a crap. No one would believe the kind of weaponry, shields, and technology we have. All that UFO crap the nut jobs talked about at Roswell? I've seen the saucer and damn, it's badass. What I find really hard to believe is how anyone on Earth is smart enough to reverse engineer. Yeah. Think about that one for a minute.

The mission went off without a hitch, but it felt wrong. We were driven to the remote location. Our vehicle was blacked out, and we arrived in a densely wooded area. We were given the coordinates and the go-ahead. The targets did not expect us. Five men, three women. Our Invisi-shields protected us and sure as hell confused the targets.

After we finished the mission, we destroyed the bodies and their campsite. As instructed, we took the infant. The little guy didn't look well. He didn't even cry. I don't know what they wanted with him. My hope is that one of the bastards I work for has a heart and plans to relocate the child.

Goddamn it! If those people were paraterrorists, I'll eat a whole pot of Henneman's diarrhea-special chili. They moved fast and they were strong. They sensed us even though they couldn't see us. Lycanthropes. But only one of them shifted—the female who protected the baby. The rest had to be Roma, cousins of the full-bloods and only able to shift during full moons. What I don't get is why a full-blood was hanging out with Roma. They're not exactly tolerant of each other—at least not according to the intel we received.

I don't feel right about what happened. We killed a goddamn mother! I want to puke out my guts. It didn't matter that she was a lycan. Shayla would hate what I did, what I've become. Hell, I hate me right now.

The other men in my unit haven't said anything. We're not a touchy-feely bunch, for Christ's sake. We know how it works. We do our jobs; we keep our mouths shut. And we never, ever tell anyone who we are or what we do.

And we sure as shit don't keep diaries.

Chapter 12

"Simone! No!" Brady wrenched away from me.

He startled me so badly, I fell off the swing. Hurt stabbed me, literally, as my ass hit the porch, and emotionally as I faced Brady's abrupt rejection. I stared up at him with wide eyes, my pride wounded.

"Don't do that. Not ever." He wiped his neck, then drew his hand away and stared at the blood. He went white. "Jesus Christ," he muttered.

Guilt flooded me. Did he have a thing about blood? Him? A big, tough soldier? It didn't make any sense.

"It heals," I said, my voice quivering. "It won't leave a scar."

"You can't drink from me. Do you understand?"

Mortified, I nodded. Fear seized my voice, my ability to move. I'd heard that same darkness in Jacob's tone, right before he hurt me. I wanted to curl up into a little ball and cry. What had I done? I just snacked on Brady, that's what. I'd assumed he was okay with me feeding on him, which was stupid. Embarrassment broiled me.

Brady surged to his feet, then leaned down. I flinched and turned my face away.

"Simone?"

All my earlier bravado (Seductress? Predator? Hah!) was gone. "I'm fine," I said, staring at the grit-covered boards on which I sat. Gran swept the porch every evening, but it was difficult to keep it clean. "You better go wash your hands."

"I'm not leaving you on the floor." He squatted next to me. I was grateful he didn't try to touch me. He sounded soothing now, his manner gentled. "I'm sorry you fell. I'm sorry I . . . overreacted."

"I said it's fine."

"Simone," he said softly. "Forgive me."

I finally glanced at him and saw how he was look-ing at me. Sincerely. With concern. He seemed to know that I didn't want him to get too close. Would I ever trust again? How much time would pass before I could forget what happened to me? To my family?

"Only if you'll forgive me," I said. "I shouldn't have done that. Rick didn't show up, and you stir my ap-petites. All of them."

I don't know why I confessed that to him. For some reason, it caused relief (yep, there was desire there, as well) to glimmer in his gaze.

His lips hitched into a grin. "Don't get me wrong," he answered. "I liked it." He shook his head. "My blood is . . . infected."

Come to think of it, Brady tasted a little metallic, like I'd licked a pipe. Yet his blood was also more deli-cious than Rick's, rich like devil's food cake slathered with chocolate icing (metal shavings on top).

"Infected?" I worried my lower lip. "Are you okay?"

"I'm fine. It's not how you think. It's complicated." He studied my face. "May I help you up now?"

He offered his unbloodied hand, and even though I didn't really need his help, I accepted the gesture. We stood, and I let go of his hand and stepped back. He seemed to recognize I wanted distance, and he didn't try to crowd me.

"Simone?" called Gran. "Guests are arriving, child."

"Be right there!" I called back.

"You . . . uh, have some blood on your mouth," Brady said. He pulled a handkerchief out of his front jeans pocket. I took it and dabbed my lips.

"Keep it," he said when I tried to hand it back. "I have a lot of those."

I studied the white cloth and saw the initials BH stitched in the corner. "It's kinda old-fashioned."

"My mama raised me right." He was trying to lighten the mood, and I appreciated it.

"We better go in," I said. Brady extended his arm in an after-you gesture. I turned around and went inside the kitchen.

I was still hungry. I hoped Rick had arrived because I really needed my pint. I didn't want to make another mistake. And I never wanted to hurt Brady again.

The party had been in full swing for more than an hour. Rick never showed up and he wasn't answering his cell phone. Even though I gorged on pot roast, green bean casserole, corn on the cob, and sweet potato pie, hunger gnawed at me until all I could think about was sucking on a juicy artery.

After returning to the house, I'd separated from

Brady and had managed to mingle with my friends while avoiding him (and trying to make it seem like I wasn't).

Nearly everyone had shown up, including Patsy and Gabriel. I'd never seen people enjoy food the way the vampires were, and since we weren't required to digest, there was no limit on what we could shove down our gullets.

Tables and chairs had been set up outside. Someone, one of the lycans, maybe, brought a grill. The scent of cooking meat seemed to entice everyone, and every so often a groan of appreciation would roll through the crowd.

The best thing about the whole event was that Glory was playing with the other kids. Firefly tag had ensued, and my baby girl ran and jumped and squealed. It didn't seem to matter to the kids that she didn't talk. And to see Glory being social and liking it brought me a heart full of joy.

"She's doing well," said Eva.

I turned and found Broken Heart's schoolteacher standing beside me. In her hand was a plate filled with three slices of pie and one slab of cheesecake. She saw me notice her dessert indulgence, and she laughed.

"Carb heaven," she said, sighing contentedly. "And it'll never glue itself to my thighs." She ate some of the cheesecake, closing her eyes as she savored the bite. Then she pointed the fork in the direction of the kids. "You thinkin' about enrolling Glory in school?"

"I don't know," I said. I watched Glory tag Jenny, who was Jessica's daughter, and giggle as she turned and ran. Flet bounced along with her, his golden light never far from her. My baby seemed so happy. "She's still not talking. This is the first time I've seen her even want to be around other people."

Eva nodded. "Our classroom is small, and even though we do a lot of typical coursework, I'm very informal. I think Glory would find it fun. Maybe, if she's around other children, she'll decide she wants to talk."

I wondered what she'd say. I wondered if all our secrets would spill from her lips, a purging of what had come before, of what had been done to her. Of what I had done to her father. My stomach clenched. I couldn't be afraid anymore. Jacob was dead. Technically, so was I. Glory deserved a life with security and love and friendship—even if that meant facing my past head-on.

"I'll talk to her to about it," I finally offered. "And if she wants to give it a try, I'll call you."

"Excellent." Eva looked down at her plate. "If you'll excuse me, I think there's a piece of German chocolate cake with my name on it."

I smiled. Across the yard, I saw Brady talking to one of the lycanthrope triplets. Considering the serious expression of the one manning the grill, he was certainly Damian. I had to assume Brady was chatting with either Darrius or Drake. He seemed to sense I was watching. He glanced up, his gaze on mine, sharing a look with me that I'd seen lovers like Jessica and Patrick share. It made me all warm inside (oh, baby), but I couldn't forget what had happened on the porch. I'd overstepped my bounds, but Brady had scared me. I couldn't let that go. It wasn't fair. He didn't know about Jacob. He couldn't begin to follow rules that he didn't know existed. But that was how I felt. It was probably best, then, that we keep our distance.

Brady clapped the lycanthrope on the shoulder and

headed in my direction. Shit. I looked around for something to do, someone to talk to, and saw Elizabeth Bretton peering over one of the tables laden with our impromptu feast.

Elizabeth kept to herself even more than I did, though she was always very nice whenever she made an appearance. She was a handsome woman, in her early forties, which was the result of vigorous self-care, good genes, and, as she once told us, "a marvelous plastic surgeon." Vampirism had made her beauty permanent—no need for any more surgical enhancements. She had shiny auburn hair cut short and designed to frame her lovely face. Her eyes were brown, and reminded me, oddly enough, of just-baked brownies—warm, inviting, and sweet. Elizabeth was the last remaining Silverstone, though she'd never tried to claim the mansion or property that rightly belonged to her family. Rumor had it that her estranged husband and daughter were in Europe. Elizabeth lived in a modest cottage inside the compound and had become Zela's (yeah, *that* Zela) assistant. She probably had better vampire training than all of us.

I glanced out of the corner of my eye. Brady had reversed directions and now weaved through the crowd of women hovering around the dessert table. You'd think there was a shoe sale over there.

I hurried over to Elizabeth. "Hey, there! How you doin'?"

Elizabeth looked up. "Just fine, dear. Oh, my. You're getting a little fangy. Haven't you eaten?"

"My donor never showed up."

Elizabeth's eyes flashed concern. "You know, I haven't seen Darlene or her daughter, either. Seems like everyone is here except those two."

And Rick. Anxiety rippled. Why hadn't he shown up or called? And where had Darlene gone off to? Surely she wouldn't miss a party. She loved parties.

"I left a message on her voice mail," I said.

Reiner had stopped Brady and engaged him in a conversation. I could see the frustration etched on Brady's features. Hmm. That Reiner was starting to grow on me. Not that he'd helped me on purpose.

"There are plenty of donors here," reminded Elizabeth. "I suggest you find one."

"Great idea. See you later." I whirled around and headed toward a knot of people by the creek. They dispersed before I could insert myself into their midst and hide. Shit.

"How's it goin' with your pixie?" asked Zerina.

I nearly jumped out of my skin. I spun around and slapped a hand to my chest. I glared at her. "Where the hell did you come from?"

"Thought we went over that." Zerina laughed. She looked like Courtney Love today: kohled eyes, pink-striped minidress, hole-filled black stockings, and pink wedge heels that were at least five inches. Her hair was spiked and the tops of the spikes were black. "What's got your knickers in a knot? Would it be that lickalicious Brady who's headed your way?"

I looked over my shoulder. He'd gotten stalled again, this time by Glory, who clung to his legs like a Lilliputian latching on to a giant invader.

"Why you runnin' away from him?" asked Zerina.

"Do you really care?"

She considered this. "Not really." Her pink eyebrows soared. "Oy. Your fangs are showin'."

"Thanks for the update." I walked away, trying to

seem casual, and headed toward Jessica. She sat alone on a fold-out chair with a gold box on her lap.

"Hey, Jess."

She looked up at me, her expression similar to that of a heroin addict who'd just shot up. (Discovery Channel, people—watch it, already.) Her lips were smeared with chocolate.

"How many of those one-pounders have you had?"

"This makes three," she said, clutching the box. "I know, I know! When you consider all that's wrong in the world, it seems completely selfish to enjoy a wish gone wrong. It's really, really wrong to suck down three boxes of Godiva truffles. But I have to say, Simone, I am sooooo fucking happy right now." She plucked a chocolate from the box. "See this? This is an edible orgasm." She shoved it into her mouth. From the look on her face, I could well believe it. I liked chocolate, too, but wow. That was some serious love right there. Her eyes popped open. "You want one?"

"No," I said. "Enjoy your diabetic coma."

She grinned. "Thanks to you and that dumb-ass Flet, I won't ever have to worry about having one."

I left Jessica to her truffles. My hunger was acute now, and I knew if I didn't find a willing neck soon, I might just gnaw on the nearest one.

"Hey, Simone!"

I might've been able to ignore the voice had it not belonged to Patsy. I trudged toward her. She and Gabriel stood near the front porch. Another gentleman stood with them. His gray hair was pulled into a long ponytail. He wore the most garish yellow shirt (with pineapples on it, thank you) I'd ever seen, and paired it with black shorts. He also wore hemp flip-flops.

"This is George," said Patsy.

I peered at him. He looked familiar. Like that comedian. I considered what I was thinking. Nah. I held out my hand. "Nice to meet you. I'm Simone Sweet."

"Groovy." He shook my hand. I considered him again, and realized he was a vampire. Holy moly. At what human age had he been Turned? He looked at least seventy.

"George will be opening up a facility here in the next year," said Patsy. Her lips couldn't decide whether to smile or to grimace.

George nodded. "It's for vampires who were Turned after the age of sixty. Not many of us, mind you—probably forty or fifty—at least in the United States."

Who would Turn a senior citizen?

He seemed to realize what I was thinking. He laughed. "Man, we all have our stories. Not all of 'em nice. But even though we have all the powers and our bodies are strong, we weren't made youthful again."

"Seventy forever?" I asked.

"Yep."

"So . . . the facility is a home for elderly vampires?"

The man hooted and slapped his knee. "No, man. We're opening up a nudist colony."

Chapter 13

"Seriously?" I looked at Patsy.

She nodded. "Broken Heart's getting ready to be the safest place in the world for all paranormals. If a bunch of old bloodsucking farts want to walk around naked, I don't give a shit." She narrowed her gaze at George. "As long as you do it only in the designated areas. I don't need children traumatized." Her brows went up. "Or me. I don't want to be traumatized, either."

George put his hands up. "Whatever you say, Queenie."

"Have you eaten?" asked Gabriel, staring at me. He tapped his mouth. "Your fangs are showing."

"So I've been told. Rick, my donor, never dropped by."

"You can have my neck," offered George. He leered comically. "I'm very well aged."

"Thanks," I said, "but I always keep my vintage blood in its original bottle."

George chuckled, then his gaze was drawn to something behind me. "Yowzer. Who's that good-looking mama?"

I turned and saw my grandmother standing on the porch steps with Libby and Ralph. Their toddler twin boys were settled in the grass a foot away, playing happily with wooden trains.

"The redhead?" I asked. "That's Libby, and that guy next to her is her *husband*, Ralph."

George shot me a look that questioned my IQ. "Not her. The other hot-looking chick."

"*Gran?*" I sputtered, my gaze swinging toward my grandmother. Her gray hair was pulled into its usual bun, her skin looking as though someone had created it out of crinkled paper. She was dressed in a blue shirt and khaki shorts. Her feet were encased in her favorite blue house slippers. I don't think she even owned a pair of real shoes. "Whoa, buddy. You better suck in those fangs. That's my grandmother."

"Her name's Elaine," offered Patsy, because she was evil. "She's really nice."

I turned to glare at Patsy. She shrugged. Her lips pressed together as if to stall a smile; merriment twinkled in her blue eyes.

George took off and I took a step after him, but Patsy said, "Oh, leave him alone. He's harmless, and your grandmother's entitled to have a little fun."

"Vampires aren't harmless." I stopped, watching George introduce himself to Libby, Ralph, and Grandma Elaine. Then my two friends defected, claiming their toddlers as they went off to the buffet.

Damn it.

George was a little too close to Gran, and I don't know what he whispered, but she actually blushed.

He didn't seem to care that she was blind (or old) or human (or old). Guilt snaked through me. She'd sacrificed so much for us. I felt protective, but also uncertain. Gran was more than capable of taking care of herself. And honestly, I hadn't seen her smile like that in a long time. I supposed that flirting didn't really have an age limit.

Defeated, I turned back to Patsy and Gabriel. Another person had joined them. I knew right away he was human. He smelled like one, and I heard the beat of his heart, the air in his lungs. I licked my lips, then realized I'd done it. I was starting to feel a little like Wile E. Coyote chasing after the Road Runner.

"This is Shawn," said Patsy. "And this here's Simone." She pushed him toward me. (Way to be subtle, Patsy.) "He's a new donor. I suggest you get acquainted."

The idea of gnawing on Shawn's neck squicked me. I mean, introducing your meal to your vampire was like that scene in Douglas Adams' *The Restaurant at the End of the Universe*. You know, the one where the cow comes to the table and insists Arthur choose his cut of meat? Yech.

Shawn was tall (but then nearly everyone was compared to me) with sandy brown hair, kind brown eyes, and a lean build. He seemed nice enough, but I wasn't too interested in his outsides. I wanted what was chugging through his insides.

"Is there somewhere private we can go?" asked Shawn.

I nodded. I was starving, but I was also nervous about taking a pint from this guy. First-date jitters, if you will.

"Simone?"

Shit. Brady had finally caught up with me. I looked over my shoulder, smiling widely. "Hi there."

He held out his hand to Shawn. "Braddock Hayes."

"Shawn Coburn." He flinched a little at Brady's hand squeezing.

Their hands dropped and then awkward silence ensued. Brady's expression was thunderous. Oh, come on. Did he really think I was gonna go off and do something sexual with this guy?

"Shawn's a donor," I said, stopping short of adding, "And I'm really hungry, so go away." I tilted my head at Mr. Don't Ever Suck My Blood and raised my eyebrows in a do-you-mind gesture.

He relaxed a smidgen, but he still didn't look happy.

"Okay, then. We gotta go." I waggled my fingers in a wave that took in Brady, Patsy, and Gabriel and got my ass outta there. I headed toward the house. No, not there. Where else? The barn. I didn't particularly like the place, but it was farther from the house and offered some privacy.

I walked through the backyard, Shawn following, and headed up the little hill toward the barn. My skin prickled the closer I got to the dilapidated building. It had once been red, but most of the paint had long ago chipped away. Here and there was a spot of color, like the damned thing had measles. The left door listed, hanging at an angle.

The dark gap looked like a monster's grin.

"Here," I said, going around the left side. We were still protected from everyone's view without having to traverse the barn. The tree line was a few feet away, which added to the ominous *Friday the 13th* feel. You know, like Jason would jump out any minute and hack us to death.

Shawn looked around, obviously nervous. With vamp vision, dark wasn't really dark. I realized to Shawn it appeared pitch-black. The kind of dark you didn't want to be alone in with a vampire.

"Let's just get this over with," I said. I felt like I was cheating on Brady because my lips would be on Shawn's flesh, and on Rick because I was sucking someone else's blood. *Good lord, Simone, you are a piece of work.*

"What do we do?"

I narrowed my gaze at him. "Haven't you done this before?"

"First time for real vampires. I used to be a donor for the wannabes."

"Wannabes?"

"Yeah. You know the Vampyre Raige?" He pronounced it "vampire rage" and spelled out the words for me.

I shook my head.

"They used blades." He held up his right arm and I saw thin white scars all over the pale flesh. "Anyway, it doesn't geek me out or anything. Though I've never had anyone use their fangs before." He thought about his own statement. "Real fangs. I've been punctured with the dental fakes."

"I don't think this is a good idea." I didn't want to pop this guy's vampire cherry. I just wanted my pint, and then I wanted to avoid Brady until I felt better about what had happened between us earlier.

"No, no, it's fine," said Shawn. He bent his neck and lowered himself so he was fang level to me.

Well, how could I resist that invitation? I sank my fangs into his artery and blood gushed into my mouth.

Ugh!

I yanked away from him so fast, blood spurted. He slapped his hand over the wound and stared at me, wide-eyed.

I spit out as much as I could. It tasted so foul . . . like I was swallowing sewage. I wiped my mouth, then glanced at him. "What the hell did you eat?"

"N-nothing," he said. Blood was leaking from between the fingers covering his neck. He looked pale and scared.

"I'm sorry," I said. "It's just . . . you taste weird."

"The Vampyre Raige loved my blood," he said, sounding offended. His lips started to tremble and his skin went even whiter.

"Your neck's still bleeding?" I asked. I grabbed at my hip to get my cell phone and realized I hadn't clipped on my holster. I figured it would've ruined my dress. Stupid girly vanity.

"Where's your phone?" I asked, panic rising. Jesus, he looked bad.

He shook his head.

"Okay. I'm gonna get help. You'll be all right."

What was Shawn supposed to say? Yeah, I believe the vampire who injured me? I had to make it right. I stumbled around the corner. My dress and hands were spattered with blood. I was feeling nauseated and dizzy.

"Simone!"

I heard Brady's voice coming from inside the barn. I really needed to put on the vamp speed and get to someone, anyone at the party.

"Brady," I managed. "Why the hell are you in there? Shawn needs help."

"So do I. Hurry!"

I stopped at the gaping doors.

Fear mamboed up my spine and did a soft-shoe on my scalp. I grabbed the right door and swung it open. I stepped inside, anxious. The dusty air was tinged with the scent of manure. It felt thick, too, like a slimy blanket dropped onto my skin. I saw moldy stacks of hay, leftover farm equipment, toppled boxes, and damaged crates.

No darting shadows, no maniacal laughter, no ectoplasm-coated walls. And no Brady.

I felt the feathery touch of evil. Light, teasing, deadly. I swallowed the knot in my throat, too afraid to move deeper into the barn. Something terrible had happened here—and I didn't want to know the details.

Metal screeched. Then I heard *crack . . . pop . . . whoosh.*

The left door had been leaning on top of its companion. Without that support, it broke free of the rotted wood and rusted hinges. Had I remembered that I was a vampire with überspeed, I might've gotten out of the way. Instead, like an idiot, I threw my arms in front of my face as it came down on top of me.

When I awoke, I was on my side, the big wooden door pressing me into the hard-packed earth. Pain attacked me with the ferocity of hungry wolves, biting and tearing every inch of my battered self.

I shoved the door off me so hard it hit the wall of the barn and shattered. Wood flew everywhere, and I turned face-first into the dirt to avoid the shrapnel. Damn it! Was it even possible to make a good decision today? Dirt plumed in the air, disturbing the mustiness that lingered in here. If anything, I'd made it smell worse. Grit sandpapered my tongue and clung to my teeth. Yech.

Aching all the way to my pinky toes, I sat up. Vampires healed quickly, but I hadn't had my pint yet tonight. Feeling better wouldn't be instantaneous. At least I hadn't broken anything, which was a miracle.

Obviously, my hearing was damaged because I'd sworn I heard Brady call me in here. Nausea still swished in my stomach and I felt off balance.

With my head throbbing and my stomach threatening the dry heaves, I got to my feet and brushed off my dress. Didn't do much good, though. I was filthy. Dirt streaked my arms and stained my dress, right along with the blood. I could only imagine what my face looked like. My right hip throbbed and I pressed my fingers against the sore spot.

The aches and twinges were fading. Pain stabbed my knees and vibrated up my spine, but at least I could walk. The way that barn door hit me, I should've been dead.

Well, deader.

But even though the ol' vampire corpse was healing itself, it wasn't doing a damned thing about how sick I felt.

I heard a pain-filled groan and realized I'd forgotten all about Shawn. Damn it! What kind of thoughtless bloodsucker was I?

I scurried out of the barn and back to the young man. I fell to my knees and gave in to my stomach's demands to vomit. Nothing came out except for spittle; leftovers from the blood still trapped in my mouth.

Shawn leaned against the barn, looking so gray I would've thought him dead if he hadn't turned his terrified gaze to mine.

That's when it occurred to me that I could pick him up and take him straight to the people who could help him. At least, I hoped I could. I felt weak and my head was spinning (figuratively, of course).

I squatted down, intending to scoop him into my arms. My vision started to blur.

What was going on here?

I'd passed out earlier and now I was gonna do it again. Had Shawn poisoned me? My heart lurched. The Taint. Oh, my God. In my twirling thoughts I heard Doc Michaels say that humans couldn't pass along the Taint.

Then what was wrong with me?

I heard rustling behind us, in the tree line. The woods curved around the property; the house and barn located in the crescent-shaped field that abutted the creek.

Even though I felt the edges of my vision blacken, I made myself turn around. "Hello?"

I heard a man's low laugh. Fear rocketed through me and I fell to my knees, trying to hang on to consciousness. God, I was scared. So scared of what I'd done and what had been done to me. "Who's there?" I whispered.

He laughed again. A shadow detached itself from the tree in front of me. Definitely a male. He retreated into the forest, whistling. Something about the tune bothered me. Familiar, that song. It made me feel even more frightened.

"Someone help us!" I cried. "Please!"

Moments later, I heard the soft thud of feet and looked up. Patrick stood there, and behind him Lorcan and Damian. God bless vampire hearing.

Patrick took in the scene and stared at me. "What the hell did you do?"

"Nothing." I didn't appreciate the looks I was getting. I didn't mean to hurt Shawn or to get smacked by a barn door. I felt like I was sitting inside a freezer. My teeth chattered together like castanets. My insides were surely getting frostbite. It was June in Oklahoma, for Pete's sake. The last thing I should be feeling is chilly.

Brady arrived seconds later. He must've run the whole way, but he didn't sound or look winded at all.

"Simone!" He picked me up, ignoring the dirt and the blood and the guy who was dying. "Are you all right? Jesus H. Christ! What happened?"

He turned his gaze to Patrick, looking at him as if everything was his fault.

One black eyebrow winged upward in disbelief. "We heard her cry for help. We found them just as they are." Patrick leaned down and scooped up Shawn. "He's still bleedin'."

Damian sniffed. "I smell death."

"Noooooo," moaned Shawn. "I don't . . . wanna . . . die."

"I'll take him to Dr. Merrick." Patrick sparkled away.

Damian hurried past us. Brady held me close. His heart was thudding and his muscles were tense, and not just from holding me. I knew the fight-or-flight response very well. Why in the world would Brady feel as if we were in danger?

"This is my fault," he murmured. "Shit."

I knew he was thinking about his blood, the blood I drank without his permission. He'd said it shouldn't affect me, but maybe I wasn't immune from his mysterious infection.

Damian returned. "There's a body back there." He held up a wallet. "I got his ID. Rick Delaney."

"Rick's my donor," I said. Horror crawled through me. No, no, *no*. "But he never showed up."

"Apparently he did. Someone drained him, Simone. There's not a drop left in him." His voice was neutral, but I saw suspicion in his jade eyes.

I felt too ill to defend myself. I sagged against Brady. My vision was getting worse, and so was the spinning. My stomach twisted again and I wanted to hurl. Stupid body! I was a vampire. None of my innards worked anymore.

"Simone?" Brady's voice sounded far away. I grabbed on to his shoulders. A black pit had opened beneath me, and even though I tried to hold on, I had to let go.

I spiraled into the endless black.

Chapter 14

Tuesday, June 18

"Simone, you have to drink."

Brady's voice.

Weird. Eyes won't open. My body felt heavy. 'Member that scene in *X2: X-Men United* when Wolverine shoved that hose into the girl's mouth and filled her up with that metallic stuff? She floated dooooooown into the water, and clunk . . . dead.

That's how I felt. Clunky and dead.

I sooooooo relate to movies, you know.

"Baby, you have to drink."

Brady's voice again. Memory flickered. I remembered the smell of his skin. The feel of it against my mouth.

No. Not right.

I was somewhere beep-y and ammonia-y. Now, where was a place like that? Been to one before, I think. Yeah.

"Drink." Warm flesh pressed against my lips.

Ah. Yes. He'd made me do this before. Couldn't open my eyes then, either. Something wrong, though.

Oh, that's right.

Never drink from Brady.

"Can't," I murmured hoarsely.

"Please, Simone."

"Brady said no! Won't hurt him." Ouch. It actually hurt to speak. I willed my eyelids to lift. Nope. No cooperation there.

"You've been feeding from me for the last couple of days. You have to, baby. Or you're not gonna make it."

Well, that didn't make any sense.

"We did this yesterday. Why doesn't she remember?" Brady sounded tired. Worried.

"I don't know." Hmm. Woman's voice. Not Jessica. Or Patsy. Heard that patient, soothing tone before. Couldn't remember her face. Her name. "Given the data and the evidence thus far, our theory is correct. One more day and she should be done with the process."

Process? I couldn't wrap my brain around all the words. Hungry. Very hungry. Weren't you supposed to get pudding or something when you were in this place?

Hospital.

Yeah. *Hospital.* Wait. I hated hospitals.

"Simone." Brady's voice was low, so smooth and sexy. "Drink."

Once again, warm flesh tempted my lips. Beneath that lovely skin pulsated the very thing I wanted. Life.

I drank.

Chapter 15

I woke up during the seizure.
My whole body shook and twisted.

"What's wrong with her?" yelled a man's voice.

"She's convulsing," said a woman. "Hold her down."

I felt hands pressing on my shoulders and grabbing my legs. Trying to keep me still. Thoughts spun away. Panic clawed.

Help me, God. Please, help me.

Band-Aid prayers, said Gran. *God don't work that way, child.*

You shouldn't stay with him, girly, said Lyle. *Nobody deserves that kind life. Especially not you.*

Nobody wants a whiny, stupid, selfish little girl like you, Simone. I'm the one who loves you, said Jacob. *You're mine, honey. All mine.*

"She might be rejecting the change, Brady."

"No," he cried. "No! Stay with me, Simone. Stay with me, goddamn it!"

*   *   *

"Oh, the shark, babe, has such teeth, dear. . . ."

Bobby Darin singing, and twining with him the deep tone of another voice.

Jacob.

I knew the words to the song. "Mack the Knife." Jacob sang it all the time. His father had taught it to him. His father taught him how to do many things: build a doghouse, shoot a rifle, punch a wife.

He was not a nice man.

Jacob spoke fondly of him, as though he were the perfect dad. By the time I'd found out about Jacob's true nature, about the drug-addict father who'd helped create the monster I married, it was too late.

Jacob's voice was louder now.

He'd turned the CD player to ear-busting volume. I heard cabinet doors and drawers opening. Slamming. Things falling, crashing. Idiot. How could I hide in the silverware drawer?

We lived in a two-bedroom ranch house about a half hour away from Nellis Air Force Base. It wasn't a large house and it was older, not as insulated as newer homes, which was why I could hear everything he was doing. He did it on purpose, to terrify me and to create multiple messes. Messes I would be expected to clean up. And it didn't matter how much my ribs hurt or if my eyes were swollen or my hands were bruised and sore.

"Mama."

"Ssshhh, Glory." My baby sat on my lap, her tiny arms clinging to me. She trembled, sniffling. We'd fallen asleep in the bed, watching *A Bug's Life*.

Jacob had come home unexpectedly. He was supposed be doing hush-hush training. Supposed to be gone a blessed week. So I'd relaxed. In the past couple of days, Glory and I had gone to the park, had dinner at Lyle's house, went to the mall, and bought Dippin' Dots. It had almost felt like a normal life.

The door had crashed open and Jacob had yelled, "Honey, I'm ho-*ome*."

I'd grabbed Glory and hidden in the bedroom closet. At dinner the night before, Lyle gave me a cell phone and told me it was a gift. We had a land line, but Jacob didn't allow any phones to be plugged in unless he was home. When he left, he took the phones with him. He wasn't worried that I might need a way to call for help in case something bad happened.

He *was* the bad.

I had no one. Not until our elderly neighbor Lyle had taken an interest in me, and despite my constant rebuffs, finally befriended me. He was a nice old man. Someone I could talk to, someone who listened, someone who cared.

"Call me, call the police, call anyone," said Lyle. "Just get some help, girly."

I'd kept that cell phone with me. A lifeline. And as Jacob tore apart our home and sang that goddamned song at the top of his lungs, I dialed 911.

"I know you're in here, oh, darling wife," called Jacob as he stumbled into the bedroom. The song ended, but Jacob had looped it, so *snap, snap, snap* . . . Bobby Darin began again, belting out the tune about the criminal Mack.

My heart hammered in my chest and perspiration dotted my face, dripped down my neck. Terror scrabbled through me like a plague-ridden rat, piercing my insides with tiny, sharp claws.

Glory pressed her face against my shoulder. She'd

never seen Jacob in a full rage. I'd managed to protect her. During my pregnancy and for two whole years, I'd made sure her father never laid a hand on her.

I wanted to leave Jacob. Lyle was going to help me escape. I just needed some time, some money. And now, as Jacob's heavy military boots stomped across the wood floor, I realized I'd been crazy to stay. Even another minute. What was wrong with me? I'd put myself and my daughter in danger. For what?

Oh, God.

"Nine-one-one, what's your emergency?" asked a female voice.

"My husband is going to hurt me. I have a toddler, and we're hiding in the closet. Please help us. *Please*."

"Stay calm, ma'am. I'm dispatching officers to your location."

Knock, knock, knock. "Ooooooh, Siiiimoooone. Sweet, sweet Simone. You've been a very bad wife. Kitchen's a mess. So's the living room. And no dinner?" He made a *tsk*ing sound.

I knew that sloppy tone. My heart turned over in my chest. Shit. Oh, shit. He'd been drinking. Nausea roiled as I clutched my daughter. Dealing with Jacob drunk was a hundred times worse than when he was just pissed off.

The doorknob rattled. There was no lock on the closet. Jacob was taking his time, tormenting me, leading up to the big show. It would be my fault. I hadn't cleaned the house well enough, I hadn't made dinner on time, or I hadn't recorded his favorite show. Was it so much to ask for me to be nice to him? Didn't he provide for us? Didn't he work hard to give me a nice home, pretty clothes, quality food? I'd heard his justifications a thousand times.

The 911 operator was still talking. I didn't shut the phone. I put it down, out of sight.

Glory's sniffles turned to wails. I patted her back. "Ssshh, baby. It's gonna be okay."

The lie felt thick on my tongue. Whatever happened to me, I had to make sure that Glory was okay.

The door swung open.

Silhouetted in the doorway was Jacob. He swayed, grabbing the frame with one hand. In the other was a half-empty bottle of Cuervo Gold. He was so tall, so broad and muscled, and handsome. Dark hair, dark eyes, slanted cheekbones, pouty lips. Underneath those devilish good looks was a real devil.

"Look what you've done," he crooned. "You've scared our little girl. Made her cry. Such a bad mother. I should take her away. Give her to someone who'll love her proper."

"Over. My. Dead. Body."

"What? What did you say?" He grabbed me by the hair and pulled. Pain raked my scalp and I screamed. I reached up and clawed his hand with my nails.

He was so stunned that I'd resisted, he let go and stared down at me. His eyes were glazed. And he smelled like he'd been rolling in garbage.

I pried Glory off me and put her down. Her arms reached up, her hands trying to latch on again. She was sobbing and chanting, "Mama, mama, mama."

I stood up and shoved Jacob backward. The tequila bottle sloshed, and he laughed as he righted himself. "Look who's grown a pair of balls."

"That makes one of us," I said.

His eyes went cold. "You owe me an apology." He pointed the bottle at me. "Shouldn't question my manhood. Maybe I need to show ya I'm all man. Whatcha think about that, you stupid little bitch?"

I didn't answer, even though I was terrified. Still, I stayed between him and the closet. He wouldn't get to my daughter. And the operator would be able to hear him.

I would keep him away from Glory until the police arrived.

All I had to do was survive long enough for someone to help us.

Chapter 16

From the field journal of Cpl. Braddock Linden Hayes
21 SEPT 98

W e've decided to end it.

We're killing innocents, or worse, bringing in the poor bastards for experimentation.

A good soldier follows his commander's orders. But I'd rather be a good man, damn it. Shayla would be ashamed of what I've been doing—and I can't stand the thought of her hating me.

There's only one reason our government would want to capture werewolves, vampires, and God knows what else. It's the same reason they've been messing around with alien technology, the same reason they do anything: to create better instruments for war, from soldiers to machines.

We have another mission: routing a nest of vampires who've settled in an abandoned farm in South Carolina.

It's the perfect cover for getting out.

Just a couple more weeks, and this clusterfuck will be destroyed. And we'll be free.

We'll run. But as Shayla once told me, I can never outrun my conscience. I can only try to do the right thing and hope that sometime down the line, I'll be able to pay enough penance for what I've done.

Chapter 17

Wednesday, June 19

I woke up feeling like I had swallowed a bag of cotton balls. My eyes felt gritty, too. I rubbed them and blinked awake.

I was tucked into a hospital bed. I leaned up on my elbows. The room was small, white, sterile. The antiseptic smell made me want to gag. God, I hated hospitals. I'd been in emergency rooms far too often, getting injuries treated and lying about how I got them.

"Simone?"

I looked to my right. Brady was in a chair, obviously having just awoke himself. He looked exhausted. He hadn't shaved, his hair was mussed, and his clothes were wrinkled. How long had he been here? How long had *I* been here?

"What happened?" I asked.

"I poisoned you."

That wasn't the answer I'd expected. He'd warned

me that his blood was different—to use his word, infected. But how could a human blood problem affect me? I was already dead.

Memories crowded into my mind, a blur of images and sounds. Poor Shawn, so gray, collapsed against the barn. "Shawn. Is he . . . ?"

"He died." Brady stood up, crossed to the bed, and took my hand.

"Oh, my God." I hadn't known him, but I still felt sorrow at his passing. "Did I . . . ? Was I . . . ?"

"He was nearly drained," said Brady. "Same as Rick."

I closed my eyes and tried to swallow the knot in my throat. That's right. My donor was dead, too. He'd been such a sweet guy. I opened my eyes. "I didn't drain Rick. Or Shawn."

"Rick probably arrived at your house and was lured up to the barn. As for Shawn . . . whoever did it got interrupted. That's why he was still bleeding. It's a wonder he even lasted as long as he did."

I remembered then the shadowy figure in the woods. The whistling as he retreated. I went cold. I recognized the tune. "Mack the Knife."

No, no. I had to be wrong. I'd been woozy, close to passing out. I'd been thinking of Jacob is all, and my mind made it seem like the whistling was a familiar tune.

"Shawn's blood tasted like I was drinking a garbage blood shake," I said. "Is that why I passed out?"

"Dr. Merrick thinks it's because of me. My blood. There's a lot to tell you." He brushed my hair off my forehead and then leaned down to kiss my temple. "I thought I'd lost you."

I didn't know how to respond, but I was grateful for

his comfort and for his vigil. He really cared about me. The idea of being Brady's girlfriend both scared and thrilled me. I needed to find a way to reconcile my own feelings. I couldn't let my past ruin my future. I had to take control of my life, once and for all.

"What about my daughter? And Gran?"

"Both fine. They've been here to see you every day."

"Every *day*?"

"It's Wednesday night, Simone. You've been in and out of consciousness for three days. Like I said, there's a lot to tell you."

Everything he had to tell me was bad news. No one had seen Darlene, her daughter, or Dunmore since Saturday. I admitted that I'd asked Dunmore to go handle Darlene's water problems.

On Monday night when Marissa didn't show up for school, and Darlene didn't answer her cell phone, a security detail was dispatched to her home.

They found Dunmore in the kitchen, facedown in two inches of water. The kitchen pipes had busted, just like Darlene had said. If I'd hoped to hear that Dunmore was just fine, it was in vain.

Dunmore, too, was dead. Worse, he hadn't met his end accidentally. No. He'd been killed and drained.

"Vampires don't feed on lycans," I said. I felt sick to my stomach. "The Ancients made a pact with the lycanthropes and Roma to never feed on their kind."

"I know. Patrick told me that most vampires uphold the pact," said Brady, "but there are those who don't."

I knew from my Vampire 101 classes that any vampire caught drinking lycanthrope blood was punished. Sometimes the offender was handed over to the lycans for judgment. No member of the Consortium would dare to drink a lycan's blood.

With Patsy birthing the *loup de sang*, everything would change. A whole new race of blood-drinking lycans would change the rules for all of us.

My thoughts circled back to Darlene. What had happened to her and her daughter? Then it occurred to me that I'd been the last person to see the woman alive.

"Maybe she left," I offered. "Just moved away or something."

"Do you really think that's what happened?" he asked.

I shook my head. "No. But it's better than the alternative."

The door swung open and Dr. Merrick entered. She smiled, her gray eyes filled with sympathy. I'd always liked her. She'd been very kind to me and Glory.

"How are you feeling?"

"Dead," I said, "but in a good way."

She chuckled. Her gaze skated to Brady. "Did you tell her?"

"Not yet."

"Does this have to do with his blood?"

Dr. Merrick nodded. "I think Brady can explain it best. I'll leave you alone for a little while. Then I'll check on you, try to get you out of here, okay?"

I nodded, feeling relieved. I did not want to have to stay in this room for another night. I wanted to go home to my family. I wanted to hold Glory and see with my own eyes that she was okay.

Dr. Merrick patted my arm, then left quietly.

"You want to call them?" He flipped open his cell phone, pushed a speed-dial number, and handed it to me.

Hearing Gran's voice was like hearing a choir of angels. "I'm so glad you're okay, honey! We're gonna come up," she said.

"I'm getting out of here. I'll call you when we're on our way. Tell Glory that I'm coming home. That I love her."

"I will. See you soon."

I ended the call and handed the phone to Brady. He put it away, then sat on the edge of my bed and held my hand. His expression was carefully blank. I hated when he did that. I had the worst poker face ever. I worked hard to maintain the facade of my happy-happy, joy-joy, but I'd never mastered the ability to show no emotion.

"This whole thing started more than ten years ago. I used to work for a covert government organization that targeted and destroyed paranormal beings."

I stared at him, openmouthed. "You used to kill people like me?"

"We were told your kind were domestic threats. It's true we killed supernaturals, but we also captured them. Instant death was preferable to being poked and prodded by the organization's scientists, believe me."

Brady clutched my hand, and I could see in his gaze that he wanted me to believe him. Maybe even absolve him. It must've been really difficult for him to talk to me about his past. I squeezed his hand, hoping to reassure him. He flashed me a tight smile.

"I got out. But not before they tried to kill me and my team. We went in supposedly to destroy a nest of vampires. Instead, my team died in an explosion set off by my superiors. That's when I found out about PRIS, and later, I joined up with Elmore and Dora.

"The night of the explosion, I snuck back into the facility and destroyed as much as I could. I set the lab on fire, shot up the computers, and stole as much technology as I could find. I promised myself to use all my training and all their goddamned toys to protect people, *all* people."

That explained his unusual weaponry and how he knew how to build the Invisi-shield.

"What does this have to do with me drinking your blood?"

"Part of the preparation was the absorption of nanobytes. Tiny robots that repaired our systems, gave us extra strength, boosted our senses."

"So you're a vampire without actually being vampire?"

"Yeah. Sorta. Three different types of these 'bots were shot into us over the course of nine days. It took three days after each treatment for our bodies to make nice with our new pals."

"I've been out for three days," I said. "I've absorbed the 'bots into my system? I'm not even alive!"

"You woke up, baby. And that means the 'bots have been accepted by your body."

"I don't feel any different." I didn't. I felt like the vampire I was three days ago. "What could they possibly be doing in there? My organs don't work. I don't have a viable circulatory system. I only have blood when I feed."

Speaking of which, I was starving. My expression must've given away my thoughts.

"You can only drink from me," he said. "Dr. Merrick thinks the 'bots have made other blood incompatible. A defense mechanism."

I leaned against the pillows and tried to absorb everything. Crap. People were dying or missing. Brady was some sort of cyborg. And now I was, too.

I'd never be able to take another donor. Brady was human. What if he died? Would I die, too?

Again Brady seemed to read my thoughts. He nodded. "I've been thinking about that, too." He sucked in a breath. "I don't see any alternative. You'll have to Turn me."

"Uh, no." I sat up and brought his hand to my lips. I kissed each knuckle. "I don't want to risk Turning you just to make sure I have dinner for the rest of my unnatural life. We'll figure out something, Brady."

"Maybe I'd want to hang around for other reasons." He took my face into his hands, his gaze tender.

"Like what?" I asked.

"You." He kissed me softly. "I think forever with you would suit me just fine."

My heart trilled. And that familiar sensation of heat (okay, lust) swept over me.

"You need to drink, don't you?" Brady lay down next to me and gathered me into his arms. He angled his neck so that it was flush against my mouth.

My fangs popped out.

I sank them into his artery and drank. Now I knew why his blood had that metallic taste. All the same, his blood was richly satisfying, and in no time at all, I'd finished my pint.

I stretched against him, languid. His erection brushed my belly. Startled, I looked down at his jeans, then back up at him.

He grinned. "You turn me on."

"Me? Or my fangs?"

"All of you." His hand fell to my hip, still tucked underneath the thin sheet. I wore one of those hospital gowns that opened at the back. I had nothing else on except my panties.

His other arm was tucked under his head. He seemed content with that one simple connection. I, on the other hand, felt like wiggling closer and doing things I really shouldn't.

"I want to talk to you about Shayla," he said.

The mention of another woman's name instantly doused my ardor. "Who's Shayla?"

Eep. I sounded jealous and suspicious.

He knew it, too. He grinned. "She was my sister. My twin. When we were seventeen, she was diagnosed with acute lymphoblastic leukemia. She should've survived it. Eighty-five percent of those diagnosed with ALL do survive. But four months later, she was gone."

"Oh, God, Brady. I'm so sorry." I kissed his collarbone and smoothed my hand over his scruffy face. He looked at me, and I saw the sorrow in his eyes.

"The day she found out, she insisted we go get tattoos."

"Really? Where's yours?"

"Used to be here." He raised the hand cupping my hip and showed me his wrist. I saw only a small mass of white scarring. "Two hearts linked together. When I joined the PET, they removed it. We weren't supposed to have any identifiable marks—plausible deniability and all that shit.

"She wanted to be a vet, and I wanted to be an architect. After I lost her, I decided not to go to college. Without Shayla, life was just gray."

"You were really close."

"Yeah. We'd been best friends our whole lives. After our parents died, all we had were each other. I never imagined that I'd have to live without her." He sighed. "I joined the Army. It was an impulsive decision, but turns out I was pretty good at being a soldier."

"I'm sorry you lost your sister," I said. "I'm sorry she died, Brady."

He brushed his lips across mine. "I never thought I'd find someone else I could talk to the way I talked to her. I could pour my heart out and know my secrets were safe." He kissed me again. Lust fluttered anew. "That's how I feel with you, Simone. Safe."

I felt such awe that he trusted me with his secrets. Yet I wasn't sure I deserved to be Brady's confidante. He didn't know about my past, and I didn't think I could tell him. I didn't want that look that was on his face now, the one that was so warm and . . . well, loving . . . to be wiped away.

"I have pictures of her," he said. "I'll show you, if you want."

"I'd love to see them. Thank you for sharing that part of your life with me, Brady."

He nodded. "What about you?"

I looked at him questioningly.

"You had nightmares." His blue gaze captured mine and I saw his concern, his curiosity. "Bad ones, Simone. Tell you the truth, I'm damned interested in knowing just who the hell Jacob is."

Chapter 18

"Is that why you told me about Shayla? So I'd tell you about Jacob?" Unease skittered through me. It was one thing to hear and promise to keep the secrets of another. And it was something else entirely to give away mine.

"No, Simone. I told you about my sister because I wanted you to know about her. You can trust me. But if you don't want to talk about this Jacob guy . . . then okay."

The only person in the whole wide world who knew about my husband was Gran. Everyone else thought I was just a financially struggling widow who moved in with her grandmother. That was true enough, I supposed. But it was only a part of the story.

I could tell Brady some of it. I could share with him what I hadn't shared with anyone else. I trusted him, too. At least, as much as I could trust anyone.

I'd been raised by two parents who loved me and who loved God. They took me to church every Sunday.

Their religion built a web of pretty lies about a beneficent deity who granted mercy and gave each of His
children purpose. I believed it all—even after God saw
fit to kill my parents in a car accident when I was only
nineteen.

I told Brady all of this. I couldn't hold his gaze, so I
stared at his wrinkled T-shirt. "That was the same year
I met Jacob. He was twenty and had already served
two years in the Air Force.

"I believed God had put Jacob into my life to heal
me. To guide me the way my parents had. I did everything he said. I gave up college. I gave him access to
my inheritance and the money from my parents' insurance."

I paused, thinking about those early days. Jacob
told me that he'd found the perfect woman. A trust-
worthy woman of faith and virtue. I was a virgin. I'd
never been in love. And Jacob was handsome, charm-
ing, and said everything I needed to hear.

"He said he loved me and that he wanted a family,"
I continued. "And I wanted to be loved and cherished.
We married, and he was assigned to Nellis Air Force
Base."

Brady tensed. I looked up at him. I couldn't really
discern his expression, but I got the feeling he knew
something I didn't. Surely not about Jacob? Or maybe
he was just getting upset on my behalf, suspecting
what was to come.

"We lived off base. I hadn't realized it until later, but
he was separating me from the other wives, the poten-
tial to make friends. Every social engagement I got to
attend was only on his terms, with his rules."

I didn't realize he was controlling me—not until the
first time I broke one of those rules, and he made sure

I paid the price. I couldn't tell Brady that. I didn't want to admit how weak I'd been.

But he guessed, anyway.

"He hit you."

I nodded. I lived day by day, scared and compliant, trying everything possible to make him happy. I believed I deserved the way he treated me. He had me convinced that I wasn't a good enough wife. Every time *he* got pissed off, the failure was mine. So I spent a lot of time trying to figure out the wants and needs of my husband without ever considering my own.

Then I got pregnant.

"Jacob seemed happy about the baby," I told Brady. "I naively thought that having a child would make everything better. I figured Jacob wouldn't hit me anymore. And Glory would fill up the emptiness inside me."

Jacob hadn't counted on our elderly neighbor Lyle Williams befriending me. Or that I might one day grow a spine. Or that he might have reason to be afraid of what I could do to him.

This was what I couldn't tell Brady. I didn't have the guts to confess what had happened that night when Jacob pushed me too far. Lyle had paid the price. And so had Glory.

I'd do it all again, in a heartbeat, if it meant saving my child. But I was ashamed. I'd built a new life, a life given to me because of the sacrifice of others.

"You left him?"

I nodded again. "I was so fucked up."

"You were terrorized by a man who took vows to protect you and honor you. At least you got out. Some women never leave their abusers."

"I got counseling. I learned a new trade. And I

made sure that Glory and I just . . . disappeared." It wasn't that I didn't want Jacob to find us. He was dead. I didn't want to be tracked by authorities. I didn't want to have to answer for what had happened. Any bravery attained by standing up to Jacob had been voided by running away from the consequences of what I'd done.

Becoming a vampire wasn't in my life plan, but overall, it worked out. Now we'd be off the grid forever. No way would the Consortium allow one of their own to be taken into the human world. We survived only because they didn't believe we existed.

"He's dead." I figured I could give Brady that much without revealing the why and the how.

"And yet you still have nightmares about what he did to you."

Only because I'd thought I heard some intruder whistling "Mack the Knife." Even the idea of that song was enough to give me the heebie-jeebies. No wonder my subconscious had gone wacky.

Why hadn't I told Brady about the figure in the woods? I didn't like the idea of being under suspicion for hurting Shawn and Rick. Telling him or anyone else that I'd seen a mysterious man would just make everyone think I was lying to protect myself.

Maybe I'd hallucinated. That thought wasn't any more comforting than thinking my dead-and-buried husband was roaming around Broken Heart.

Brady rubbed my back. "Everything's going to be okay."

That remained to be seen. But for now, everything *was* okay, especially since I was snuggled in Brady's arms.

Brady's fingers slid down the gap in my gown. His

fingertips hesitated on my bare skin. I waited, expectant.

"I should probably get up," he murmured. "Dr. Merrick will be back soon."

"Yeah," I agreed, not meaning it.

He didn't move.

Instead, he shifted so I was pressed fully against him. His erection (whoa, baby) rubbed my belly. I felt my breath catch (or would have if the whole breath thing actually worked).

I wrapped my arms around his neck, lifted my face as his lips descended toward mine.

He went in for the set-her-on-fire kiss. No gentle persuasion this time. His tongue pierced the seam of my lips, and I eagerly met his invasion.

I let myself get lost in the moment. No more denials, no more doubts. Only me. And Brady. And *this*.

He rolled me onto my back and covered me. His hard-on slid between my thighs, putting delightful pressure on my clit.

I trembled. I was so uncertain about these feelings Brady caused, but really, I was responding to that hot ache inspired by him. His kisses and touches made promises I hoped he'd keep.

He had that guy essence, not cologne, just power and sex and yum. His body covered mine, and I felt a split second of panic before forcing myself to relax.

If I knew anything at all about Braddock Hayes, it was that he wouldn't hurt me. He was not Jacob, and I would not allow my old fears to spoil how I felt about this man.

We kissed until I ached with yearning I'd never known. It wasn't just the raw need for sexual mating, but the desire for a genuine connection. Human beings always searched for that mythical romance-novel intimacy, where sex wasn't just about the physical enjoyment but the melding of souls.

I don't think I wanted soul melding so much as I wanted affection. I didn't realize how starved I was for the touch of another. What pleasure was derived from the simplest gestures: laughing together, holding hands, kissing.

I didn't stop him when he pushed the bedcovers down and tugged up my hospital gown. I was awash in sensations. I couldn't stop quivering.

No one had seen me naked since Jacob.

Three years was a lifetime as a single woman with no dating prospects.

Anxiety wrestled with lust. Lust won easily enough.

Brady skimmed the underside of my breasts; his thumbs brushed the edges of my areolas.

"Brady?"

He looked at me, his blue eyes dazed with such tender longing that I lost my ability to speak.

"You're beautiful," he said, his voice husky. "I don't think I've ever wanted a woman the way I want you."

He punctuated that statement by suckling one turgid peak into the warm cave of his mouth.

Pleasure bloomed, a fire flower that burned all the way to you-know-where. I weaved my quaking fingers into his thick, soft hair.

He let go, licked the hard nipple, and blew on the crinkled flesh until the peak tightened even more.

Butterflies danced in my stomach.

He moved his attention to my other nipple. But while his mouth worshipped my breast, his hand clasped the one he'd tortured, pulling on my aching nipple.

Holy freaking fuck.

My body was having one helluva of a party and made it clear that the brain was not invited to attend. My mind clouded. No more thinking.

Click. Click. Click.

What the hell was that noise?

Brady rose above me and attacked my mouth again. I couldn't resist the urge to touch his cock. I maneuvered my hand between us and stroked the poor trapped thing.

Brady moaned. He tore his mouth away from mine. "God, I want to be inside you."

"We can't," I whispered.

"I know." He rested his forehead on mine, trying to gather his breath. I heard the frantic pounding of his heart, and knew he was tormenting himself as much as he was me.

Click. Click. Click.

The damned sounds were familiar.

High heels on laminate flooring.

Shit! Dr. Merrick was headed down the hallway. I looked at Brady, my eyes wide.

"Goddamn it." He rolled off the bed while I got retucked into the covers. Brady dragged the chair as close as he could to the bed and sat in it. I'm sure he was trying to hide his erection, but that thing wasn't easily disguised.

Dr. Merrick entered the room a few seconds later. I felt like my parents had caught me necking with my boyfriend. That had never happened, given that I hadn't dated in high school.

The doctor, however, gave no indication that she

knew what Brady and I had been doing. She came around the other side of the bed.

"You seem to be doing well," said Dr. Merrick with no hint of irony. If I could blush, I'd be as red as a cooked lobster. "Brady, why don't you excuse us for just a minute? I'll examine Simone, and if all is well I'll discharge her."

Brady took my hand and squeezed. "I'll go to the vending machines and get some of that bad coffee."

He left, in a hurry, I might add. I bit my lip, trying not to laugh. Poor Brady.

"He's a good man," said Dr. Merrick. "You're very lucky."

I didn't know how to respond to that. There was no point in denying Brady and I were (gulp) together. All the same, I didn't much feel like talking about it. "So, what are you going to do? It's not like you can check my pulse or listen to my heartbeat."

"True." Dr. Merrick sat on the edge of the bed. "Frankly, vampire bodies rarely require medical treatment. Even the most grievous of injuries can be healed with enough rest."

"How will the nanobytes affect me?"

"I don't know. Maybe not at all, except that they are rejecting any blood but Brady's. No vampire has ever had to deal with this particular situation."

"Vampire cyborg. Sounds like a late-night horror movie."

She chuckled. "Yes. But you survived the trauma." She looked down at me, her eyes questioning. "I examined you when they brought you in. Your Turning did not erase all the signs of abuse. Whatever happened to the person who hurt you?"

I killed him. I put on my brightest smile. "I took my daughter and escaped."

"Where is he now?"

"Dead." I sat up and clutched the blankets to my chest. "I really don't want to talk about it. My past is my business."

"Only if the actions wrought three years ago do not return to harm all those you know and love."

I stared at Dr. Merrick. No one really knew much about the doctor, only that Patrick and Lorcan vouched for her. The Consortium had brought her in to run the newly built hospital. She was the only medical professional on call. It was not easy to find a physician who could treat humans and parakind.

I had the very uncomfortable feeling that she knew more about me than I wanted anyone to know.

"Are you familiar with the stories about the Fates?" she asked.

Talk about a change of subject.

"There were three, I think. Something about spinning the threads of life?"

"Ah, yes. And when it was time for a human to die, one sister would cut the thread with her shears." She chuckled. "The Greeks. Such wonderful storytellers, but they so often got it wrong.

"Fates are immortals, Simone. We were created by the gods to help keep balance in the world of humans."

I swallowed the knot in my throat. Fear beat a tattoo in my nonexistent pulse. "You're one of those?"

She nodded. "Yes. I'm a Fate. And I know what you did to Jacob."

Chapter 19

Horror shot through me, and I clutched the blankets. Well, shoot, what was I gonna do? Duck under the covers and hope she went away? Damn. Dr. Merrick was the last person I'd ever believed would figure out my secrets.

"What are you going to do?" I asked. I couldn't stop the quiver in my voice.

"Nothing." She shrugged. "It's not my job anymore. You see, the Fates weren't three sisters or witches, although it's true that we are all females. In the beginning of the world, there were many of us.

"The Germans called us *norns*. I always liked that term best. We determined the course of a human's life. And of course we could be bribed with offerings. A reversal of illness, a healthy child born, a lover returned." She looked at me. "Can it really be called fate if our gifts could be purchased? Give us enough gold, enough blood, enough slaves and we might give you want you asked."

"Band-Aid prayers," I whispered. I felt like weeping, but I didn't know why. I could feel those fictional threads of my life unraveling. Did Dr. Merrick hold the shears that would clip the thread? "What about God?"

I wanted so badly to believe again in the beneficent deity I'd grown up praying to, the one I had loved until He'd taken everything from me, even my own life.

"What is God—the one or the many? Is it not all the same? We are energy. We are joined by the very essence of life in all its form. God is not one thing. The father-mother God is *all* things."

"You sound like my parents."

"Then they were wise."

She didn't say anything for a minute, maybe to give me time to gather my thoughts. What could I say to her? She was telling me about herself for a reason. We weren't exactly friends. We were barely even acquaintances.

"You said you knew about Jacob."

"I was created as a Fate, and even though it is no longer my purpose on this Earth, the powers are still mine. I see into the hearts of humans, especially when an injustice has been wrought. What you did, Simone, was wrong."

I had no words for her. I'd justified what I'd done a million times. And honestly, I'd probably do it again, only I wouldn't hesitate. At least then I would save three lives instead of just two.

"Can you decide not to be a Fate?" I asked. "Flet is a pixie, and he says the rules of magic cannot be changed."

"The gods realized we were abusing our privileges. What they wrought, they can destroy."

Not according to Zerina. "You can't destroy energy."

"True. Think of it more as a reabsorption. The gods, or as you like, God, creates the all-in-all from the Source. He's the source and everything we are, everything that lives, is part of the Source. The Fates returned from whence they came. All but a few us. Those who were allowed to stay were directed to find ways to help the creatures we had harmed by our selfishness."

"You became a doctor?"

"Healing was a specialty of mine. I've been a healer ever since the gods decreed that we would no longer control the lives of mankind. Man became in charge of himself. Your decisions create your life. No one else, not God and not the Fates, can be blamed for where you are and what you are doing."

"Why are you telling me all of this?"

"The ripple effect. You throw a pebble into the water and it creates ripples. Your action was to throw the pebble—the representation of your choice. That's all that you can control. But not the ripples—those are the consequences of your choice. And that you cannot control."

Getting a lecture from a Fate was scary. She was delivering bad news like a teacher trying to teach calculus to an English major.

"Sometimes, what you've done in the past is still rippling . . . right into your present."

"You're saying that what I did back then is about to catch up with me now?" This terrified me in a way nothing else ever could. I didn't know how such a thing could occur, unless the authorities finally found me. And even if they did, what could they do? I was a vampire. My heart sank to my toes. Would the

Consortium, or, worse, Queen Patsy, judge and punish me instead?

"What will happen is unclear," said Dr. Merrick. "The future is never written. But I do know that evil is here in Broken Heart. And that whatever has been unfolding these last few days is because of you. Retribution is at hand, dear girl."

Was she saying I was the indirect cause of the deaths? Or of the disappearance of Darlene and her daughter? Impossible. I didn't believe her. At least, I didn't want to believe her. The truth of her words weighed heavily on me.

"I'm giving you this warning, Simone. You cannot escape what you have started, but you may be able to save those you love."

"And myself?"

Dr. Merrick looked troubled. "I don't know. What will find you? Revenge . . . or justice?"

After Dr. Merrick finished giving me her doom-and-gloom predication, she said I was okay to go home. I wanted to see Gran and Glory. I wanted to drink some of Gran's lemonade and have a warm chocolate chip cookie and pretend like everything was okay.

I got dressed in the clean clothes that Gran had apparently brought on her last visit. My cell phone was clipped to my denim overalls.

I was more subdued when Brady returned, but he didn't call me on it. Instead he tucked me into a wheelchair and rolled me to the front doors of the hospital. I could walk just fine, and I was glad when Brady took my hand and held it all the way to his truck.

As he drove out of the parking lot, I opened my cell

phone and called Gran to let her know that we were on the way.

"Oh, honey, I'm so glad!" Her voice held relief. "We were worried."

"I'm all right now. Let me talk to Glory." I waited a few seconds, then said, "I'm coming home, baby! I love you."

She tapped the receiver—her little way of saying, *I hear you and miss you, too.*

Gran took the phone again. We talked for a bit longer, then hung up.

"What did Dr. Merrick tell you?" asked Brady.

"I told you. I should be okay so long as I just drink your blood."

There's something else. Why won't you tell me? Why won't you trust me?

"I do trust you."

Brady glanced at me. "What?"

I turned toward him, my seat belt pulling against my shoulder. "You asked why I didn't trust you. I do."

He was silent for a long moment. "I didn't ask why you won't trust me, Simone."

"Yes, you did. I heard you."

He pulled off the road, parking the truck on the shoulder. The engine rumbled. I was so glad Brady kept the air-conditioning on high. The summer heat was atrocious; the humidity felt thick in my useless lungs. He turned toward me. "I didn't say it," he repeated. "I *thought* it."

Jesus. He'd thought the question, and I'd heard him. "Maybe it's the blood. Or the nanobytes working their science mojo."

"Maybe." He took my hand and looked deeply into my eyes. "Or it's an indication that we're mates."

It was true that vampire mates shared the ability to read each other's thoughts. But there was a problem with Brady's theory.

"You're human."

"So what?"

"*Vampire* mates share a telepathic bond, Brady. It makes more sense that the nanobytes are somehow linking us." It made me nervous that he'd even suggested the whole we're-mates idea.

Don't get me wrong. I liked him. A lot. And I owed him for his kindness and care of me and my family. But I couldn't commit to the *L* word, much less the whole let's-get-married-for-a-hundred-years thing.

"Don't you think we should try for a second date?" I asked, smiling. I was trying to lighten the mood, but Brady didn't seem to appreciate the attempt.

"I know what I want, Simone." He straightened and started driving again.

Neither one of us bothered making small talk. We settled into the uncomfortable silence, which made the rest of the trip oh, so fun. Brady pulled up to the house, then turned off the truck. He unbuckled his seat belt.

"I want you, Simone. I'll take as much time as you need, but I'm not going anywhere." He sucked in a deep breath. "I'm not Jacob. I swear on my life I would throw myself into a pit of rusty spikes before I hurt you or Glory."

"I know." I unbuckled my seat belt and slid across the space between us. He took my hands and held them tightly. I didn't know how to reassure him. I wanted him, too. But I was scared of commitment. Of making another really big mistake. That wasn't fair to

Brady and I knew it. Yeah, I knew it, and it didn't matter.

"You're still trying to decide if you can confide in me," he said softly. "There's nothing, Simone, *nothing* you could do that would change how I feel about you." He kissed me gently and pulled back. "Is that it? Are you afraid to tell me what happened with Jacob?"

No, I was afraid to tell him what I had done *to* Jacob. Brady could say whatever he wanted. In the end, how could he look me in the eyes as I confessed the details of that night, and say that he still lov— I mean, respected me?

"I just need time," I said. "We have that, right?"

"Yeah." He smiled and then kissed me again. I melted against him and took all the solace I could from his embrace. God, he made such wicked promises with that mouth.

Finally, we pulled apart. He was panting and dazed, and I was all hot and bothered. Oklahoma summers had nothing on this man. Hoo, boy.

"I need to get back to the Invisi-shield. It's almost done. It should be operational before the festival begins."

"That's good news." And it was. More protection we'd need if Dr. Merrick was right about the lurking evil. (Why did evil always lurk?)

Brady kissed me good-bye and left. I felt torn up inside, knowing I'd disappointed him. He'd wanted more of a commitment from me. He deserved as much—the whole damned truth, for one thing.

You know what? I'd disappointed myself, too. As I walked up to the porch, I realized that I had to take Dr. Merrick's warning seriously. Maybe the ripples of past events had caught up with me. Had I really believed I could escape from what had happened?

What could I do? Take Glory and Gran and go somewhere else? Yeah, and leave Brady and the citizens of Broken Heart to their fates. Why should they bear the consequences of what I had set into motion? No, I couldn't do that. The alternative was to admit to everyone the truth, all of it, and hope we could find a way to deal with whatever was coming for us.

I paused on the porch steps, clutching the railing. I had to get my emotions under control. Acting rashly wouldn't get me out of trouble. In fact, anger and anguish had been the key ingredients to the biggest fuckup of my whole life.

Maybe working on one of my little projects would clear my head. I kept several in the house, just things to tinker on during my free time. I needed to think this through before deciding what to do next.

I entered the house. Glory sat on the couch, watching television, Flet glowing gold and sparkly on her shoulder. I heard the SpongeBob Squarepants theme song blare.

Glory noticed me. She squealed and scrambled to her feet, running toward me. I picked her up and hugged her tightly.

"I love you so much."

Glory leaned back and cupped my face. Then she gave me a big, sloppy kiss. I longed for the day my little girl would speak again. I wanted to hear her voice so badly. That anxious-love-ohcrap-whoawow mommy feeling flowed through me. I wanted to laugh and cry. God, she was precious. She deserved to be in a safe and loving environment. If I did nothing else, I would ensure that for my daughter.

I hugged her again, but she was already wiggling out of my arms. She took my hand and led me across the living room. I entered the kitchen, my greeting to Gran dying on my lips.

Opening-a-nudist-colony George sat at the kitchen table with Gran, drinking coffee. To my utter shock, he was *holding my grandmother's hand.*

"Simone!" Gran popped up from the table. She swung around and with her usual unerring aim (did she have sonar, or what?), grabbed me into a hug. "I'm so glad you're all right. When you called and said you were okay, I thanked God."

I hugged her back, very glad I was still around to do so. Then I let her go and looked at George. Well, maybe I glared. His guileless gaze met mine. He smiled. *You don't fool me, buddy.*

"So, what's been going on since I've been unconscious in the hospital?" I asked. Yikes. Did that sound like an accusation?

Gran's cheeks went red. Oh, my God. What had she been doing? No, wait. I didn't want to know.

George patted her hand. "Well," he said, grinning up at me, "the best news is this: I'm courting Elaine."

Chapter 20

"You're what?" I screeched.

"We're dating, honey. George's been here every day, just helping out and . . . well, being real nice."

I. Just. Bet. I stopped short of demanding more information, too afraid of what they might tell me. What if they kept dating? What if Gran moved into the nudist colony?

I felt woozy.

Okay. Way to project, Simone. Calm down.

"He's a vampire." Sheesh. I sounded like I'd implicated him as a serial killer.

"Yes, dear. So are you." Gran was using her patient tone. "I'm blind, and he drinks blood for dinner. We all have our little quirks."

Oh, gawd. Did we ever.

"By the way, Reiner was asking after you."

"He was here?"

"Just about everyone dropped by and checked on

us. We have so many casseroles that I don't think we'll be able to eat them all."

Well, that was the Oklahoma way. Tragedy + comfort = casseroles.

Obviously, I'd missed my Monday night appointment with Reiner to help him complete the queen's gift. I wondered if he'd gotten someone else to fix it. Or maybe he was still hoping for my help.

"I need to go, buttercup," said George. "I'm meeting with the construction team."

Had he just called Gran *buttercup*? Ew.

"You don't let the grass grow under your feet, do you, George?"

"Nope. I see what I want and go for it." He was looking at my grandmother when he made this announcement. "See you later, ladies."

He leaned down and kissed Gran right on the lips. He saluted me, then patted Glory on the head. I hadn't seen another vehicle parked in front of the house, so I could only assume George liked to walk.

He left through the back door, whistling softly.

"He's Family Ruadan," said Gran, as if she'd realized that I'd been wondering about his mode of transportation. "He took me up."

"In the air?" I asked, trying not to flip out. "You went flying with him?"

Glory returned to the living room. The annoying giggle of SpongeBob floated into the kitchen. Thank goodness my daughter was more interested in the sponge that lived in a pineapple under the sea.

I turned to stare at Gran, unable to form any words.

She shook her finger at me. "Don't you give me that look, young lady. I'm a grown woman."

I didn't bother to ask her how she knew she was

getting The Look. "If you tell me you have needs, I'm going to yark."

"Well, I do, Simone. Seventy-three isn't dead, you know."

Vampires didn't get headaches, so the pain throbbing behind my eyes wasn't real. I couldn't blame my body for trying to deal with its stress in human ways.

The phone rang, saving me from having to respond to the whole needs comment. I flipped open my phone. "Hello?"

"Ah, Simone. I heard you were released from Dr. Merrick's tender care. How are you feeling?" asked Reiner.

"Just dandy. What can I do for you?"

He paused, maybe to consider if I was being sarcastic or not. (I was.) "I still need your help with the project we discussed on Saturday. Is it possible for you to meet me at the garage this evening?"

"Yeah," I said. "Sure."

"Very good. Half an hour?"

"See you then."

Gran was frowning at me. She rose from the table and took the empty mugs to the sink. "You're not leaving, are you?"

"Just for a bit. Reiner needs my help with something."

"Three people dead and two missing. Damian's got guardians patrolling our property, so we're safe. But you, all alone in that big ol' garage . . . it makes me worry, child."

"I'm sure the guardians are in town, too." Now I was feeling nervous about leaving my family. I had no doubt that the lycanthropes could kick just about anybody's ass, but Gran was right. And the two dead bodies had been found on our property. The possibility of the shadow man lurking in the woods, watching the house, made me sick to my stomach.

"You feel safe here?" I asked Gran. They'd done well enough without me for the last three days.

"Always have, always will," said Gran. "You going to the garage?"

"I'll get done quick as I can, promise."

"All right." She walked to me and gave me another hug. "I love you, Simone."

"I know," I whispered into her hair. She smelled like talcum powder. Like a grandmother. She was soft, too. How could I be angry that she was dating? She deserved some happiness. We all did.

I let go. I was feeling all weepy, and for a vampire who couldn't shed tears, it wasn't exactly satisfying to cry.

Before I left, I called Flet to me. "I want you to stick by Glory, no matter what. Protect her as much as you can."

Flet nodded. "Is this the favor I owe you for the wrongdoin'?"

"Yes. If you keep Glory safe, all debts are paid."

"All but one," he reminded me. "I prefer her company, you know." He cleared his tiny throat. "All the same, I'm glad you are . . . still among us."

I was surprised at the fairy's admission. "Thanks, Flet."

"Yes, well, don't get used to it. You're still a pain in the ass."

"So are you."

I saw the quicksilver smile before he whirled around and buzzed back to Glory. I guess the little bastard wasn't all bad.

I went out to my truck, which was parked in the front yard. It seemed weird that I'd woken up in the hospital—what?—an hour or so ago, and now I was carrying on with my life like usual. But then that was the natural order: The world didn't stop just because you did.

I was almost to town when my phone buzzed. Wow. I was popular tonight.

"Hey," said Brady. "How are you doing?"

"I just talked to you twenty minutes ago."

"I know. I missed you."

Aw. I grinned and my insides went all ooey-gooey. "I miss you, too. What are you doing?"

"I'm nearly to the build site. In a few minutes, I'm going to get all sweaty and use my manly muscles."

I laughed. "I wish I was there to see that."

"If you're good, maybe I'll show 'em to you later."

"Promises, promises."

He laughed. Then in a voice that made my womanly parts clench (yowzer, he was go-od at that), he asked, "Can I tuck you in tonight?"

Ooooh, baby. My mouth went dry, and my undead heart turned over in my chest. "Yeah," I said softly. "I'd like that."

"Okay. See you an hour before dawn."

We said good-bye. Five minutes later, I arrived at the garage.

Reiner was waiting for me.

I didn't bother with opening the office. We went directly into the garage and over to my worktable. Reiner unloaded the box he'd brought with him.

The statue was in three pieces: the base, the Moon Goddess and Tark, and the crystal orb.

Two hours passed, and all I managed to do was put

the pieces together. The staff wouldn't lift at all, much less light the damned orb. I shook my head. "I hate to say it, Reiner, but I think you might need magic to make this thing work. I'm sure Zerina or one of the Wiccans could create a spell that would do the trick."

"Perhaps you are right." Carefully, he boxed the statue. Then he held out his hand. "Thank you, Simone. You have helped me more than you know."

"No problem, Reiner."

He held my hand for a little longer than was comfortable; then he let go. He said good-bye, then took his precious gift and left the garage.

As I cleaned up my workstation, I puzzled over the strange icon. Its metal was odd. I'd never worked with it before. I wondered if Zela, or even Elizabeth, would recognize it. Maybe the stuff was somehow made by lycans, or something particular to Germany.

I was bummed I hadn't been able to figure out how to do more than just put it all together. It wasn't really designed to include clockwork pieces. It didn't look as if it was meant to move at all. Magic was probably exactly what Reiner needed. I wondered if he'd thought of it before, but if so, why drag me into the process?

My brain was starting to cramp. Too much was going on, and the stress was making my shoulders bunch and my neck tingle.

I no longer had the ability to suck in a deep, calming breath. Maybe when Brady came to tuck me in, he'd be willing to do a little massage. He could start at the top and work his way down.

Heh.

I locked everything up and headed around the back to where I'd parked my truck. The night air was thick with humidity. It was the kind of quiet I noticed before a thunderstorm rolled in.

I put my hand on the door latch.

The scrape of a boot against gravel. Behind me.

I whirled around, adrenaline driving a spike of terror into my belly.

No one was behind me. But I still felt as though someone were nearby, watching. The hair rose on the back of my neck.

"Who's there?" I yelled. I didn't exactly sound brave or confident.

Screw it. I jumped inside my truck, locked the doors, and jammed the key into the ignition. The engine roared to life, and I felt immediately better.

I shifted into reverse and looked over my shoulder as I started to back up. A man stood behind the truck. I slammed on the brakes. What the hell?

I swear my poor, dead heart wanted to leap out of my chest and crawl away. The man was dressed in black from head to toe. He was big, tall, and broad shouldered. There was a familiarity to him, but I couldn't place him. Not Brady. He wouldn't stand there scaring the crap out of me.

"Simone," he taunted. "Sweet, sweet Simone."

My vampire ears had no problem hearing him. That voice sounded like . . . oh, hell, no. No! I didn't care who the guy was, I was getting the hell out of here. I pressed the gas, and the truck fishtailed.

The man jumped, and I mean *jumped*. He went over the top of the entire vehicle and landed on the other side. The black outfit shone oddly in the headlights. And his face was covered in the same material as his outfit. Only his eyes were showing, and I couldn't really discern their color.

The truck bounced out of the driveway and onto the road. I rammed the gear into drive and sped down Main Street. All I wanted to do was go home.

Brady! I need you!

I wanted to feel safe. I wanted someone to stop that horrible man from chasing after me, from catching me. Fear made my hands shake. I was trembling so badly, I couldn't keep the wheel steady.

I was too afraid to pull over, but I wasn't doing too good a job staying on the road, either. I looked behind me.

The road was empty.

I turned back and screamed.

A big, black truck barreled toward me. I realized I was on the wrong side of the road, and I overcorrected, swinging too far to the right. I stomped on the brakes.

My truck slid down the gravel shoulder.

Oh, my God. Oh, my God.

I couldn't get ahold of myself. I was shuddering and cold and nauseated.

"Simone!"

I screamed and threw my arms over my head.

"Honey, it's Brady. It's okay."

I dared a glance out my window. Brady stood there trying to open the door. "Let me in, baby."

I unlocked the door and fell into his arms. I pressed my face against his shoulder and stood in his embrace, quaking like I was having a seizure.

"Why aren't you wearing your seat belt?" he asked. "You could've been killed."

I snorted a laugh. "Are you kidding me?"

"Sorry. I'm just a little freaked out. When I saw the truck go off the road . . . Jesus." He held me so tight.

I needed him. I wanted him. I didn't care what it took to keep Brady. I'd do it.

"How did you get to me? How did you know?"

"I heard you cry out for me."

We really were connected. Thank God for that. I might've smashed into a tree before I made it home. At least I was starting to calm down. I felt safer now.

"I was headed into town with Damian. We were going to pick up some food for the crew." He leaned away just enough to look at my face. "It was lucky we were so close."

"Thank you," I said. I pressed my face into his chest. His heartbeat reassured me.

"What happened? Why are you so scared?"

"There was someone at the garage. In the back lot. He . . . he jumped over the truck, Brady."

"Vampire?"

"He was wearing this black, shiny outfit. He looked almost military."

He tensed. "Shit."

Dr. Merrick had been right. Whoever was sneaking around town had targeted me. And if she was right about that, then she was surely right about why he was here.

"Everything okay?" The voice was Damian's.

"She's fine," said Brady. "I'm going to take her home."

"I'll meet you back at the build site, then."

Brady shook his head. "No. I'll return tomorrow."

I sensed Damian wasn't thrilled with this news, but he seemed to accept it. He walked away, then I heard the truck start and drive away.

I don't know how long Brady stood on the side of the road and held me, but I took every bit of comfort I could from him. Then I made the decision. I would tell Brady everything. Give him the truth and the trust he'd asked for. And then hope that he'd meant what he'd said earlier. His feelings wouldn't change. . . . He would still want me. Maybe he would even (gulp) love me.

Finally, I pulled free from his embrace. "I have something to tell you, Brady. Well, more than one thing. It may change us . . . if you know what I've done."

"I told you already, there's nothing that will change how I feel about you, Simone. There's no way you can top my past—you know what I did."

"I understand it," I said. "And I don't judge you for it."

"Then expect the same from me."

I nodded. As I tried to gather my courage and figure out what to say first, my phone rang. I groaned. "This thing has been ringing all night." I took the phone out of the holster. Caller ID showed my grandmother's number. I tried to steady myself. I didn't want to sound freaked out when I talked to her.

"Hi, Gran."

"Baby, you need to come home quick," she said. Her voice shook. "Glory's missing."

Chapter 21

From the field journal of Cpl. Braddock Linden Hayes
30 OCT 98

Everything went wrong. We walked into a trap.
Worse, we ran into a group of paranormal re-
searchers who lost one of their own in the explosion.

ETAC fucked us. And for what? Having a conscience?

Screw those bastards.

I'll give them payback. Then I'll spend the rest of
my life trying to make up for what I've done.

I can't write in the journal anymore, but I'm keeping it. I'll put it in a safe place with a few other key
items. If ETAC ever tracks me down . . . hah! I'd like to
see them try. I dug out that tracker myself and destroyed the tattoo. If they try any damned thing, then
I'll make sure the whole world knows who they are
and what they do.

I think Shayla is cheering me on now. I can hear her voice in my head, in my heart, yelling, "It's about time, you silly bastard."

She's right. She was always right.

Chapter 22

Brady insisted on driving my truck, mostly because I couldn't keep my hands steady long enough to put the key in the ignition. I sat in the passenger's seat and stared out the window, grateful he'd pressed the accelerator to the floor.

A mother's worst nightmare was losing her child. In a way, I'd already lost Glory. Her desire to speak had died the same night as her father. She shut off a part of herself that no one could reach, not even me.

I knew that kind of hiding. To survive, some folks had to wrap up a little part of themselves and tuck it away. Life with Jacob required such sacrifice. So either I gave up my sanity or I shut off my emotions. It was easier to be a robot—at least until Glory was born.

"Start from the creek bank and work toward the forest behind the barn. Use the sensors. Call if you find anything. We'll be there in ten."

I looked at Brady and frowned. He wasn't using a cell phone. "Who're you talkin' to?"

"My team. They're already at your place. Damian's got a team there, too." He glanced at me, then took something from his right ear and gave it to me. "It's a communication system. A com link."

The device was the size of an earplug, except that it was silver and had a blue light on its top. The light flickered off. "How does it work?"

"It turns on when you put it in your ear. You can hear others with the same device and talk to them. It also translates everything it hears into English—or whatever language you request."

"I've never seen anything like it."

"No one has." He took the com link from me and returned it to his right ear. "Shit!"

He swerved to avoid the rusted RV that hadn't quite parked on the *side* of the road. Then Brady hit the brakes so he wouldn't plow into the rambling truck in front of us. It pulled onto the shoulder, joining a long line of cars, campers, and trailers. We were near the turnoff that led to my house, and over here the forest was thick. Firelight danced between trees, flickering yellow fingers that clawed apart the darkness. People carrying sleeping bags, equipment, and sleeping children streamed into the woods.

"Roma," I said. "Seems like they're all showing up for the festival."

"Does Broken Heart even have a hotel?"

"Not anymore. The only one we had was torn down by the Consortium. Though I hear a couple of Wiccans might open a bed and breakfast."

"At least you can go there and eat now."

Yeah. What a thrill. Brady's attempt to lighten the

mood was so not working. Argh! I could kill Flet for giving away my goddamned wish. I could've had it and used it to find my daughter. I clenched my fists so hard my nails dug into my palms. I had to settle down. Get my mind off worrying.

"The Roma are all about communing with nature," I said. "They don't like hotels."

"You sure know a lot about Roma."

"The Consortium educated us. Just like going to Turn-blood college." God, this conversation was moronic. We should be talking about Glory, about how to find her. I knew that I couldn't do anything, and that was what drove me crazy. Brady and Damian's men were the best in the world. If they couldn't find her, I had no chance of tracking her. But I had to do something. Anything. *Oh, Glory, baby, where are you?*

"Almost there," said Brady, his voice strained. He turned onto the dirt road and accelerated. I glanced at him. His hands gripped the steering wheel, and I saw a muscle working in his jaw. He was worried about her, too. I had the strangest urge to reassure him. Then I realized he hadn't done much to reassure me.

"Why haven't you told me everything's going to be all right?" I flinched at the accusation in my tone.

His gaze flicked to me. "I don't say things I don't mean."

I felt like he'd socked me in the stomach. I pressed a hand against my quivering belly. "Thank God you didn't go into social work. You really suck at the comforting thing."

"You want me to lie to you?"

Yes. No. I gritted my teeth and returned to looking out the window. Silence fell between us like a bag of rusty razors. I felt cut up and wounded by Brady's choice to keep things real.

Moments later, we pulled into the gravel driveway. My grandmother stood on the porch, her sightless eyes aimed at us. I jumped out of the truck and ran to her. "Gran!"

"Oh, thank God, Simone." She wrapped her spindly arms around me and squeezed. It was like getting hugged by a willow tree. I squeezed her back, envying her tears. I didn't get to cry anymore, but I sure wanted to. In my mind thrummed a terrifying beat of *findGloryfindGloryfindGlory.*

"I don't know what happened," she sobbed. "We were sitting by the creek. I heard her moving around. She don't talk, you know, but she's restless. I can always hear her. And then . . . there was nothing. I called and called for her, and she never came. I dialed Damian right away, then you."

"You did right." We didn't have police anymore— we had the lycans. Damian and his crew were our 911. I led my grandmother to her favorite rocking chair. "Go on and sit."

"I can't." She faced me. "I gotta do something, baby."

"How about making some lemonade? Glory loves it, and those men will be thirsty when they bring her home."

My grandmother smiled. "I got plenty of lemons, thanks to our trees."

Just like everything else that had ever been planted near the house, the lemon trees refused to thrive. So I sectioned off part of the back porch and built Gran her own little grove. We went online and bought a lot of damned dirt from an out-of-state gardening supply place. The three lemon trees bloomed and bore fruit. Gran made the best lemonade, lemon pies, lemon bars, lemon anything you ever ate.

If you were the kind of person who could still eat.

It had been seven kinds of wrong to be able to smell a freshly baked chocolate chip cookie from five blocks away, only to never be able to taste it. That was the true vampire curse. Now I could eat, but I couldn't find my kid.

"Better make several pitchers," I said, watching Gran walk to the front door.

"Maybe I'll whip up some lemon bars, too," she said.

"Sounds good."

She smiled at me, and even though we both knew it was busy work, at least making lemonade and cookies was better than standing around worrying.

Brady was gone. He'd probably joined his team. I felt bad about how our conversation had ended. I shouldn't expect so much from the man, but I did. I wanted him to make everything all right.

I'm sorry, I sent out tentatively. Being able to send thoughts into Brady's head was kinda freaky.

I'm sorry, too. I'll find Glory, I swear.

Thank you.

I wished I had a com link so I could hear what was going on. Even though I knew it was useless, I walked around the house. Nothing. No one. Just me making sneaker prints in the useless dirt.

I walked into the front yard and stood there, listening. Even twenty yards away, I heard the water's quiet burbling. It seemed such a harmless thing, that creek. It was maybe ten feet wide and probably no more than six or seven feet deep. Glory could swim, so even if she'd accidentally fallen into it, she could've gotten back out. And Gran would've heard the splash.

No, Glory had wandered off—something she'd never done before. Why had my little girl left? Had she seen something? Or had someone stood at the edge of the woods and beckoned her? Dread pulsed at the base of my spine, and chills shot through me. I couldn't think the worst. She hadn't even been missing an hour. The only silver lining, or should I say gold lining, was that Flet was with her. It wasn't much of a comfort, but it was something to hold on to. He had to be with her, otherwise he'd be here. *Please keep her safe, Flet. Keep her safe, and you can have anything you want.*

I stopped walking. What would happen if I called Flet to me? If I asked him to show us where Glory was?

"Flet," I called. "Come to me."

Seconds stretched into minutes. Shit. Either he was ignoring, something he wasn't supposed to be able to do, or he was fulfilling my directive. Or, he was . . . well, he couldn't be dead.

I was afraid to call again. If he was with my daughter, then at least she wouldn't be as scared. I couldn't help but think someone had taken her. But who? And why?

I studied the little pier jutting into the stream. It was old and the wood faded, but it was sturdy. Many evenings, I'd sat next to Glory on the end of that pier and dipped my feet into the cold water. She held my hand, content to just *be*. Glory had given me courage—and then she'd shown me how to find peace.

I couldn't face the water, or those memories, so I rounded the house again.

I stood in the backyard and stared up at the barn. Had the door fallen because the hinges had finally rusted through? Or had someone tossed it onto me?

The mystery man.

"Hey, Simone."

"Aaaahhh!" I spun around.

George stood behind me.

He threw his hands up in the air in a gesture of surrender. "Sorry, man. Didn't mean to startle you."

"Why would you startle me?" I yelled. "Just because my daughter's now among the missing and people died right here!" I jabbed my finger at the ground. "*And* there's a crazy guy running around town, doing his best to scare the living hell shit out of me. Yeah, *George* . . . why could you possibly *startle* me?"

"Sor-ry. Whew. Somebody needs a Valium." He spread his hands out. "Chillax, man. I just wanted to see how you guys were doing. Elaine's really freaked out."

"She called you, didn't she?"

He nodded. Then he jerked a thumb toward the back porch. "I'm gonna go in. Maybe you should go with me."

I shook my head. I knew I should apologize to him, but I couldn't get the words out. He'd scared me by dropping into my yard without warning. I hadn't decided whether or not I liked him.

He said nothing else, just did that little salute thing again, then went into the house.

I walked up the hill. My hearing was good enough that I could hear their smoochy-smoochy, and I couldn't handle it. It was wrong to not want my grandmother to be enamored of George. I supposed that I had created expectations for Gran. She'd been my rock, my sounding board, my saving grace. Being disgruntled that ol' George was interrupting the status quo wasn't fair. I'd been reminded that Gran was a person with the same kind of needs and hopes as everyone else. I was finding love (Did I really just think that?) with Brady. Why couldn't Gran find the same with George?

By the time I wrestled free of my tangled thoughts, I found myself standing at the spot where Shawn lost his life.

I smelled the old, rusty tang of his blood. My vampire vision easily picked out the smear of red on the sun-washed boards. Guilt pierced me, as sharp and deadly as Jessica's swords.

What had happened to him? Who had drained him? And Rick? Was it the same person, or was there a group? A year earlier, we'd been plagued by vampires known as Wraiths. As far as anyone knew, they were history.

So much had happened here. Like Gran said, with the sweet came the sour. We'd fought Wraiths, Ancients, dragons, and zombies. When would we finally be able to rest? To create a haven for our kind? A place of safety for our children?

I didn't know if it were possible. The Invisi-shield offered the best hope. Keep us in and everyone else out.

I sighed, kicking at a clump of earth, which rolled a few inches and landed on something shiny. I kneeled down and retrieved the silver object.

A brooch.

Had the ripples reached Glory? Was she the first to pay the price for my failures?

"I told you, Mr. Silverstone, I'm not interested in anything you have t'offer."

The female's Irish brogue was rife with irritation. But I heard fear quiver in her voice, too. In front of me two figures appeared, wavering like ghosts in a Scooby-Doo cartoon. The woman faced a tall fellow whose polish and wealth were obvious in both his old-fashioned clothing and his mannerisms.

"If you don't want your husband to lose the farm, I suggest you reconsider."

"I'd rather have me respect and the love of me husband than the whole of Broken Heart tucked in me pocket. You won't sully me, Mr. Silverstone." She whirled around, and he grabbed her by the wrist.

"Let me go," she yelled.

He captured her other hand and yanked her to his chest. "I will have you, Mary McCree." He brought his mouth down on hers.

She plowed her knee into his groin.

He cried out, letting her go and grabbing at his crotch.

"Do it again, you filthy bastard, and I'll cut 'em off." She turned and ran.

The images faded to nothing.

I shoved the silver ornament into my pocket, my chest tight with grief and worry. I squeezed my eyes shut and pressed the heels of my palms against the growing ache.

I wept as only a vampire can. My throat constricted and pain stabbed my eyes. But I had no tears. Only the anguish.

That's probably why I didn't sense the danger until it slammed me into the barn.

I went through the wall.

Shoulder first.

Skidded across the ground.

On my side.

Smacked into a moldy pile of hay.

And collapsed.

Dust plumed and caught in my lungs. Hay exploded into the air, falling on me, clinging to my hair and clothing.

I scrambled to my feet, my hip throbbing.

No one was there.

Whoever had shoved me through the wall had disappeared. I stood in the barn, trying to regain my composure. I listened as hard as I could, but heard nothing. No heartbeat, no heavy breathing, no slide of shoes on dirt.

I was alone.

I grabbed my cell phone, indulging in the automatic human reaction to call someone for help. I was a vampire, damn it. I didn't need 911.

The phone was a mangled mess inside the holster. Shit. I used my vampire speed to return to the house. Fear pounded inside me like a heartbeat.

I expected to find my grandmother and George in the kitchen, but I found only three pitchers of lemonade and a mixing bowl filled with batter.

"Gran?"

She didn't answer. Foreboding crawled through me. I hurried through the living room. The TV and lights were on, but my grandmother wasn't in here, either. The screen door banged shut behind me as I stepped onto the front porch.

Men were gathered on the bank of the creek. Some stood back, while others kneeled at the edge.

"I tried to call your phone, honey," said Gran. She stood next to the railing, her fingernails digging into the wood. George had his arm around her, his gaze solemn. Tears rolled down her cheeks. "They found . . . something in the creek."

"It's not her," I said, fighting off the hideous suspicion clamoring through me. "It's not Glory."

I didn't hear her response because I was running. To the creek. I shoved through the ring of men standing watch, and tried to pry myself between those kneeling. They wouldn't let me through.

"Move, goddamn it!" I grabbed one by the shoulders and yanked him backward. He flew into the knot of men behind me, knocking them over like bowling pins.

Then I saw. Brady in the water. Holding her. Her face cradled to his shoulder. Her skin waxen, her body limp, her dress shredded. Her bare feet dangled in the water.

"Simone," he said. "Stop, honey. Please."

My grief was a living, breathing entity. It reached out and punched at the water. The creek churned and swirled. Water geysered and lacerated the muddy banks.

Brady shifted and her arm slid free of his grasp. The hand falling, falling into the water . . . and my mind snapped. I'd seen her tiny hand falling, falling into the blood. *I didn't mean to do it. I didn't mean to do it.* I couldn't move, and there she was, two years old, in her footie pajamas, squatting next to me, her tiny fingers dripping red.

Someone was grabbing me, holding me back. I slipped to my knees, my gaze on that small, still form, and screamed.

Chapter 23

I heard Brady's voice, but couldn't comprehend his words. Then what he was saying penetrated my anguish. "She's not Glory, sweetheart. She's not Glory."

When I came out of the fog, I stared into the jade eyes of Damian. He was the one who'd blocked me from going into the water and still held me by the shoulders. He glanced at the girl and grimaced. "It's Marissa." He dropped his head.

Darlene's little girl. Oh, God. Oh, no. Relief shuddered through me and drifted like snowflakes through my horror. My gaze skidded toward the creek. I watched Brady relinquish the girl to a dark-haired man, who gently lifted her into his arms.

"Did she d-drown?"

He shook his head once, and suddenly, I didn't want to know any more about the child. Another mother had lost her baby tonight. I knew it was wrong to feel so happy that Glory wasn't the lifeless one in Brady's arms. But I felt that way all the same.

"What about Glory?" I clutched Damian's shoulders. "Where is she?"

"We're expanding the search. We will not stop until she is found, Simone."

Then Brady was there, lifting me away from Damian's arms and into his. He scooped me up and strode toward the house. His jaw was clenched, his brown eyes dark with pent-up emotion.

I smacked his chest. "What the hell are you doing?"

"Taking you home. Where you'll stay with your grandmother. Do you understand me?"

"I'm short, not stupid. And here's a news flash: You don't get to tell me what to do."

He put me on the porch and gripped my arms. "Until I know what's going on here, I want you and Grandma Elaine safe. I won't be able to focus unless I know you're all right." Frowning, he studied me. "What the hell happened to you?"

"I got in a fight with the barn. It won."

Any other time, he might've laughed. Instead, he had the nerve to look even more concerned about me. He kissed my forehead. "Please, Simone," he whispered. "Stay here."

It was the "please" that did me in. That and the intensity of his stare. And maybe that little kiss of comfort. He really did care about us. I knew if anyone could track down my daughter, it was Brady.

"All right. When you find Glory, call Gran's cell phone. Mine's broken."

He nodded. Then he whirled around, reinserted his com link, and started giving orders to his team. Gran put her arm around me and squeezed.

"What was all the fuss?" she asked.

"Nothing." I couldn't bring myself to tell her that

another little girl was dead, one who looked a helluva lot like my daughter. "She's not there."

I looked at George and silently asked that he not tell her the truth. He nodded in acknowledgment.

"Brady will find her," said Gran, her voice all kinds of relieved. "I'm gonna go finish the lemon bars. And I'm gonna pray."

I wanted to pray, too, but God and I had a parting of ways even before I'd become a vampire. I still went to church every Sunday, hoping to find forgiveness. To find my faith again. Then I'd gotten undead, which was the reason of all reasons not to go to church anymore.

Gran and George went into the house, and I looked at the awfulness going on in my front yard. Most of the men dispersed, reengaging in the search effort. Four others took the girl to a black Ford F-350 truck. Three got into the bed with their precious cargo; the other swung into the driver's seat.

In no time at all, everyone was gone.

I stood on the porch, listening to the wind rattle through the trees of the nearby woods. I heard faint sounds—pants scraping bark, grass slapping at boots, voices murmuring. After a moment or two, even those noises faded. . . . And I heard only the water's quiet burbling.

"Where the hell are they?" I cried in frustration. It had been almost three hours since Glory had gone missing. Dawn was a little more than an hour away. I already felt the tug of slumber. I didn't want to go to bed without knowing Glory was all right.

I wouldn't have a choice. My body did whatever the hell it wanted when it came to sleep. There was no

Jolt for us undead, nothing in the world that stopped us from our daily rest.

I paced the living room, feeling frantic and helpless. Brady had called Gran's cell phone once, just to let us know that they hadn't found a damned thing.

"They'll find her." Grandma Elaine was sitting in her rocking chair, humming as she knitted another blanket. George was in the kitchen, cleaning. Apparently, the man reacted to stress by turning into Mr. Clean. He'd mopped, swept, taken out the trash, and was currently scrubbing out the refrigerator.

Gran always knitted blankets, mostly for Christmas presents. She also gifted her famous pepper-raspberry jelly—the only time you could ever get the stuff. Once you had a taste, you craved it all year long.

I had tried to fix my cell phone, tried to use it as a way to get my mind off Glory. My hands were shaking too much, and my brain refused to work. Gran had found some comfort in her knitting, but watching her be patient and steady just jangled my nerves more.

"Simone, you gotta have faith."

"You think God is gonna save her?" I asked, tasting bile. "You think if I pray hard enough, He'll bring Glory home? He didn't seem all that interested in saving us when we needed His help the most. She almost died then, too. You know what I had to do. You know what happened. God wasn't there." I smacked the arm of the couch. "We're just lab rats in a maze, looking for the fucking cheese. And He keeps moving the cheese."

"You're the only one who can figure out your relationship with our maker, child." She sighed and turned toward me. "Are you really going to blame God for the choices you made?"

We'd had this conversation before, and it always hit

the same wall. And if I were to believe Dr. Merrick and Zerina, then God was not just some all-powerful guy who helped one person but not another. He was life itself. And my life was created by my choices.

I think I might be able to live with that concept of God. I couldn't blame Him for what I had set into motion. Lyle showed up with the gun. Jacob had laughed, even after Lyle shot him in the shoulder. Laughed as he wrenched it out of the old man's hands and put it to Lyle's forehead.

"Simone?"

I heard the concern in Gran's voice. Being blind had in no way inhibited her ability to see the truth about people. She knew I was skipping down the dark side of memory lane.

"I'm okay." I stood up, trying to shake off the willies. Thinking about my old life, about when I was the Other Simone, always gave me the chills. "I need some fresh air."

"Really?" said Gran, smiling. "Since when?"

"Oh, ha." I leaned down and kissed her cheek. "I'm too restless to just sit here. I'm going for a walk. I'll be back in a few."

"All right, baby."

She went back to knitting, and I left the house. I sure as hell didn't want go to the barn again. I hadn't quite processed what had happened to me there. When Brady came back, when he brought Glory to me, I would sit down and tell him everything.

Going to the creek didn't hold any interest for me, either. I didn't want to relive those moments when I thought Brady was bringing Glory out of the water. That poor girl. What had happened to her? And what about Darlene? Was she dead, too?

Stupid as it was, I walked toward the water, inexplicably drawn to the place. Before I knew it, I was already halfway down the pier. I stopped, looking out to the water. It didn't look so calm and friendly now. I doubted I'd ever stick my toes in there again.

I walked to the end of the pier and looked down. I saw nothing in the muddied water. Just the usual debris—sticks, leaves, and there, a candy wrapper. Baby Ruth.

Squatting, I peered down. The disturbed silt hadn't yet resettled, and it left the water murky. Gray clouds had scuttled across the moon, only half-visible, leaving very little light.

The Baby Ruth wrapper twirled around, just out of my reach. With everything that was going on, picking up litter was the least of my worries. I studied the gently sloping banks. The section near the pier had been gouged by boots and hands.

Wait a minute. Baby Ruth? That was Reiner's favorite candy. What the hell was it doing floating in the very creek where Marissa had died?

My whole body froze. No—no way. Granted, I didn't have good feelings about the man, but I couldn't see him killing a little girl.

Then again, I'd already shown what a bad judge of character I could be.

"Simone?"

I almost jumped out of my skin. As it was, I nearly fell into the water.

Reiner grabbed me by the shoulders and pulled me backward, preventing my headfirst splash into the stream.

"Shit!" I shrugged off his hands and struggled to

my feet. "You scared the hell out of me! Why did you sneak up on me like that?"

His eyebrows almost touched his hairline. "I did not sneak up on you. You were . . . occupied."

I couldn't hide my nervousness. "Sorry! It's just . . . I'm crazy worried about Glory."

"Understandable, *Liebling*. You are all right?"

"I'm fine, just fine." I managed to push my lips into a trembling smile. "Is that why you're here? To join in the search?"

He shook his head. "I am here for Marissa."

For a shocked moment, I couldn't speak. Finally, I managed to sputter, "What?"

He tapped his nose. "It's what I do, Simone. I'm a tracker. The best."

"Better than Damian and his brothers?"

"The best," he repeated. "I can track anything, anyone. I will find the one who strangled the little girl."

My stomach clenched. "Strangled? Sweet Jesus."

Had he done it? Perfect cover if the murderer was the one searching himself. Still, Reiner's eyes held no guilt. To my überears, his heartbeat and breathing remained normal. He didn't flinch away or try to avoid the subject of the dead girl. I couldn't believe he was *that* cool under pressure, so I was left with one conclusion: He hadn't hurt Marissa.

"You understand the importance of finding the killer, *ja*? It is the only reason why I do not join the search for your daughter." He looked empathetic. "Do not worry, Simone. Your Glory will be found."

"Of course she will." I wanted so badly to cry again, but I swallowed the knot crawling up my throat. I had no tears. And dry-weeping in front of Reiner . . . well,

I just wouldn't do it. "I'll leave you to your work, then."

I engaged my vampire speed and reached the house in no time flat. I went inside, feeling more agitated than ever. Maybe if I liked the guy better, I wouldn't feel so offended by his need to create a connection with me. Reiner had some sort of agenda here in Broken Heart. Obviously, he didn't like that the princes had abdicated their political positions. Then again, he'd gone to all the trouble of making that expensive statue. Surely such a gift meant he was embracing the future of his people. Was he here to support the new direction? Or was he here to thwart it?

I rolled my eyes. *What next, Simone? You wanna study the John F. Kennedy case files and form another theory about the magic bullet?* My paranoia only subsided after I got undead. Having supernatural abilities certainly made me worry less about the past catching up with me. Broken Heart had unknowingly become the ultimate Witness Protection Program.

I heard the trill of Gran's phone. I hurried into the kitchen. Gran leaned against the counter, her face red from crying.

George held her cell phone up to his ear. "Yes, Brady. She's here."

He held out the phone and I took it.

"Please tell me you found her."

"Two men will arrive in approximately five seconds. You will go with them." His voice was as hard as granite.

"Oh, my God." My undead heart did a loop-de-loop. "What aren't you telling me?"

He didn't respond.

I tried to draw in a breath, which so didn't work. "It's close to dawn, damn it!"

The back door opened and two men, dressed head to toe in black uniforms filled with all kinds of scary equipment, entered. Their faces were covered and they wore goggles.

I looked at the strangers who stood sentinel in my kitchen. They each raised their rifles and pointed them at my head.

"What's happening?" asked Gran, her blind gaze tracking the intruders. "Who are you?"

George stepped in front of my grandmother, and she grasped his shoulders.

"Hey, man," said George, his arms rising. "Chillax."

The man on the right swung his rifle and aimed it at the vampire.

"No," I cried. "Please!"

A beam of blue light issued from the gun. It struck George in the heart and lasered straight through him into my grandmother.

They were knocked backward, George's eyes wide as he fell to the floor. He landed next to Gran, who was moaning, blood burbling from the wound in her chest.

I screamed and moved toward them. George would be okay; he was already dead. But Gran . . . oh, my God, Gran! I could smell her blood and her fear. George wasn't moving, but Gran had the presence of mind to press one of her hands against the laceration.

The other man grabbed my wrist and jerked me toward the door.

His grip was like iron, and no amount of pulling and clawing at his gloved hand made him let go. They couldn't be humans, not if their strength matched mine. Usually it was easy to pick out who was human, lycan, or vampire. It appeared they'd somehow managed to shield me from determining species.

I couldn't glamour them because they had on black goggles, which completely covered their eyes.

For all my vampire perks, I sure was sucking ass right now.

I fought and yelled and begged, but they dragged me out of the house. The one who'd shot George and my grandmother pulled a small silver gun from his weapons belt.

Brady! Goddamn it, Brady!

"Hold her."

His partner grabbed both my arms and twisted them behind my back. I yelped. Then his asshole friend placed the tiny gun against my neck.

Simone? What the hell is going on?

I heard a small hissing sound. The world went soft, and my body liquefied.

Everything went dark.

Chapter 24

Thursday, June 20

When I opened my eyes, Jacob leaned over me, stinking of booze and eau de sewer. The tequila bottle was still in his hand. He swigged it, his throat moving as he gulped the poison down.

Confusion splintered the images dancing through my skull. Kitchen. Men with guns. Gran getting shot. The odd memories spun into blackness.

What's going on? Where am I?

Glory was crying. She'd stayed in the closet, obviously too afraid to come out. Jacob ignored her sniveling, her gulping cries for mama. It was almost as if he couldn't hear her.

My cheek throbbed where he'd backhanded me. My face felt wet. He watched, smirking, as my trembling fingers swiped at the moisture. Blood.

"What'd you say to me?" he asked, his mouth

curling into an even uglier sneer. "Say it again, bitch. I fucking dare you."

"I-I'm sorry."

"You're goddamned right, you're sorry."

Slowly, I sat up, cradling my sore cheek. My jaw throbbed. I knew from experience a bruise would bloom there as ugly and obvious as a black rose among the white.

Jacob straightened. "Get up."

My whole body quivered, pain and terror weaving thorny tendrils inside me. It hurt to move, but I managed to get to my feet.

"You really sorry about what you said?"

I nodded, trying to adopt a penitent expression, gasping as agony stabbed me.

He reached out, and I couldn't stop the flinch. He cupped the side of my face he hadn't bashed. "You're so pretty, and now look at you. Face is all messed up." He grabbed my chin and yanked my face to his. Pain screeched through me; I bit my lower lip to keep from screaming.

"Get your hands off her!"

Startled by the sound of Lyle's voice, Jacob let me go and stumbled around to face the old man. He was pointing a .38 Special at Jacob. And he'd brought Roogie Roo with him. The little terrier stood next to his master, baring his tiny teeth and growling at my husband.

"Lyle, no!" I cried.

He might've been in his seventies, but his grip was steady and so was his aim. Jacob seemed to find the situation more amusing than worrisome. He tossed the bottle behind him. It spun across the carpet, its amber liquid splashing out.

"Get the baby, Simone," said Lyle. "Then you're gonna leave, and this son of a bitch is goin' to jail."

I couldn't make my feet move. I knew Jacob wouldn't let us leave. Lyle could be waving around an Uzi and Jacob wouldn't have cared. He was well trained in combat and weaponry and didn't scare easily. Hell, he didn't scare at all.

"Please, just go," I begged my friend. "We're okay. Really."

Lyle's blue gaze hardened. "This is for your own good, Simone. Now get the baby."

"Yeah, honey," said Jacob lazily. "Get our darling girl and go with this silly old bastard."

He grinned, and I knew we wouldn't make it out the door. He'd rather kill me himself than let me go. And what about my daughter?

I looked at Lyle. I wanted, more than anything, to pick up Glory and run. All I had to do was to accept his help and take the risk.

That was the problem. I wouldn't risk Glory. If there was any way to get her out alive, I'd do it. Even if it meant not going with Lyle.

I knew why he was doing this. He was a retired police officer who'd seen domestic violence end in tragedy too many times to count. Worse, his only child, his daughter, had died at the hands of an abusive boyfriend.

He'd shared those stories with me, hoping to encourage me to leave Jacob. I'd started making plans, but not much else. I was too intimidated to stand on my own two feet, not to mention apprehensive of what life would be like in the world that allowed men like Jacob to thrive. No matter how many times he hit me or threatened me or made me feel like shit, at least I had a roof over my head, food to eat, clothes to wear.

At that moment, I understood how pathetic those excuses were. How I let my own weakness and fear control me. Jacob beat me because I allowed it. Somehow, somewhere, I believed I deserved to be terrorized.

I glanced at Jacob. His gaze was on me, waiting for me to move, to decide. My heart jackhammered in my chest, and sweat slicked my spine.

"I can't live this way anymore," I whispered. I turned toward the closet.

Jacob leapt toward Lyle and wrested his hand. The old man went down on one knee, trying to keep hold of the weapon. He balled up his free hand and hit Jacob. None of his blows affected my husband.

Jacob wrenched the gun free and twisted Lyle's frail arm. I heard the snap as Jacob broke it. Lyle screamed and fell to the floor.

Roogie Roo launched himself at Jacob, tearing into his leg. "Goddamned dog!"

He kicked the terrier hard. Roogie Roo yelped, flying across the room and smacking into the wall. The poor little mutt slid to the floor, limp.

Jacob aimed the gun at Lyle, who raised a shaking hand in a weak show of protection.

"Jacob! No!" I leapt onto his back, trying to grab for his arm, but it was too late.

He shot Lyle. Three times the gun went off. Three times Lyle's body jerked as metal pierced his flesh.

The first bullet killed him.

I let go of Jacob, falling to the floor. I sobbed into my hands, praying with every breath in my body for God to help me. *If it's my time, Lord, so be it. But please, please help me save Glory. She's just a baby, God. She deserves a safe, happy life.*

Jacob dropped the gun and staggered to the bed. He sat down heavily, his gaze taking in the destruction he'd wrought. "Fucking bitch. Look what you made me do."

Blood from Lyle's body ribboned toward me. The gun was wet with it. Six bullets. Lyle had told me that a .38 Special had six bullets.

Three were expended.

My hand trembled as I picked up the gun. It felt heavy, the weight of the world in my palm. I got to my feet and swayed there, trying to dig past the pain, the weariness.

I aimed the gun at Jacob. "You're going to let us walk out of here."

"Or what? You gonna kill me?" He laughed. "You can't even kill a bug, Simone. You'd rather set them free in the yard than crush one with your dainty princess foot."

"The police are coming."

He shook his head. "Don't lie to me."

Sirens sounded in the distance. What the hell had taken them so long? A few minutes earlier and Lyle might be alive.

Jacob's gaze pinned me. "You called the fucking police?" He shot to his feet, his expression all menace. "You ungrateful bitch."

He ignored the gun shaking in my hand. He put his hands around my throat and squeezed. His eyes were wild, his face red with fury.

I couldn't breathe.

The barrel of the gun pressed against his heart as he choked me. My vision grayed and my heart pounded in my ears. The room was spinning, and everything seemed to be falling away from me.

I squeezed the trigger.

Jacob released me and careened backward. His eyes went wide and he fell, landing on his side. He was still breathing as the blood poured from his chest.

I fell to my knees, coughing, wheezing, trying to get air into my lungs. Glory crawled out of the closet and climbed over her dying father.

I couldn't move, and there she was, two years old in her footie pajamas, squatting next to me, her tiny fingers dripping red.

That's when I heard the police sirens roar up our street. The cars screeched to a stop, doors banged open, feet pounded up the concrete walk.

Too late.

I awoke chained to a wall.

Reliving that night was like being thrown into hell. Why was my conscience tormenting me anew? Here I'd thought I'd dealt with my past.

Turns out, not so much.

I'd been stripped down to my bra and panties. The room was as dark and stuffy as a basement. Not even my vamp vision could discern anything, not windows or furniture or even other walls.

I struggled, straining as hard as I could on the chains. The manacles that surrounded my wrists and ankles glowed blue. Then it seemed as if dozens of tiny nails were simultaneously shoved into the flesh bound by the shackles.

The pain was excruciating.

I screamed.

Memories flashed. Intruders busting into my

kitchen. Gran and George being shot. Oh, God. I squeezed my eyes against the ache. Was she alive? *Please, please, let her be alive.* Grief settled around me. How could she survive? That blue beam had taken down a vampire. Surely a human had no chance.

Suddenly, I realized that someone else was in the room. It wasn't that I hadn't sensed a presence before. I'd been alone. Whoever this was had just appeared without sound or movement to give him away.

"Simone Sweet," said a voice. "Sweet, sweet Simone."

Everything went still. My body went cold, clammy. "Jacob."

"I'm disappointed that you didn't keep my last name."

"You're dead."

"So are you. And yet here we are, having a conversation."

Dread pulsed through me. He sounded so calm, so in control.

"What? Disappointed you didn't kill me?"

"Deeply," I said.

He laughed in that hard, mean way I remembered. Jesus, Mary, and Joseph. My undead heart tried to claw its way out of my throat.

I heard a click. My worst nightmare stood a foot away, shining a flashlight on me. He wiggled the light in my face, forcing me to narrow my gaze to avoid being blinded.

Then he put it up to his chin. He looked the same. How could someone so handsome be such an evil bastard? The yellow beam lit his features eerily. "Boo!"

He laughed, then danced the beam across my body.

"Looking good, honey. Blood diet sure is doing you wonders."

He knew I was a vampire.

Suspicious, I glared at him. "You were the one in the woods," I said. "And at my garage."

"Yeah, I shoved you through the barn wall—don't forget that." He looked at me, his enjoyment plain. "Simone, it's Brady."

His voice sounded just like Brady's. He'd lured me into the barn, probably setting it up so the door would fall on me. And then he called on the cell phone and made me believe Brady had taken custody of me and tried to kill Gran and George.

"I've learned some new skills, honey." He laughed again. "I bet you wet your panties when you saw me. Aw. C'mon, now. I couldn't resist visiting my wife." He tsked, tsked. "Imagine my surprise when our newest mission to rid the world of paraterrorists brought me to my old hometown. And not only do I discover Broken Heart filled with vampires and lycans, I find my long-lost family."

My heart dropped to my toes. "You shot Elaine!"

"Wasn't my finger on the trigger. Besides, every war has collateral damage."

He didn't have a soul. He was a fucking sociopath who liked to hurt people. How could he not be upset that Gran was injured, or worse?

"I never figured you for a mechanic. My guess would've been stripper. I mean, you don't really have brains, but oo-wee, you got a smokin' body."

"Shut up, you prick!" Pain vibrated in every nerve ending, but my fury was even greater. "You took Glory, didn't you?"

And Flet. What had happened to the pixie? I was afraid to ask.

"She's my daughter, too. And since her mother won't be around much longer, she's gonna need me."

Several thoughts whirled. Jacob was out of his freaking mind if he thought I'd die like a good little vampire. I had to find Glory and get her to safety. And Jacob was flinging around the same kind of military terms as Brady. No wonder he'd tensed when I talked about Nellis Air Force base. Duh. Nellis and Area 51 were both in Nevada. Where else would the government take and train an elite group of soldiers to fight paraterrorism?

Prior to the night that I shot my husband, Jacob said he'd been transferred into a new unit. He was training for something big, he'd said. Something I'd never believe. At the time he was bragging about it, I remember feeling only relief that he would be gone more often.

"You're with ETAC," I accused.

"Guilty." He turned off the flashlight. "And your new boyfriend is on ETAC's most-wanted list. You've been unfaithful, Simone. After all, we're still married."

My stomach squeezed, and bile rose in my throat.

"Oh, and FYI . . ." His voice was a purr and too damned close. He turned on the flashlight again and aimed it between us. He was mere inches from my face. He grinned at me and revealed a set of gleaming white fangs. "I'm a vampire, too."

Chapter 25

Shit. Oh, shit.

Jacob hissed as he pressed his fangs against my neck, his tongue flickering like a slimy snake's.

"Stop it!" I strained against the bonds. "Get away from me!"

The manacles glowed blue, and once again pain screamed into every nerve ending. I sucked in a useless breath, my eyes aching with the need to cry.

"Would it help," he said in Brady's voice, "if I sounded like this?"

His hand cupped my breast.

I wanted to vomit. "Get. The. Fuck. Off. Me!"

He laughed and backed off. "Darlene wasn't nearly as . . . resistant."

I realized what he was saying: He knew Darlene. And now she'd disappeared.

"You remember what it was like when you disappointed me?" Jacob reached out and stroked my cheek with one finger. His nail scraped my cheek. "She was weak, Simone. But you, you surprised me."

"How long have you been here?" I asked, my voice trembling. And then another more terrible thought occurred. "You . . . killed Rick and Shawn!"

He didn't answer, but his eyes flashed with malice. Oh, Jesus. He'd killed my donor and poor Shawn. And God knew who else. My gorge rose. "M-Marissa," I whispered. "Did you hurt her, too?"

He shrugged. "She looks a lot like Glory, doesn't she?"

Dumbfounded, I stared at him. Did he mean Marissa had been killed because someone thought she was Glory . . . or that she wasn't?

A door opened on the opposite side of the room. Jacob turned off his flashlight and moved away. Thank God. I sagged in relief. The sharp projections inside the cuffs eased up. Ah. I got it now. No struggling equaled no pain.

I heard a buzzing noise, and the overhead lights flickered on.

"What the hell are you doing in here?" asked the man striding into the room. "I told you not to have contact with the prisoner."

Jacob stood at attention and saluted. "With all due respect, General, she is my wife."

"Out. Do not disobey my orders again or you'll find yourself pinned to the wall."

Jacob saluted the man again, then marched out of the room. I felt a smidgen of satisfaction at Jacob's upbraiding. But I didn't fool myself that I'd seen the last of him, or that he wouldn't find another way to torment me.

I studied this new threat. He was short and squat,

his face as flat as an iron. He had steely gray eyes and a haircut that made the top of his skull look like a wire brush. He was dressed in the same black outfit as the others.

"I'm going to give you a choice, Simone. You help us, and you get your little girl back and relocation to a safe house."

"Or?"

"Or I kill you." His tone held neither persuasion nor threat. He merely expected me to do what he wanted. Well, hell. Why bother with the illusion of choice?

"What, exactly, would I be helping you with?"

"We are executing a plan that will protect this country from the terrorist threat presented by supernaturals. The biggest congregation of parakind ever in the United States will happen in two days. We must nullify this menace."

"It's a religious gathering," I said, horrified.

"We are aware of Patricia Marchand and her . . . condition. We cannot allow two of the most powerful segments of supernaturals to unite. Or breed." Disgust wormed across his face.

He was crazy. Not once in the history of humans had parakind attempted to take over. Granted, the Wraiths wanted to rule over their human prey, but they never made it past warring with other vampires. Parakind took care of their own problems. Besides, there weren't really enough of us to take over the state of Texas, much less all of America.

I felt chilled to the bone, and not because I was hanging from the wall in just my underclothing. Jacob was a vampire. Someone had Turned him, knowing what he would be doing as part of ETAC. "You're using supernaturals to fight on your behalf. Isn't that hypocritical?"

"We utilize the enemy's tactics in order to defeat them." He stood before me, his eyes as hard and flat as pebbles. "I assure you that we will be victorious."

"Then why do you need me?"

"Your vampire gifts, in particular your water powers, will help us implement certain strategies. In addition, you are in close contact with Braddock Hayes, a man we intend to reacquire."

They couldn't have Brady. I'd give them everything else, but not him. He'd escaped from ETAC and tried to make up for all that he'd done.

Maybe it was time that I did the same.

"If you agree to our terms, you'll be released from your imprisonment and briefed. After you complete your mission, you and your daughter will be relocated."

Where? To Guantánamo Bay? I didn't just fall off the turnip truck. Even if he kept his word, he wouldn't let Glory and me go off on our own. The relocation would surely be somewhere they could control our movements. Or worse, we could be the next in line for experimentation.

I hated to think what he had in mind if I chose death before dishonor.

I did not want to betray my friends. I didn't want anyone else to get hurt. But most of all, I didn't want my daughter to pay the price for my mistakes. I would do anything for Glory. All I had to do was figure out a way to save Broken Heart, too.

Yeah. Easy peasy.

"All right," I said. "But I want to see my daughter."

"That can be arranged." The General grabbed a

wrist chain, yanking on it. The nails jabbed my wrist, and I yelped. Damn it! "If you do not do exactly what you are told, both you and your daughter will die. I do not give second chances, Simone."

I nodded. The General terrified me. He was as cold and methodical as a robot, no more interested in emotion than a lycanthrope was in eating a salad.

I had no idea how I was going to help ETAC complete its insane mission *and* save everyone I cared about. Maybe it wasn't possible.

But I had to try.

I'd been allowed to dress in the clothing they'd confiscated from me, everything but my shoes. Like I had a knife or a mini-C4 explosive tucked into my Nikes. Paranoid freaks. I was a mom and a mechanic, not James Bond. Besides, a vampire's weapons were part and parcel of the whole blood-sucking gig: fangs, speed, strength, and glamour. That explained why, as I followed the General down the dimly lit hallway, two men dressed like cyborg Rambos marched behind me. They both carried the black rifles that probably issued blue beams of death.

Gran. My heart clenched. Was she really dead? Or had she survived? And poor George. He could've turned to ash after I was carted away.

We stopped in front of a door. It looked as thick and secure as a bank vault. He pointed to the slit in the middle.

I had to stand on my tippy-toes, but I managed to look through it. Behind the sliver of glass, I saw two children. They each occupied a bed. Tubes were placed in their nostrils and an IV snaked from their left arms.

Helpless rage pounded like primal drums. My

daughter was in the right bed, her eyes closed, her small chest rising and falling under the thin covers.

The other bed held a boy with shaggy blond hair and Brad Pitt looks. He looked eleven, maybe twelve years old. He reminded me of someone, but I couldn't place who.

"What the hell is this?" I gritted out. "What did you to do them?"

"They're sleeping. The drugs are harmless, at least in their current dosage."

Oh, my God. I lowered to my feet, my palms flat against the door so I could stay upright. My legs felt like wet noodles.

"If you fail, we will turn up the dosage to a fatal, irreversible amount. Your end will not be as . . . easy."

Terror paid me another visit. It settled heavy and icy in the place where my heart used to beat. My daughter was in danger, danger that her own father put her in *again*, and here I was, wishing I'd shot my husband with all three bullets. In his head.

"You son of a bitch!"

"I suggest you rein in your temper, Simone," said the General curtly. "You don't have the luxury of being an emotional wreck. I'll take you to the briefing room, and you'll memorize everything I tell you. You will do each thing in order and at the correct time."

What choice did I have? They had Glory. I'd make nice until they returned me to Broken Heart. Then I would find a way to communicate with someone. No, with Brady. He would believe me. He would help us.

I could rely on him.

"One more thing," said the General as he led the way into the briefing room, "if you tell anyone about our agreement, the deal is off and your lives are forfeited."

I said nothing. I cast my gaze to the table as I sat in a chair across from his. It was the same kind of threat Jacob used to issue—as if guilt, low self-esteem, and base fear weren't enough to keep me in line. *If you tell anyone, you'll wish you hadn't.*

That bullshit didn't work anymore. The General could blather on all he wanted about ultimatums. I'd find a way out, and this time, I would ask for help.

"Listen carefully," said the General.

I did.

I woke up on the pier, my hand dangling over the side. They'd used the silver gun on me again, all in the name of protecting their location. Why dump me here? Why not inside my house? Or even at my garage?

Water splashed against my hand. I rose to a sitting position and stared down into the shimmering water. Everything would be all right. So long as I killed everyone in town, betrayed the man I was falling in love with, and threw every one of my principles out the window. I—

"Simone."

I was so relieved to hear Brady's voice, I scrambled to my feet and turned, intending to . . .

Brady stood on the pier, staring at me like he didn't recognize me. He was dressed in his ETAC uniform. The belt around his trim waist was filled with gadgets—and weapons.

I walked toward him, my hands out in supplication. I could trust him. He promised that nothing would change between us. And I believed him. "Brady."

"Why did you disappear?" His words were clipped.

Do not reveal to anyone where you've been or that you've been in contact with ETAC. The General had offered the warning in his concise, empty tone. They'd stuck a tracking device in my shoulder, in the unlikely event I got a case of the stupids and tried to run away. Worse, they could hear everything I said.

When I offered no answers, his lips thinned and he shot me a look of disgust. "How could you, Simone? She was your grandmother. And George was just a nice guy."

My belly shook with nausea. Foreboding clambered up my spine. "What are you talking about?"

Regret sliced his expression, but only for a second. He removed a pistol from his belt and aimed it at me. "You shot them," he said, "with a gun you stole from me."

Chapter 26

I couldn't explain how George and Gran got shot, since that would mean admitting that ETAC was in Broken Heart. I'm sure it was only a matter of time before someone realized it, though with all the paranormals streaming into town and the festival preparations, everyone was preoccupied.

I couldn't figure out how to communicate with Brady—at least not without giving myself away to the assholes listening in. Then I remembered: We shared a telepathic bond.

Brady?

Get out of my head.

Hurt, I stared at him. His face was as hard as granite, and the gun pointed at my head was rock steady. He looked as though he might actually pull the trigger.

I couldn't bear to see the judgment in his eyes. I didn't understand why the guys who grabbed me used a gun stolen from Brady. If they could get to his weapons cache, why the hell couldn't they get to him?

"Brady," I said. "Please."

He shook his head. "No more lies, Simone."

Lies? What lies? I looked at him, helpless.

"C'mon," he said. "Let's go."

I believed that ETAC had a backup plan if I failed. All I knew for sure was that if I didn't complete the three tasks by tomorrow at midnight, it was all over for me and Glory.

You will disable the Invisi-shield, said the General, *but without destroying it. We want the posts intact. The damage should be incurred during the last hour before dawn.*

I didn't see how I would complete the first directive, and I was trying really hard not to panic. I had to figure a way out of this. Now.

Apparently, there *was* a gun missing from Brady's personal arsenal. The blue beams were not bullets. All laser signatures were the same. I'd never been to Brady's quarters, much less to the facility that housed his weaponry.

I hadn't expected to be accused of trying to shoot Gran and George, much less be targeted as the prime suspect in the murders of Rick, Shawn, and Dunmore. In addition, they'd thrown in the missing Darlene as Murder Victim #4.

The only person I had not been accused of killing was Marissa. That one they couldn't pin on me for a variety of reasons, so the theory about my killing rampage now included the idea that I had a partner.

I sat as a hostage in my own living room as Brady explained everything to me in a voice so devoid of emotion he reminded me of the General.

Damian and Patrick had arrived, along with Patsy and Gabriel. I supposed we didn't need the full

complement of Broken Heart citizens to watch my ac-
cusers humiliate me. Besides, the queen had all seven
powers of the Ancients. She could boil, fry, or freeze
me at her discretion.

"I would never, ever hurt a child, nor be associated
with someone sick enough to hurt a child." I glared at
everyone. Look at what I had done to protect Glory
from her own father. Not that anyone here knew it.
"You really, truly think I did this? That I not only killed
people—for no apparent reason, but that I also con-
sorted with a child murderer?"

"No," said Patsy. "I've been in the presence of true
evil, Simone. And that's not you. But we gotta figure
out what's going on here."

"Consider the victims," said Damian. "Rick and
Shawn were both your donors. Your phone call sent
Dunmore to Darlene's. And Darlene disappeared that
same day."

And Marissa had been found in the creek by my
house. I got it. I did. I had a connection to everyone
who'd died. But I'd watched enough *CSI* to know that
they were missing one important element: motivation.

"Why would I kill them?" I asked.

"Maybe someone forced you," said Brady. His gaze
burned with fury. Was that righteous anger at me . . .
or for me?

"Or someone is trying to frame me."

And yet, either way, the question remained: *Why?*
ETAC needed me mobile. I had no known enemies in
town. I almost always kept to myself; Brady was the
first person who'd visited the farm for any length of
time. He had opened the door to hosting the potluck,
to connecting with the others who lived and worked
here.

I remembered Dr. Merrick in the examination room, her brown eyes filled with worry as she warned me about the unfolding events.

Revenge . . . or justice.

Jacob.

I went cold inside. He'd been watching me, shadowing me for who knows how long. ETAC didn't come up with this whole blow-up-parakind idea out of the blue. Had he killed Rick? And then gone for Shawn? He'd lured me into the barn, and he'd made the phone call as Brady. Had he been at the garage on Saturday? Heard me talk to Darlene, and later somehow knew I'd called Dunmore?

The three men were drained. Jacob was a vampire. As a human he'd had a difficult time controlling his base urges. He damned sure wouldn't control his blood hunger.

Shit. I took a sec to gather my composure. Did they somehow suspect that my husband was alive? Worse, did they think that I was in collusion with him? The idea made me sick to my stomach.

Damian and Brady exchanged a look, and Damian shook his head. What the hell did that mean? What were they communicating about? The scenario was going bad, and fast. How the hell could I disable the Invisi-shield tonight if I was under suspicion of murder? If they knew he was lurking around town, did they suspect that ETAC was here, too?

"Why didn't you tell us that your married name was McCree?" asked Patrick.

Crap. They knew that Sweet was my maiden name. Only Gran could've told them, so that meant she was alive. At least, I hoped so. And now, because it appeared I'd lied to protect myself (duh), they'd have less reason to believe I wasn't running around town, acting like Freddy Krueger.

"Elaine is my husband Jacob's grandmother," I admitted. I explained that Elaine's dead husband was Jessica's great-uncle, the half brother of Jessica's grandmother, who'd passed away some time ago.

Jonathon was the result of an affair between his mother and Jessica's great-great-grandfather. He'd given the property to Jon and Elaine, but neither one had claimed it. Not until the car accident that killed Jon and took Gran's eyesight. She reverted to her maiden name, which is why no one knew her connection to Jessica's family.

"Jess doesn't know, then?" asked Patrick.

I shook my head and looked at the carpet. My stomach roiled. How did I reassure everyone that I wasn't the problem? How was I supposed to tell them about the real threat?

I thought about Gran, the woman to whom I owed so very much. She never admitted it, but I think the name change helped her keep her distance from her only son: Mack. He'd been a drug addict who often blacked out; he usually didn't remember that he'd beaten his wife and son.

"Elaine was the only family I had," I said. My tone was pleading, but I couldn't stop it from cracking. I felt the ache behind my eyes for tears that would never flow. "I couldn't make it on my own. It wasn't just the financial difficulties, but my emotional instability. I needed the support. I went to therapy for almost two years—in Tulsa. Then I was Turned, and, well, I guess I was strong enough by then to stand on my own two feet."

"You told me that Jacob was dead." The suspicion in Brady's voice was a dagger in my soul.

"I shot him in the heart," I said, knowing my confession would reinforce their suspicions. "So yeah, he's dead."

"Why did you shoot him?" asked Gabriel softly.

"Apparently I just like to kill people." Anger vibrated in my voice. These people were supposed to be my friends. And Brady . . . he was supposed to be even more than my friend. The one I trusted. The one I could depend on.

"The bastard hit her," said Brady.

Too little, too late. I felt like his support was reluctantly given; his tone revealed frustration and doubt. I don't know why he even bothered to defend me that tiny bit. As much as I hated to admit it, he was the only one who could help me.

Brady, please!

Stay out of my head, Simone. I mean it.

Stoic, he stood on the other side of the coffee table, his arms crossed. I caught his gaze and rubbed my wrist.

Would he get the implication?

Frowning, he gazed down at his own wrist, which his black glove covered. But at least he was looking at the wrist scarred by the removal of his tattoo. He glanced at me and I tilted my head to the left, lifting my shoulder as if trying to shake loose some of its tension.

He gave a slight nod, then looked away. I could only hope that he meant he understood.

Patsy sat on the couch. She took my hands into hers and stared at me. Her eyes glowed red, drawing me deeper into her gaze. I felt my mind go fuzzy.

"Tell us about the night your husband died."

I started talking, but it was like someone else revealed what had happened. I felt outside myself, watching at a distance, vaguely interested. I told them everything, from the moment Jacob arrived to the moment I killed him.

"The police were coming," I said. "I don't know if they heard the shots. I stole Lyle's wallet, grabbed Glory, and ran out the back door."

Our yard was fenced, but Lyle's was not. I swung Glory over the chain-link and tumbled over myself. Lyle's home was unlocked.

While the police busted into my house and found the bodies, I took precious moments to wash off the blood from me and Glory. I took the cash from Lyle's wallet and left it on his dresser. He'd told me about his cookie jar fund, so I went into the kitchen and took all the money from it, too.

Then I wrapped up my silent daughter in one of Lyle's jackets and snuck out. Had I more presence of mind, I might've stayed there and tried to bluff the police. Say it was my house so I could wait and take Lyle's Cadillac. Later, I realized I'd left a blood trail in the backyard and in Lyle's house, too. Irrational fear had worked in my favor.

I had $234. I carried Glory all the way to a seedy roadside motel—the kind of place with hourly rates and a clerk who smelled like pot. He didn't look twice at me.

I soaked our clothes and scrubbed out as much of the blood as possible. Called a cab. Bought bus tickets and got as far as Laughlin.

"How was it that you came to Broken Heart?"

Patsy's voice was soothing. It seemed to promise relief from my guilt, if I'd only tell her what she wanted to know.

In Laughlin, I met Joe Montresso, who took one look at me and Glory and decided we needed rescuing. We did. He owned a garage in town with his life partner, Avery, who rebuilt motorcycles. They gave me a job, helped with Glory, and let me rent the room above their garage. Joe and Avery taught me all about mechanics, said I had a natural talent for putting things back together. Everything except myself.

Four months passed, then five, and then Elaine's birthday came around. I took a chance and called her.

Though the Air Force had informed her of Jacob's death, they had not told her the circumstances. I cried as I admitted everything, and she told me to come to Broken Heart.

I said good-bye to Joe and Avery, packed up Glory, got into the truck Joe had fixed up for us, and drove to Oklahoma.

Patsy knew the rest of the story.

"Did you kill Rick or Shawn?" she asked.

"No."

"Do you know what happened to Dunmore and Darlene?"

"No."

"Where did you go after Elaine and George were shot?"

I opened my mouth, but someone grasped my shoulder and startled me. I looked up into the worried face of Brady.

"Enough," he said to Patsy. "Quit grilling her."

Patsy's blond brows rose nearly to her hairline, but she lifted her hands in an *okay* gesture, and the redness in her eyes faded to their natural blue color.

I shook off Patsy's glamour, feeling a mixture of gratitude and resentment. At least they knew I wasn't a cold-blooded killer.

But I didn't appreciate the mind-fuck.

Brady released me and retreated. Damn. He couldn't get away from me fast enough. I didn't want to be judged by these people. Still, what the hell did I expect? This kind of interrogation and suspicion was my nightmare come to life.

Dr. Merrick had been right. All my choices had led to this moment. To this place.

I was so screwed.

Chapter 27

No matter what anyone thought about my guilt or innocence, I was housebound. Patsy said Gran and George had survived the shooting, but she didn't tell me much else except that I could visit Gran tomorrow night.

Brady made a big deal about telling me the search for Glory was ongoing. I realized I'd been stupid. I should've asked about her and played the panicked mom. I knew where she was, and that her very life depended on me, but no one else did. However, there was more on the plate of the queen than what I'd been doing. Or not doing.

Looking exhausted and irritable, Patsy said her good-byes and left with Gabriel.

I sat on the couch with my knees pulled up to my chin and listened to Brady, Patrick, and Damian decide what to do about little ol' me. My thoughts circled round and round. How could I get to the posts and sabotage the shield? How could I talk to Brady and ask for his help? He was shutting me out in every way, including more mental rebuffs.

Way to be on my side, asshole. He'd said there was nothing I could ever do to make him turn away. Liar. I was really starting to hate anything that produced too much testosterone. So I was overreacting. It's not like I didn't have a reason or three.

Raised voices brought me out of my reverie. Brady was arguing with Damian and Patrick.

"You're too close," Patrick said. "Having you stay with her is like asking the fox to guard the chickens."

Wow. Patrick using farm analogies? He'd been living in Oklahoma too long. Brady looked as though he wanted to plant his fist in both Damian and Patrick's faces. He had no qualms about kicking paranormal ass.

"Add whatever security measures you want," said Brady. "But I'm staying."

I wondered why he was even bothering. He could be out of here, no obligation to me, and on to something else. I don't know if I felt relieved or apprehensive that he was being all dutiful. Maybe a little of both, with some resentment and panic thrown in.

Crap, crap, *crap*! I already felt the tug of dawn, and damn it, I still had my task to accomplish—and it had to be done an hour before dawn. I wasn't naive enough to think I could sneak away from a lycan, a vampire, and a military-trained counterterrorist.

But I did have an idea. It was a long shot, one I was willing to take. Otherwise I would have to outwit the Three Stooges.

Hmph. Really. How hard could that be?

"I'm goin' upstairs," I said, unfolding myself from the couch. "It'll be lights-out soon, anyway."

Three suspicious gazes swung in my direction.

"What are you going to do up there?" asked Damian.

Several rude responses tried to crowd out of my mouth, but I swallowed 'em down. "Pray," I said. "Maybe God'll see fit to help me. Maybe He'll see fit to help us all."

That declaration stunned them into silence. Trying not to feel too satisfied that I'd gotten them to shut up, I went upstairs to my room and closed the door. I locked it, too. Not that doing so would do any good.

My room used to have double windows, but they were covered over; the walls had been sprayed with a special metallic substance perfected by the Consortium. Basically, it kept the sunlight from getting into my room. I'd always slept safely here, even though I wasn't friends with the dark.

I turned on the light and got onto my bed, a full-sized white four-poster that looked like it belonged to that girl from *Labyrinth*. All I needed was piles of stuffed animals and posters of unicorns and rainbows. The bed was whimsical and so not my choice. I guess I'd never thought about redecorating since maybe, somewhere in the back of my mind, I thought I'd get my own house. My own life.

I sat in the middle of the bed and crossed my legs. If I wasn't already slated for hell, telling that lie about praying might put me on the fast track. Of course, if I was wrestling with my beliefs about a higher power, then I supposed that threw the whole heaven-and-hell theory out of the mix. Not to mention, death wasn't exactly a problem for most vampires.

I waited for a few minutes, just to make sure no one was going to check on me. No one came. Not even

Brady. I tried not to think about him or how I felt about his abandonment.

Then, softly, I called, "Flet. Come to me."

No annoying gold sparkle arrived. One minute blended into the next. I was getting more and more tired, and I fought the instinct to lie down and close my eyes. Time. Damn it, I still had time.

"Flet," I said again. Desperation weaved into my words. "Come to me!"

For a breathless moment (well, I guess every moment for me was breathless), I waited, and then . . . gold sparkled in front of me.

Flet.

He put tiny fingers to his lips, then sent a poof of gold magic all around us. We were encased in a big, sparkling bubble.

"They cannot hear us," said Flet. "And when I go, you must act as though I did not arrive."

I nodded. What a clever pixie. I'm glad at least one of us was thinking straight.

"Where have you been?" I asked.

"I've been watchin' over Glory," he said, sounding miserable. He heaved a tiny sigh. "I failed to protect her. 'Twas all I could do to hide and follow the men who took her."

"I didn't see you there."

"I'm only visible to those I wish to see me," he said. "I saw you. And I know what they asked of you."

"You didn't leave Glory." Marvelous little Flet had stayed close to my daughter.

"Not until this moment."

"Do you know how to get into ETAC?"

He nodded. "They aren't far, and they are hiding,

too. In a shield like the one you are building for Broken Heart."

It must be really good if not even the lycanthropes could sense it. ETAC had been in and out of town without detection, either. Or had they? Maybe the Consortium knew more about what was going on than what they were telling me.

"I need you to sabotage the Invisi-shield," I said. "You'll need to disable four posts, one in each quadrant; that way it can't be easily fixed."

"This is one of the things we must do to keep Glory safe?"

"Yes." I looked at him. "Can you do it?"

"Of course I can! I'm a pixie, aren't I?"

He sounded so offended I wanted to laugh. When had I become fond of the little bug?

"Is there more to do?" he asked, anxious. "Or will Glory be freed after I disable the Invisi-shield?"

"I still have to trap the attendees at the festival, so that a bomb can take them all out." I swallowed the knot in my throat. "And then I have to kill Brady. They want me to drain him so they can Turn him."

"These humans know how to make the undead?" Flet sounded horrified.

"Yes," I said, thinking of Jacob. ETAC had taken his body into custody. He was dying from the bullet lodged near his heart, bleeding out. Somehow, some way, they had Turned him.

"Will you do these things?" asked Flet. He floated close to my face, his tiny eyes assessing me.

"Yes," I said, my entire being aching with despair. "For Glory, I'll do anything."

Flet placed a tiny hand on my forehead. "Be well, Simone Sweet."

A feeling of peace washed over me, a gift from the pixie—the last being on Earth who I thought would understand my torment.

"When I'm done," said Flet, "I will return to Glory."

"Thank you, Flet."

In the blink of an eye, he disappeared, and with him, his bubble of protection.

I lay down, giving in to the exhaustion washing over me. Vampire sleeping habits were nearly absolute. I would pass out soon, whether I wanted to or not.

"Oh, Flet," I called out, "why didn't you come?" I pounded the pillow as if angry. "He must've run away, the ungrateful snot."

I didn't know whether the General would believe my act. "At least the shields will go down tonight," I said, hoping the General heard me. "It's a good thing I know how to do that remotely."

I hoped he believed me. I hoped Flet did as I asked. Mostly, I hoped that I could still figure out a way to save my daughter *and* my friends.

That was my last thought before I fell into the deep dark of vampire sleep.

I awoke suddenly.

"Simone."

Brady sat on the bed, a tiny silver gun in his hand. It looked like the one ETAC had used to knock me out. I felt really weird. I was wide awake, but I shouldn't be. I knew this, but I didn't know how. I felt like I'd been hooked up to an IV filled with Jolt.

"The drug will only last two hours," said Brady. He showed me the tiny gun. "Experimental. I wasn't sure it would work." He'd turned on the small lamp on my side table. He pointed to a silver cone sitting on its edge. "That will block the transmissions to ETAC. They won't suspect anything because you're supposed to be asleep."

"You knew about ETAC?"

"I suspected."

I wrapped my arms around myself and scooted away from him. "Did you believe I killed those people? Or that I would shoot Elaine and George?"

"No. Never." He sighed. "I couldn't give myself away, Simone. There's too much at stake. And I didn't know how far their technology has advanced." He tapped his head. "They have telepaths."

If that were so, they might've heard our conversation. Brady had been protecting me.

"They have Glory, and if I don't do exactly as the General tells me, he'll kill her. If I step one inch out of line—"

"I know their methods." He grimaced. "How the hell did they find us?"

Chills rippled up my spine. Finding out that Brady believed me and was trying to help me soothed the hurt. But I had trust issues, damn it. How could I believe that he would really help me?

I'd have to take a risk.

"Jacob," I whispered. "He'd been transferred into a new unit. I . . . I thought I'd killed him. But ETAC took him." I looked down at my toes. "They made him a vampire."

"Your husband is alive?"

I nodded, unable to look at Brady.

"Good. Then I can kill him myself."

Startled, I looked up and was shocked to find Brady just inches away. He cupped my chin and gazed deeply into my eyes. "If it's the last thing I do, my beautiful, brave Simone, I will make sure you and Glory are safe. He won't touch you ever again."

I couldn't tell Brady how Jacob tormented me when I was chained, helpless, to a wall. Brady's expression was already filled with determination, and yeah, I saw the hatred there, too. I recognized that emotion easily enough.

Brady kissed me. Every doubt melted away under his tender assault. I felt my whole body kick into a new kind of awareness. Heat flickered in my belly. I moaned and wiggled into Brady's embrace.

He wrapped his arms around me, not asking for anything else, just to be kissed, to be held. At that moment, I realized my world had shifted. The wall I'd so carefully built around my heart crumbled into dust.

I supposed it was the wrong time and place to realize that I'd fallen in love with Braddock Hayes.

Stupid, stupid, stupid.

"I would really love to continue this," said Brady, his tongue flicking against my earlobe. "But the clock's ticking."

I sat on Brady's lap, secure in his embrace, and told him everything I knew, from being taken to ETAC's cloaked facility to Flet's help with disabling the Invisi-shield. According to Brady, the pixie had succeeded in taking out the posts.

"It had been ready to go online tonight," said Brady. "In time for the festival. There's no way to fix those posts, not with all the damage he did."

Good. I nibbled my lower lip. Brady brushed my hair away from my face. "What is it?"

"Something Jacob said about coming to his old

hometown and finding his long-lost family. I don't think he's the one who brought ETAC here, Brady."

I wasn't sure that my suspicions were correct, but I'd learned to trust my instincts. Well, mostly.

"There was a boy in the same room where they're holding Glory," I said. "He reminded me of someone and I hadn't figured out who it was until just now."

Brady nudged me. "Well?"

"Reiner Blutwolf," I admitted. "Do you think that boy might be his son?"

Chapter 28

Brady inhaled a sharp breath. "Shit."

"I'm probably wrong."

"Maybe not." He looked at me. "I told you that ETAC sometimes took in paranormals. Many of those were children. The first one I ever took in was a lycanthrope infant. A boy."

"You think it's the same child?" I shook my head. "I don't know, Brady. I guess the age would be about right, but still . . . it seems like a long shot."

However, if ETAC had Reiner's son, it would explain why I felt like the lycan was such a fake, but why his sorrow had seemed real. Maybe he felt guilty about betraying his people, about setting them up to die just so his son could live.

"What a clusterfuck!" Brady rubbed a hand over his hair. "What else are you supposed to do?"

I licked my lips. "There are several small tributaries that crisscross under the town. The General wants me to use its waters to trap the festival attendees—right before the bomb goes off."

I rubbed my fingertips across Brady's jaw. As my forefinger slid by the corner of his lip, he sucked the digit inside and flicked it with his tongue.

I quivered and heat flooded me. One simple gesture and I wanted to leap on Brady and just . . . lick him.

I'd once thought I'd experienced love with Jacob. I'd believed that I understood the beauty and pleasure of making love—at least in the early days of our marriage.

I'd been so, so wrong.

Brady was love. Brady was lust. Brady was . . . everything.

"I have to do something else," I said, reluctant to admit it. "One more task."

His eyes had gone dark, and I knew he was thinking about kissing me. Maybe never stopping. And I wanted that. If my daughter and friends weren't in imminent danger, well, I'd gladly give up a hundred years to be with Brady.

"What?" he asked.

I pulled away and looked him in the eyes. "I have to kill you."

Tension stretched. I was afraid to keep eye contact, so I looked at the flowers on the bedcover. Brady gently cupped my chin and tilted my face up.

"That would certainly put a glitch in our wedding plans."

"Wedding plans?" I squeaked.

He smiled. "Too soon?"

"We haven't even had our second date," I pointed out.

"I told you, I know what I want. You." He kissed me

lightly. "I'll give you as many dates as you need, Simone."

Yeah. About that love thing. Wow. It had really blindsided me. So had Brady. I was giddy and freaked out and not ready for any of this.

I tucked it all away. We had much more to worry about.

Almost an hour was gone, and if Brady was right about the effectiveness of the drug, only one remained before vampire sleep claimed me.

"We can't do this on our own," I said. "We need help."

"We have to be careful," said Brady. "If ETAC suspects we're mounting a counterattack, they'll forego the subtle approach. It'll be a bloodbath."

Queen Patsy was the opposite of subtle. So was the town's lycan security. Brady was right; we had to handle the situation on our own.

"We need Dr. Merrick," I said.

Brady looked at me in amazement.

I nodded. "Trust me. She's perfect."

Brady flipped open his phone and dialed. I could only assume the silver cone blanked cell phone calls, too. He spoke briefly to the doctor, and within moments she appeared in my bedroom. No sparkles like when the vampires and *sidhe* disappeared and appeared. She just blinked into existence.

"Hello, Simone. Brady." She smiled. "I understand that you need a little help from Fate."

For the next hour we made our plans. If we could pull it all off (and if four million things didn't go wrong) then we'd rescue the kids, destroy ETAC, and prevent disaster from befalling Broken Heart.

It was a tall order for three people.

I didn't have much choice. I was already sinking back into sleep. Dr. Merrick winked out, using her beam-me-up-Scotty powers.

Brady kissed me good night.

And I fell into the dreamless dark.

I woke up Friday night after eight p.m., no doubt because I'd spent those extra hours awake with Brady. My tummy got the butterflies just thinking about him, and then the butterflies turned into rocks. I would have to do something terrible tonight.

Could I kill Brady and drain him?

You must use your water powers to trap the festival attendees. After the bomb destroys the abominations, you will take Brady into the woods north of your house and drain him, directed the General. *Leave his body there.*

I took a shower and got dressed. Because I could, I went downstairs and brewed up a pot of coffee and poured in some chocolate creamer. Nectar of the gods. I drank two cups, ignoring the lycanthrope that stood in the kitchen doorway.

Finally, I took mercy on him. "Just have a cup already, Darrius. What am I? The java police?"

"It's your home," he said. "I didn't want to presume."

I was under house arrest. He'd been tromping all over the place in big biker boots, not to mention taking over the couch and TV in the living room (presume, my ass).

I went back upstairs and once again locked myself in the bedroom. I turned on the cone, and since my phone had been confiscated, I used the one Brady had left me.

"Hi, Reiner," I said. "If you don't want me to tell

Damian about your plan to blow up the queen and half of Broken Heart, you'll get your furry ass over here."

I hung up on him, hid the phone, turned off the cone, and stuck it in my pocket. Then I returned to the kitchen. I was in the process of mixing up a batch of chocolate chip cookies when Reiner arrived. To me, he looked as though someone punched him in the stomach.

He gave Darrius a too-bright smile. "I came to take Simone to see her grandmother," he said.

Darrius gazed longingly at the mixing bowl. I put plastic wrap over it and stuck it in the fridge. He sighed mournfully. "*Ja.* Damian called and told me. One hour, Simone," he said. "Then you must return."

"Are you saying that so that I'll come back and make those cookies?"

He grinned sheepishly. "That is merely a perk." His expression turned serious. "We still search for your Glory. I pray to the Moon Goddess she is well."

"Thank you, Darrius," I said sincerely. I waved good-bye and followed Reiner to his sedan. We got inside and put on our seat belts. I turned on the cone. I loved that I could use the General's technology against him. I just hoped that we could best him.

"You do not understand," said Reiner as he put the car into drive and backed out of the gravel drive. "I do not have a choice."

"They stole your son, just like they stole my daughter."

He glanced at me sharply. Then he nodded.

"How long have you given up paranormals to ETAC?"

He didn't answer right away. Wrestling with his conscience, perhaps?

"Too long," he finally admitted. "Ten years ago, they killed my mate and her cousins. Then they stole my infant son. Like most lycan babies, Adaulfo was not doing well." He tapped his nose. "I am the best tracker, Simone. I did not lie about that. I tracked my son all the way to the ETAC facility in Nevada. The General offered me a deal—if I would help him find paranormals, they would save my son, and I could raise him."

I empathized with Reiner. He thought he'd lost everything until he'd been offered what he couldn't resist. And if others paid the price so that his son could live, then so be it. I knew the feeling well, though I was going to try my damndest not to sacrifice others in the process.

"Why Broken Heart?" I asked. "Why give them this town?"

"To get out," said Reiner. "I have been the General's *bitch*." He paused, his fury so palpable I could feel the air vibrate. "I'd been in touch with Damian and knew he had settled here with his brothers. They are, as you say, old school. Guardians of the undead. An outdated notion, if you ask me.

"When I found out the Moon Goddess festival would be held here, I made a deal with the General. I would give him the biggest gathering of parakind in the United States—and he would let me and Adaulfo go live among our own kind. We would be free."

"I think it would be hard to live among your own kind if you kill them all."

He had the grace to look ashamed. Well, he *should* feel shame, and guilt, and just plain ol' terrible.

"You really think he's going to let you and your son off the hook?"

His hands clenched the steering wheel, and I saw a muscle working in his jaw. I realized that Reiner had probably suspected as much. Did he have a plan to get out, anyway? Or was he relying solely on the General to keep his word?

"Do you know what *Adaulfo* means? 'Noble wolf, noble hero.' I am so proud of my son, but not of myself. I once thought of myself as noble, but no longer." He sighed again. "What can I do, Simone?"

"Disable the bomb," I said. "Help us destroy ETAC and save our children."

For a moment, Reiner looked hopeful. Then he shook his head. "ETAC is like the hydra. You cut off one head, and two grow back. You may get rid of them for a while, but not forever."

In the distance, I saw the squat white building of the hospital. My stomach squeezed as I thought about Gran lying gray and sickly in a bed, fighting for breath, for life.

"Do you think, if something should happen to me, Damian would raise my son?" He sounded far off, lost in his own thoughts. "Damian has lost much, too. He is a good leader, a good friend."

I wasn't sure what to make of Reiner's musings. Tell the truth, this turn in the conversation was making me uncomfortable.

We pulled into a parking space a few feet from the entrance to the hospital. I turned to the stoic lycan, apprehension swirling in my gut.

"You have a noble heart, like my wife. She would not approve of all that I've done. She would be disappointed." He turned to look at me, his blue eyes tinged with regret.

Reiner had already sacrificed so much for his kid. He'd gotten caught up in a bad situation, one that he'd perpetuated, and now it was time to do the right thing. I knew exactly how that felt.

I didn't know what to say to Reiner. He jerked his head toward the entrance doors. "Go see your grandmother. I'll wait for you."

As I crossed the parking lot, I turned off the cone because the General may have been maniacal, but he wasn't stupid. I don't know what he'd think about not hearing me and Reiner interact for the whole drive, but really, what was he going to do? He needed my water skills to make his plan work, and even if he was a liar, he wasn't the type of man to act rashly.

No, he was all about premeditation.

I walked into the hospital. As usual, it felt cold and empty. Dr. Merrick herself was behind the information desk in the lobby. She looked up from a clipboard and smiled.

"Elaine is on the third floor. Room three-oh-three."

"Is she okay?"

"Go see for yourself." She paused. Then she mouthed, *Are you ready?*

I nodded. Physically, yes. Psychologically, no. I wasn't looking forward to putting our plan into action, but at least it was better than following through with what the General wanted.

I didn't have much time to enact my part of the plan. I felt guilty that I wouldn't be able to hold Gran's hand the way she'd held mine so many times. I didn't like to think of her being alone tonight, when the world had a serious shot of going all to hell.

I took the elevator to the third floor and found Room 303.

I knocked lightly. "Gran?"

I didn't hear a response. I knocked one more time, then I slowly opened the door, thinking she was probably resting.

Yeah. Not so much.

George was stretched out next to her in the hospital bed (fully clothed, thank God) and Gran was pressed flush against him, her mouth on his neck. Granted, I had been in the same position with Brady not long ago, but still . . . c'mon. It totally geeked me out to see Grandma Elaine macking on her new boyfriend.

I cleared my throat.

I heard a *slurp-pop* sound, then Gran turned to me. George's eyes opened, and they looked a little dazed (um, ew). Gran wiped her mouth, but it didn't matter.

I could see the blood.

The fangs.

Holy fucking shit.

My grandmother was a vampire.

Chapter 29

"Hello, sweetheart," said Gran.

"Oh, my God." I pointed at them. "Oh. My. God!"

"Calm down, Simone."

This directive came from George. I turned my gaze to him. "You Turned her?"

"Only because I asked him. I was dying. I wasn't scared, child. I just wasn't ready to go."

I didn't really have the right to consider the natural order of life for her when it didn't apply to me. The only difference was that I hadn't been given a choice to Turn. The Consortium made that decision for all of us.

Then I realized she was looking right at me. As if she could see me. "Gran! You got your sight back?"

She nodded, her eyes crinkling as she smiled. Her fangs had receded, thank goodness. While her pale skin seemed smoother and her gray hair shone like silver, she still looked like a human grandma.

"I'm fit as a fiddle, honey," said Gran. "Now, how about you tell me what's wrong with you?"

This was the woman who not only accepted my confession about killing her grandson, but also offered me shelter and support.

And I couldn't tell her what was going on.

"I'm fine," I said. "I'm just so glad you're alive. That you're okay."

"What about those awful men?" asked Gran.

"Brady rescued me," I lied. "I couldn't get here any sooner because the Consortium is being really picky about my safety."

"Good." Gran sighed. "They told me they hadn't found Glory." George took Gran's hand and squeezed. "But I think she's gonna be okay, our girl. I really do."

"Me, too." I wanted to hug her, but George was clinging to her like Jessica grasping the mall's last box of Godiva truffles. I crossed the room and kissed Gran on the forehead. "I'm glad you're still around, Grandma Elaine. Life wouldn't be the same without you."

"Thank you, baby. Don't worry. I'll be home soon."

I leaned down to kiss her one more time. Over the top of her head, I saw George peering at me. If I didn't know better, I'd think that was suspicion lurking in his gaze. I didn't know him well enough to assume anything about the man. Who's to say I shouldn't be the one suspicious of *him*?

I went to the door, waved good-bye, and left Gran's hospital room. I untucked my cell phone and glanced at the display. It was already past ten o'clock. Time was slipping away from me.

I hurried down the hallway and felt a touch on my

shoulder. I whirled around. Dr. Merrick put her finger to her lips and gestured for me to follow her.

We went behind the empty nurse's station and through a door, which Dr. Merrick closed behind us. Brady waited in the small office. I saw a silver cone on the desk, its blue light glowing.

Brady met me halfway. He gathered me into his arms and kissed me. Wow. Had I once thought he wasn't emotive? He had no problem showing affection or letting others know how he felt about me.

"Everything is in place," said Dr. Merrick. "I've spoken to Patrick and Damian and convinced them you might be suffering from post-traumatic stress disorder. I see no reason they won't call me first after . . ." Her gaze moved to Brady.

Yeah. That was the one glitch in the plan.

"We don't have another option," said Brady. "You'll have to Turn me."

"It's not an easy process," I said. "I've never done it. I don't think any Turn-blood in Broken Heart has." I placed my palm against his cheek. "If I do one wrong thing during the Turning, you'll die."

"It's true, Brady," said Dr. Merrick. "There's a reason only one in ten humans transition to vampire. The process itself is a delicate one. It's why only Masters do it, and even then they don't always succeed."

"If she drains me," said Brady, "I'll be dying, anyway."

Dr. Merrick shook her head. Her eyes gleamed with an emotion I couldn't decipher. "There is another way." She lifted a gold necklace from her collarbone. The chain had been tucked under her shirt. The piece she clutched between her fingers was a gold circle. In the harsh glow of the overhead lights, I could see writing on the circle.

She kissed the circle and whispered, "Ruadan."

Ruadan? As in Ruadan—the first vampire *ever*? He was the father of Patrick and Lorcan, former leader of the seven Ancients, and one of the most powerful beings on Earth.

He sparkled into the office within seconds. His sons had obviously gotten their good looks from him. His hair was as dark as a raven's wing, his eyes as silver as new dimes. He was tall, well-built, sexy. And even in jeans, a T-shirt, and Converse sneakers, he was damned intimidating.

"Fate," he said, inclining his head. His expression was blank, but I sensed an undercurrent of tension. Maybe it was in the way he held himself, almost as if he expected an attack.

"Vampire," responded Dr. Merrick, her voice holding a trace of humor.

Ruadan listened as Dr. Merrick started the explanations. He remained stoic, his face expressionless. Only his mercurial eyes hinted at emotion.

When she finished telling Ruadan all that had transpired and outlining our plan, she asked, "Will you Turn Brady?"

"For you," said Ruadan, "I would do anything."

His words wore the mantle of tenderness, which slipped just a little to reveal the bitterness underneath. Why would Ruadan agree to help Dr. Merrick if he resented doing so?

I glanced at Dr. Merrick. For the briefest of moments, I saw the longing in her gaze, and I knew that there was something more between her and Ruadan. I had the oddest impression that she wanted to touch the vampire, but her hands stayed at her sides.

Ruadan agreed to be in the woods at the correct time. The idea was to Turn Brady before ETAC could get hold of him and use their technology to do the same.

Killing Brady was the key to returning to ETAC's hidey-hole. I would meet my contact at the designated time and hopefully get to the facility to rescue the kids before the General figured out he'd been had. To that end, Brady had given me some techno-whatsits that included a personal Invisi-shield, a handheld laser gun (think *Star Trek*), and the little silver gun that dispensed drugs.

"I have to go." I kissed Brady, thinking about the circumstances of our next meeting. My stomach squeezed.

"It's okay," he murmured. "Trust me."

You know what? I did.

Reiner took me home. The drive was quiet, probably because each of us had our own worries to chew on.

I was afraid to use the cone again. I didn't want the General to catch on. I could only hope that when the time came, Reiner would help us.

Reiner and I said our good-byes.

Instead of returning to the house, I took a walk by the creek. Darrius stood on the porch, watching me, his arms crossed as he leaned casually against the post. I had no doubts he could be off those steps and changing into a wolf in no time flat. Say what you will about the furred ones, but they had some seriously badass skills.

I sat at the end of the pier and looked down into the water. I'd never tapped my full powers. Like I said, as the Turn-blood of an Ancient, I had more mojo than most. I'd just never needed it before—and now I had to use it to frighten and trap innocent people.

I turned and made my way back to the house.

"Ready to make those cookies?" asked Darrius.

I laughed. "Yeah. Sure."

I managed to bake a dozen cookies for Darrius. Then I claimed I had some sewing to do. Yes, I sewed. My mother taught me how to use a machine (as well as plain ol' needle and thread), and everything.

Once again, I activated the signal disrupter. Then I called Dr. Merrick. "I need you to ask Ruadan to do one more thing for me."

She listened to my request and promised to contact Ruadan. I really wanted to ask what had happened between her and the vampire, but this was neither the time nor the place.

I locked myself in the bedroom, inventoried my equipment for tonight, added one more item, and then went to the mirror.

I looked really stressed. Well, duh. I sat on the edge of the bed and spent a few precious minutes calming myself. It made me feel a little bit better. Maybe I should take one of those yoga classes that Libby had been teaching at the compound. I sure could use some inner peace.

Not having a heartbeat was really weird. As I returned downstairs, mine should've been trying to beat out of my chest. But no, I didn't have the physical responses designed to give me away to overly sensitive lycans.

Darrius was on the couch, stuffing another cookie into his maw with one hand while the other used the remote control to flip channels.

It was easy to stick the little silver gun against his neck. He passed out almost instantly. Whoa. Brady had some powerful toys in his possession. No wonder he was so ape shit about protecting them all.

The digital display on my cell phone read eleven forty-three p.m.

Queen Patricia sat in the middle of a dais with her husband, Gabriel, and waited for the blessing of the Moon Goddess.

The festival had been in full swing all day and all evening. Almost two thousand paranormal beings had come to Broken Heart, most of those Roma and lycan-thropes. They were gathered here, on the old location of the town's high school, waiting to accept Patsy as the new sovereign leader of vampires and lycan-thropes.

Damian and Drake stood sentinel behind Patsy and Gabriel. On the left end of the stage stood two women dressed in long silver robes. Between them was Reiner, holding the statue. I realized now why he wanted me to work on it. This whole time ETAC had been setting up things so that I looked culpable. Even if I refused to cooperate with the General, I'd get blamed for a myriad of other offenses.

My stomach squeezed. It was a few minutes before midnight, nearly time for the priestesses to come onto the dais and offer the blessings of their goddess.

Underneath the town crisscrossed the sewer system. All I had to do was call the water forth and trap all the happy attendees. Then Reiner would do his part.

I hoped, for the sake of us all, he would do the right thing. I moved through the festivalgoers until I was at the back part of the field. Nearly everyone crowded toward the dais, wanting a look at the drama unfolding on stage.

The priestesses moved onto the stage and Reiner followed with his gift. It seemed as though the statue was part of the ceremony, and not just a little trinket for the queen.

Using my power the way Velthur taught me, I put my arms down and aimed my flat palms at the earth. I felt the water, even though it was deep, deep under the ground. I connected with it, drew its power to me, and pulled it . . . up . . . hard . . . fast.

The earth shook beneath our feet.

It was difficult to focus the water. I hadn't done anything of this magnitude, and if I wasn't the Turn-blood of Velthur, I probably couldn't have done it.

Dirt detonated. Walls of brown water shot up around the perimeter of the throng.

Screams erupted as everyone pushed toward the dais.

No safety existed there, especially with Reiner and the bomb.

I stayed outside the ring of violent blasts of water. Even with my vamp vision, I couldn't see much through the liquid explosions. But I heard the continued screams, and sensed the confusion, panic.

I hated that I was part of this travesty. I hated that I had to rely on Reiner to keep his word. Would people die?

Had I done the wrong thing?

Of course I had. Terror reigned. For a split second, I considered letting the water fall away and taking my chances.

Glory.

What wouldn't a mother do for a child?

My eyes ached with tears I couldn't shed. My chest was tight with anguish, regret.

Please, Reiner. Do the right thing.

Then the bomb detonated.

Thunder. Fire. Smoke.

I clenched my fists and broke the connection. The fountains dropped away; water sloshed over the ground.

People ran. Lots of people. Relief cascaded. The General would be pissed, but I didn't care. I did my part. On the dais, I saw Gabriel and Damian helping the queen off the stage. I didn't see Reiner or the priestesses.

I wouldn't know the extent of the damage until much later, but I couldn't hang around to help.

Didn't I mention that four million things could go wrong? I didn't want to think too hard about what would happen if I failed.

Now it was time to do something much worse.

I had to kill Brady.

I crept into the woods.

"Simone," whispered a man's voice.

I turned right, toward the words, and froze. The shadowy figure that separated himself was the last person I wanted to see in this world or the next.

Jacob.

Chapter 30

"What the hell are you doing here?" I hissed.

"Making sure you do what you're supposed to." Jacob sounded bored, like he was stuck babysitting his sister on a Saturday night instead of going out with his friends. Aw, poor Jacob. He couldn't pillage and kill with his ETAC pals.

He made me sick.

"I've done everything the General asked," I said. "I don't need you to remind me what else I have to do."

"Oh, don't worry," he said. "I know that you'll do exactly what you're told. You're very good at that."

I gritted my teeth and swallowed my retort. He was wasting my time. Was he doing it on purpose? Trying to make me fail? Was he really the General's insurance? Or was he the cleanup crew? Fear stroked my spine with chilly fingers.

"If you or the General harm Glory, I will kill you both."

"She's my daughter, too," he said.

"You're a sperm donor. That's all."

His eyes flashed, but I couldn't believe he was really angry about my comment. He didn't give a shit about his daughter. Never had. His whole method of operation was fear, intimidation, and control. He didn't have that power anymore.

"I'll be watching," he said.

No, he wouldn't. I couldn't bear the threat of Jacob reentering my life. After I thought I'd killed him in Las Vegas, underneath all that guilt and self-immolation was relief. He could never hurt me or Glory again. We were free.

And then the bastard had the audacity not to die.

I turned on the cone in my pants pocket, hoping the General would remain clueless. Was I using it too often? No way to tell, and now the stakes were too high not to risk.

The object I'd stored with my other tools was in the front pocket of my overalls. I hadn't thought I would have to put this idea into play so quickly, but at least I was prepared. Jacob looked disinterested when I pulled out the silver letter opener.

I used my vampire speed to zip to him and shove it into his heart. He looked down, surprised. "What the hell are you doing?"

"Ruadan!" I cried. "Ruadan!"

Jacob grabbed the opener and fell to his knees.

Staking doesn't kill vampires, but the heart is still a vulnerable spot. Damaging it slows us down. Way down.

Ruadan sparkled into sight on my left. He looked at Jacob.

"I ban thee, Jacob Mack McCree," he said. His voice held the judgment of gods. "I ban thee from our world.

We will never hear you. We will never see you. We will never know thy presence on this Earth so long as your heart bears any ill will."

"Fuck you, vampire!" sneered Jacob. "I'm not like you. Your magic bullshit won't work on me."

His exclamation made fear dance through me, but Ruadan remained undeterred.

"Walk in the place between worlds, Jacob. This is your punishment for cruelty and for murdering innocents. So do I will it, and so mote it be."

Jacob snarled, trying to climb back to his feet. I don't know who was more shocked when he started to fade—me or him.

Within seconds, he was gone.

Ruadan turned to me, then one black eyebrow winged upward. "Well, love? You've more work to do."

I nodded. "Thank you."

I put on the vamp speed and kept going until I reached the clearing where Brady waited. Had Jacob been my ETAC contact? If I believed that the General had a sense of humor or even irony, then I'd think he'd get a kick out of sending my asshole husband to guard me. But somehow, I think Jacob was a wild card—following his own urges instead of orders.

So long as the General had my daughter, I had to follow through—or at least appear to follow through. I remembered that I'd used the cone to cover up what we'd done to Jacob. So I turned it off again.

Brady was already in the clearing.

"You said you wanted to meet me?" he asked, following the script we'd set up last night.

"Yeah. I know where Glory is."

"Where?"

"Don't worry," I said. "You'll find out soon enough."

I pushed him onto the ground and sat on his chest. I hadn't fed yet, in preparation for feasting on Brady. I was a vampire now, and certainly had the hunger. I felt it building inside me, a beast I had controlled. A beast that sensed it could finally take all that it wanted from its prey.

I pinned Brady's shoulders, put my fangs against his neck, and drank.

I knelt before my sacrifice, penitent and yet darkly thrilled by what I'd just done. My gaze drifted up past the pine trees. The moon was out. It shone down through the feathery branches like the bright eye of the goddess, the one the lycanthropes worshipped. She had surely witnessed my act and was passing judgment on me. Could a deity that wasn't mine punish me?

The black wolf skidded into the clearing. Damian, the leader of the guardians. He sniffed Brady, his big furred face swinging toward me. He barked at me, his jade eyes glittering in accusation.

It hadn't taken them long to find Darrius. To track me.

Then he lifted his snout into the air and howled. Patrick and Ruadan sailed into view and landed between me and Brady. Patrick crouched near Brady, but there was nothing he could do. I'd made sure of it.

I returned my gaze to the sky. A circle formed around the moon, its red glow staining the white orb just like the blood I'd just spilled. It was almost time. I just had to wait a little while longer.

"Why, Simone?" Patrick asked quietly. "Why did you kill him?"

*   *   *

I was hollow inside, but at the same time, the power within was an uncurling viper, readying to strike. Brady's blood throbbed inside me, giving me more strength than I'd ever had before.

It was his gift. His sacrifice.

"We'll take her to the hospital," said Ruadan. "Dr. Merrick wants to see her."

Patrick and I arrived in the secured hospital room. Scrambling my atoms across time and space was the opposite of fun. He let me go as soon as we appeared, and I stumbled backward, still trying to assimilate our arrival.

Dr. Merrick took charge of me, guiding me to the examination table. The wax paper crackled as I climbed up to sit.

"You didn't have to do it." Patrick's voice held such sorrow. After everything, he still felt pity for me. He nodded to Dr. Merrick and sparkled out of sight.

Dr. Merrick studied me, then went to the cabinet that occupied the left corner of the small room. She pulled open a drawer. She took out a rubber tourniquet and a syringe with a long, wicked needle.

"Are you sure you want to do this, Simone?"

I nodded. I was, if anything, resolved. "It's too late to go back now."

"That's always the problem with choices," she said softly as she inserted the needle. "There's no going back if you've made the wrong one."

I flipped on the cone in my pocket. No need for the General to hear the rest of my conversation.

"You really think my blood can help cure the Taint?" I asked as she filled up the tube.

"The nanobytes replicate quickly. If we can figure out a way to combine the nanobytes with the royal lycan blood, we might be able to create a viable cure. One that doesn't mean a full transfusion."

"At least some good will come out of this mess."

Dr. Merrick filled up three tubes, which seemed to take forever.

"Do you think Ruadan Turned Brady?"

"Yes." Dr. Merrick removed her latex gloves and put them into a red bin. "He'll take Brady to a safe place and Turn him."

"Okay," I said. But I wouldn't believe it until I had seen Brady undead and well with my own eyes.

"Are you ready?" asked Dr. Merrick.

I nodded. I flipped off the cone, and we picked up the earlier conversation. I unloaded all the contraband Brady had given me, and put it next to me on the examination table. "It's not a wrong choice, Dr. Merrick! You have to let me go."

"So you can hurt more people? No." Then she flew backward as if someone had punched her. She hit the wall and slid down it.

I stared at her in amazement.

Her gaze met mine, widening a little, and I realized I was supposed to be making a break for it.

I left the room and stood in the hallway. I pulled out the electronic device given to me by the General. It was the same shape as the signal disrupter, but smaller.

When all three tasks are complete, use this to return to base. You'll be reunited with your daughter and given your freedom.

I pressed the button.

It felt like my whole body was set on fire. For a terrifying moment, I thought the General had detonated me. Then I found myself in the same interrogation room I'd been taken to before.

The device in my hand glowed and pulsed and got so hot, I tossed it onto the table.

It exploded.

I scrambled back as a puff of smoke wafted toward me. Damn. I walked to the door and tried to open it. Locked tight. No surprise there, not really. I looked over my shoulder at the chains on the wall. My stomach flip-flopped.

I was trapped.

Okay, Simone. Relax. Think.

The General had eyes and ears in this place, I was sure. However, I had to take one final risk.

"Flet," I called. "Come to me."

The pixie arrived in the blink of an eye. "We must rescue Glory," he said, his voice vibrating with impatience. "I do not like that awful place!"

"Go get Dr. Merrick. Show her where Glory is."

"Who's Dr. Merrick?"

Oh. Right. He'd never met her. "She's at the Broken Heart hospital. She's a Fate."

"If she's a Fate, then I can find her," he said. "What about you?"

"Save Glory, Flet. Please."

"As you wish."

The door opened, and the General strode into the room. "It won't matter who your pixie friend brings back," he said in that awful monotone. "No one can save you."

Chapter 31

"I did what you wanted," I said, turning to face him. "I want my daughter!"

The General's gaze pinned mine. "It seems Braddock Hayes has disappeared."

Woo-hoo! I looked down at the floor, lest I give away my joy. "So what? You didn't say I had to babysit him."

"You really think you can fool me?" asked the General. He gave a humorless laugh. "The bomb didn't kill anyone but Reiner. And that waterworks show you put on? Weak." He shrugged. "I admit, I expected better from you, Simone. Don't worry. I always have contingency plans. ETAC teams are already sweeping Broken Heart and wiping out the paranormal threat."

God, I hoped not. I didn't exactly trust the source of the information, either. If the General was telling the truth, then all our planning and sneaking around wasn't worth a damn.

"I'm terminating our agreement," said the General. He didn't look smug, just resolved. He was the most single-minded man I'd ever met. "And your lives."

If my life was forfeited, then it totally sucked, but okay. Whatever.

But the bastard couldn't have Glory.

"You're a mother," he said, almost conversationally. "So you understand that actions have consequences. Because you chose treachery over your daughter's life, you'll have to watch her die first."

We stood in the room where Glory and Adaulfo slept artificially. I hurried to the bed where my daughter rested peacefully. I looked at the machines pumping drugs into her and I wanted to weep.

The General stood about a foot away, letting me soak in the situation. I knew he wanted me to suffer and fret and mire myself in guilt. Then he would kill my kid. And me. Then probably go have a bowl of Wheaties.

Where the hell were Dr. Merrick and Flet?

Then . . . *blink, blink* . . . they appeared. In the middle of the room. Flet zipped to Glory, hovering anxiously above her. Dr. Merrick looked around calmly, like no one was in actual jeopardy of losing their lives.

"How do we get them out of here?" I asked frantically.

"You don't," said the General. If he seemed surprised by the sudden appearance of a Fate and a pixie, he hid it very well.

"You have no power here, mortal," said Dr. Merrick. The Fate pointed one hand at each of the children. They disappeared. Just . . . *gone*. The General actually had a moment of surprise before he pressed a tiny button on his collar and called in additional men.

Four black-garbed soldiers rushed into the rooms with guns pointed at us.

Dr. Merrick reached for my hand. Her fingertips grazed mine as several beams of blue light issued from the guns. It was as if someone had flipped off the light.

There was no sparkling, no dizziness, no weirdness. The Fate had some serious juju in the power department.

Blink. Dark.

Blink. Light.

Good thing we ended back at the hospital. I don't know who held me or where I was being taken. My shoulder, chest, and stomach burned like hell, like someone was dripping acid in ever-widening circles.

"Simone." Brady's voice. But how? He was being Turned. "Why aren't the wounds healing?"

"I don't know," said Dr. Merrick. "Those weapons are obviously designed to work against paranormal beings, even vampires. I had the same problem with George and Elaine when they were shot."

"Well, do for her what you did for them!"

Vampires weren't big on temperatures. Once your body shuts down, hot and cold don't mean much. All the same, I was feeling as though my insides were icing over. My teeth started to chatter.

"She has too many wounds," said Dr. Merrick. "A blood transfusion saved George, and Elaine was Turned."

I could barely make out the two faces above mine. Dr. Merrick. And yes, Brady. He was okay. Relief flooded through me.

I was lying on something soft. A hospital bed. Damn, the room was so cold.

"Glory," I whispered.

"She's all right," soothed Dr. Merrick. "She's with Elaine."

"Brady."

"I'm here, sweetheart," he said.

"I think I love you," I said. "Even though we haven't had our second date."

"Oh, baby." He kissed me. "I love you, too."

My vision was graying on the edges. The voices continued talking, but were fading in and out. So was I.

I knew that something was very, very wrong.

"Save her!"

"I'm sorry, Brady." Dr. Merrick's voice got softer, fuzzier. "I don't know how."

I woke up and realized two things. First, I was not in my bed. And second, I was not alone.

I turned to face my companion and found myself gazing into the blue eyes of Brady.

"Hey," he said.

"Hey." I licked my dry lips. "What happened?"

"My debt is paid," piped a voice above me. I looked up and saw the gold sparkle that was Flet. "I saved your life as you saved mine."

"Thank you," I said sincerely. "But you know if you wanted to hang around . . ."

Flet nodded. "I'll keep Glory company. She's doin' just fine."

He popped out of sight before I could respond.

"Glory is okay?"

Brady nodded. "And Adaulfo. And the queen. The

whole bomb incident started her labor. She had her triplets last night: two boys and a girl."

"Wow," I said. "Are they . . . human?"

He laughed. "They're *loup de sang*. But lycans are typically born in human form."

"And ETAC? Did we kick their butts?"

"From what I understand, yes, we did. Although a few got away, including the General."

Well, that news sucked. A lot. But we'd get the Invisi-shield working again, and even if ETAC or the General tried to come back, they wouldn't be able to breach the borders.

"Zerina gave me an idea," I said. "I think we should combine our technology with magic. Otherwise, ETAC might find a way to breach the Invisi-shield. It's not like they don't have the same kind of devices."

"Good idea." He kissed me.

I really loved it when he did that.

"I really want to see my daughter."

"She's resting in a room down the hall." Brady stroked my hair away from my face. "Your grandmother's with her."

That reassurance made me feel better. But still I wanted to hug her and kiss her and make sure she was all right.

"How did Ruadan Turn you so quickly?"

Brady shook his head. "He's Ruadan. And the nanobytes probably had something to do with it."

"I'm just glad you're okay." I kissed him. "Everyone else is safe?"

He grimaced. "All but Reiner."

Of course, I had already known that. What I would never know is if Reiner meant to sacrifice himself or if he'd just made a mistake. I think I'd rather believe he did it to make up for all the bad he'd done.

Brady helped me sit up, and I was relieved to see that I was wearing a pair of my own pajamas. "C'mon," he said. "Let's go see our girl."

When we arrived in Glory's room, Gran stopped reading the storybook. She put it down, gave us both a hug, and left, promising to return later.

Glory lay in her bed, looking wide awake and happy to see us. Her grin made my mommy heart thud in relief. I hugged until she protested with a loud grunt.

Then Brady hugged her, and she squealed.

"I love you," I said, showering her face with kisses. "I love, love, love you."

She kissed my cheek, then patted it, her eyes showing what her voice could not say. I wondered whether this latest trauma had hurt her emotional healing even more. Would she drift away again into that awful place where no one could reach her?

Then she turned to Brady and tapped his hand. She cocked her head and smiled. "Wanna play Candyland?"

I stared at Glory. Oh, my God. My baby was *talking*. She had the sweetest little girl voice.

Brady couldn't speak for a minute; I saw his Adam's apple bob as he swallowed. Softly he said, "Yes, honey. I'd love to play Candyland."

Gran had brought the game along with some of Glory's books. So we took out the board and played. And Glory talked to us like she'd done so all her life.

I felt such love and hope. Was this a God-given miracle? I didn't know. But maybe whatever good there was in the universe had touched us.

And so I said a little prayer of thanks.

We promised to bring Glory some ice cream from the cafeteria, but on the way we decided to search out Dr. Merrick. I wanted to thank her for all that she'd done for us.

Instead, we found Ruadan. He stood in the hallway a couple doors down from Glory's room. He leaned against the wall with his arms crossed, watching us approach.

"Have you seen Dr. Merrick?" I asked. "I wanted to thank her for all that she did for us."

"She's gone."

"When will she be back?"

Ruadan shook his head. "She's not coming back," he said. "She broke faith with the one who holds her life."

"I don't understand. Who holds her life?"

He smiled bitterly. "My grandmother, Morrigu. An' believe me, she's not the kind of woman you cross—not ever."

I knew a little about Morrigu; it was her dark blood that had Turned Ruadan. She was one of the oldest goddesses in the world. And apparently, one of the scariest.

"Couldn't you save her?"

"Before I was vampire, before I was married and fathered my sons, I met Ion. I was the son of a goddess and she was a Fate, but the heart does not care about such matters. Never have I loved one like I loved her.

"When the gods revoked the lives of the other Fates, Ion was among those saved. Y'see, I went to Morrigu and begged for her life. And my grandmother agreed, so long as Ion gave up her soul—and her love for me."

I was horrified. "But why?"

"She's called the queen of chaos for a reason, you know." He shook his head, as if to clear away his resentments. "Ion dedicated her life to healing others, but it was not her only purpose. The pact she made included the condition that she never use her powers as a Fate to help or hinder humans."

Oh, no. "Is she . . . dead?"

"There is no death for one such as her."

"And we got her in trouble? Because she used her powers to help us?"

Ruadan smiled wearily. "No." He turned and opened the door next to him. He gestured for us to look. Brady and I took a peek.

Marissa Clark lay asleep in the hospital bed. Holy hell. I glanced at Ruadan. "She's alive?"

"Ion used her powers to draw the child's spirit back from the veil. Then she healed her body. Changing the course of a human's life that dramatically is a no-no."

"Is . . . Ion gone for good?" I asked. I was truly sorry that Dr. Merrick would no longer be among us. Fate or not, she had been a good person. She deserved mercy from Morrigu. And I hope she got it.

"Who's to say?" asked Ruadan. "No one can ever know the mind of Morrigu." He looked again at the child. "Darlene's ashes were found in her house. We've made arrangements to deliver Marissa to her human father."

I was sad that Darlene was dead. She was ditzy and often self-centered, but those qualities shouldn't merit the death penalty.

I laid my hand on Ruadan's arm. "I'm sorry."

He seemed to understand my sympathy even as I wondered why I felt like he needed any. Still, he flashed another smile, though there was no joy in it. I had a feeling there was more to the story of Ruadan and Ion than he was willing to share.

I thought about all the sacrifices others had made so that we could live.

Now, more than ever, we needed to adhere to vision of the Consortium and our queen. Once the Invisishield was operational, everyone who lived here would be safe.

I vowed, right then, that Broken Heart would offer sanctuary to all who needed it—just as it had done so for me as human and as vampire.

"C'mon," said Brady. "Glory wants ice cream." He leaned down and nipped my ear. "And I want you."

"You missed the opportunity to make a lewd comment about licking me."

He chuckled. "I'll save that for date number ten."

Chapter 32

Three months later

"Are you sure that ninety-two dates is enough?" asked Brady.

We stood in my bedroom, toe-to-toe. Lit candles lined my dresser and the nightstands, casting a romantic glow against the silver sheen of the walls.

"Honestly, I think one date was plenty. But I had to make you work for it."

Brady laughed; then he looped one finger under my spaghetti strap and lowered it off my shoulder. "You look beautiful in this dress."

"And yet you're trying to take it off."

"You know that look that Jessica gets when she unwraps one of her truffles?" he asked.

"Like she fell into a pool of chocolate with Keanu Reeves and Hugh Jackman swimming toward her?"

He looked at me, his lips quirking. "Have that fantasy often?"

Heh. Who, me?

"Nope. Why would I, when I have you?"

"Nice recovery." He kissed my shoulder, and lust bloomed in my stomach. "Anyway, that's how I feel about getting you out of this dress."

We were alone in the house. Ever since Glory decided to start talking, she never stopped. I had the pleasure of being annoyed by her questions and worn out by her storytelling. I loved every minute of it.

I had asked her about her visits to the creek. She said she went down there to talk to Mary, who lived *in* the water. Doc Michaels seemed to think Mary was an imaginary friend. He seemed to think that Glory would let go of her imaginary friend as she started socializing with real kids. She was in school now, and it was true: Her visits to the creek had lessened over the months.

Damian had taken on the role of raising Adaulfo, a hard task for a boy who still mourned his father. At least Adaulfo had a more normal (well, for this town) childhood. School. Friends. Freedom.

Earlier, in the front yard of the house, we'd had a good old-fashioned wedding. Phoebe Allen, who now had a booming business for the Old Sass Café, thanks to Flet's wish, catered the meal. She'd made our wedding cake with devil's food—a little joke about her own demon powers.

Sometimes I wondered about that girl.

Ruadan presided as our preacher, and he did a fine job. Binding was three steps: the word giving, the claiming, and the woo-woo. Brady and I had done the first two steps.

Now, we were at step three.

Brady unlooped my other strap, and I wiggled out

of it. The dress fell and pooled at my feet. I stepped away from the material.

"Wow," he murmured as he looked over my white lace bra and matching panties. I wasn't a fancy-lingerie kind of girl, but I had to give Victoria's Secret some props. The money spent on my wedding under-clothing was worth it when it put *that* look in a man's eyes.

Brady was still in his tuxedo, though he'd taken off the tie. I unbuttoned the white dress shirt and slid my hand along his muscled chest. Yowzer.

I made short work of his clothing, though I was slightly (okay, *overwhelmingly*) nervous about seeing his you-know-what.

I'd been with one man my whole life. Even though Brady and I had gotten hot and heavy during our courtship, we'd never gone this far. I felt like I was a virgin all over again.

I'll be gentle.

Hey! No fair, mister!

As one of the few men on the planet who can literally read the mind of his wife, you better believe I'm taking advantage of it.

I grinned. Then I cocked an eyebrow and focused on a particularly naughty thought.

His smile was all wicked.

As he slid off those boxer shorts, my undead heart went *boom, boom, BOOM.*

Then . . . whoa. Wow.

Brady was broad and muscled, with curly hair on his chest and legs. His shaft was already hard. Okay. In for a penny, in for a pound.

I stepped close to him and gripped his member, sliding my fingers over the velvety skin. My whole body went on alert, heat pouring through me like a four-alarm fire.

Brady took my hand and led me to the bed. I scooted onto it, and he did, too. He lay next to me, his fingers dancing on my bare skin.

He skimmed the underside of my breasts, and I gasped. He teased my areolas with delicious strokes. Then he leaned down and suckled one nipple.

Sensations rocketed through me.

He paid homage to the other breast. I wiggled against him, my hands reaching again for his manhood. I gripped it and stroked.

Brady liked it. He responded in kind by cupping my breasts and licking, sucking, tormenting.

Lust liquefied me. I released his shaft, then stroked up his rib cage, my fingers running through hair on his chest. Then I found *his* nipples. I lightly twisted.

Brady lifted his head. "You drive me crazy," he murmured, "but in a good way."

I grinned.

Brady cupped my sex and caressed my outer lips. He pierced me with one finger, then two, and curled those fingers upward.

And stroked.

Pleasure spun out a web that crept from my sex to my womb to every nerve ending.

He stroked in and out in a rhythm that made me gulp and gasp and moan. My whole body tightened and I spun away and up and reached for that rapture he promised.

He kissed me, his tongue mimicking those wicked fingers, the crisp curls on his chest rubbing on my nipples, and then . . . oh, then . . . I fell over the edge.

And as I rode that wave of bliss, Brady lifted away

from my body, kneeling between my legs and pushing them up until my feet rested on his chest.

He angled his shaft to my entrance, and slowly, while I still pulsated with that incredible orgasm, he pushed inside.

I gripped the covers as he created a rhythm that pressed that wonderful spot again.

"Touch yourself," he demanded, his voice hoarse. His greedy gaze was on my breasts.

Feeling oh, so naughty, I cupped my breasts and tweaked my nipples. Razor-sharp pleasure zapped me, and Brady's eyes went dark and his rhythm went wild, and he groaned and I groaned and then . . .

He shuddered. Stilled. Then he was groaning. Spilling his seed inside me, his hands clutching my calves.

I went over the edge again, this time with him, my hands clawing at the bedspread as I arched, trying to take him deeper.

A minute later, he collapsed next to me. "What do you say to the person who gave you the best orgasm of your life?"

"Thank you, Keanu?"

Brady barked a laugh, then tapped my nose. "Try again."

I cupped his face and said, "How about I love you forever?"

He smiled. "I love you forever."

Well, then. There's just not much more to say, is there?

ABANDONED TOWN DESTROYED BY GAS LEAK

By Susan Rickerson, *Tulsa Tribune*

One of the oldest cities in Oklahoma, which had been abandoned by the last of its residents more than a year ago, was destroyed by a major gas leak.

Officials are unsure what the ignition source was; however, they confirmed that nearly everything in the small town was demolished.

"There's not even a road," said Fire Investigator Samuel Waters. "The highway is being rerouted to go around the damaged area. We don't recommend that anyone approach the city limits. It's dangerous."

Waters also insisted that the explosion was not related to the arson fires that plagued Tulsa in February of this year. The last fire attributed to the still-at-large arsonist was at the Crowne Plaza Hotel.

The new section of the freeway will be built at least ten miles around the town.

There are no plans to rebuild Broken Heart.

THE SEVEN ANCIENTS

(In order of creation)

Ruadan: (Ireland) He flies and uses fairy magic.

Koschei: (Russia) He is the master of glamour and mind control. He was banned to the world between worlds.

Hua Mu Lan: (China) She is a great warrior who creates and controls fire. She was killed during her attack on Queen Patricia.

Durga: (India) She calls forth, controls, and expels demons. She was banned to the world between worlds.

Velthur: (Italy) He controls all forms of liquid.

Amahté: (Egypt) He talks to spirits, raises the dead, creates zombies, and reinserts souls into dead bodies.

Zela: (Nubia) She manipulates all metallic substances.

THE BROKEN HEART TURN-BLOODS

*Jessica Matthews: Widow (first husband, Richard). Mother to fourteen-year-old Bryan and nine-year-old Jenny. Stay-at-home mom. Vampire of Family Ruadan.

Charlene Mason: Mistress of Richard Matthews. Mother to one-year-old Rich Jr. Receptionist for insurance company. Vampire of Family Ruadan.

Linda Beauchamp: Divorced (first husband, Earl). Mother to eighteen-year-old MaryBeth. Nail technician. Vampire of Family Koschei.

MaryBeth Beauchamp: Single. Waitress at the Old Sass Café. Vampire of Family Ruadan.

*Evangeline Louise LeRoy: Single. Mother to fifteen-year-old Tamara LeRoy. Owns and operates the town library. Vampire of Family Koschei.

Patricia "Patsy" Donovan: Divorced (first husband, Sean). Mother to sixteen-year-old Wilson. Beautician who owns and operates Hair Today, Curl Tomorrow. Vampire of Family Amahté.

Ralph Genessa: Widowed (first wife, Teresa). Father to toddler twins Michael and Stephen. Fry cook at the Old Sass Café. Vampire of Family Hua Mu Lan.

Simone Sweet: Widowed (first husband, Jacob). Mother to six-year-old Glory. Broken Heart's mechanic. Vampire of Family Velthur.

*Phoebe Allen: Single. Mother to two-year-old Daniel. Waitress at the Old Sass Café. Vampire of Family Durga.

*Darlene Clark: Divorced (first husband, Jason). Mother to seven-year-old Marissa. Stay-at-home mother. Operates Internet scrapbooking business. Vampire of Family Durga.

*Elizabeth Bretton née Silverstone: Separated (first husband, Carlton). Mother of seventeen-year-old Venice, who lives with her father in Los Angeles. Socialite. Vampire of Family Zela.

---

*Direct descendents of the first five families to found Broken Heart: the McCrees, the LeRoys, the Silverstones, the Allens, and the Clarks.

BRIEF HISTORY OF THE CONSORTIUM

In 1556, brothers Padriag and Lorcan (now known as Patrick and Lorcan O'Halloran) created the Consortium to facilitate education, communication, and support among parakind. They used their wealth and contacts to aid research in medicine, technology, and the arts.

At the time Padriag and Lorcan created the Consortium, most humans were aware of paranormal creatures, though any discovered living among them were cast out at best, or hunted and killed at worst. Part of the Consortium's mission became to protect nonhumans.

Largely because of their efforts, many otherworldly creatures and humanoids learned to survive by camouflaging their true natures or by hiding in areas without human populations. The Consortium was instrumental in creating myths, legends, and cryptozoology to reinforce their efforts to protect parakind from human discovery.

The Consortium's first meeting commenced in France at Clos Lucé—the home of Leonardo da Vinci (his human death was recorded in 1519). Though da Vinci was instrumental in creating the moral codes, member guidelines, and innovative direction of Padriag and Lorcan's vision, he declined to be named part of the ruling board. (No one knows where da Vinci is now, or even if he still walks the Earth.)

Although Padriag and Lorcan, as founders of the Consortium, are permanent members of its ruling board, a new chair is named every hundred years. Only the thirteen members of the ruling board can offer nominations for a new chair. While the nominated chair is not required to be part of the current board, he or she must be an active, full member of the Consortium with at least one hundred years of service. The ruling board then votes on the new chair. Board members must serve at least one hundred years and can be reelected for a second term. The only permanent members of the board are Lorcan and Padriag. All full members of the Consortium can nominate and vote in a new board.

The Consortium stayed in France until 1788. That year, on-staff psychics began predicting the French Revolution. So the Consortium moved its offices, libraries, and council members to Ireland. In 1849, after working four years to halt the An Gorta Mór (the Great Hunger), the Consortium's headquarters were discovered by a group of vampires known as the Wraiths.

After fighting off the attackers, Consortium members moved to New York City, in the United States of America. Later, the Consortium found out that the Wraiths had facilitated the potato famine to increase its access to food (Wraiths often drain humans to death) and to create drones, minions, and Turn-bloods. It is still unknown how many of the Irish really died and how many are, even today, Turned by the Wraiths.

The Consortium still has a headquarters in New York City, but constant discovery and attacks by the Wraiths and other enemies have forced the board and active members to keep subsequent locations secret. To protect its ongoing projects, the Consortium keeps its information, scientists, and key staff split into several locations around the world.

Currently, the Consortium has two major projects:

1. Searching for information (including ancient spells and incantations) and magical artifacts from archaeological sites in the Sudan.

2. Creating the first community for parakind in the small, secluded town of Broken Heart, Oklahoma.

There are a few parakind villages throughout Europe, but most of these towns have not been created or endorsed by the Consortium. It is the Consortium's hope that Broken Heart will one day be the prototype for humankind and parakind to live together in peace and prosperity.

THE CONSORTIUM GUIDELINES

1. The Consortium is a five hundred–year-old, not-for-profit organization created to facilitate relations between humans and nonhumans. It is run by a council of duly elected officers who serve on the board for one-hundred-year terms.
2. The Consortium's primary purpose is the betterment of all Earth's creatures through advances in science, technology, and medicine. Its secondary purpose is to build bridges between parakind and mankind so that one day, all sentient beings can live together in peace and prosperity. Our "bridge-building" is accomplished in many ways, and includes financing archaeological and historical research, creating safety zones for parakind, and donating funds to charitable causes.
3. Paranormal individuals interested in supporting the Consortium's goals and submitting a financial donation of $100,000 or more may apply for full membership. All full members, once accepted, must also take a blood oath to uphold the Consortium's code.
4. Humans may apply for associate membership if they will take an oath to keep the Consortium a secret, to never reveal the true nature of any

paranormal creature among nonenlightened humans, and to protect the identities of the ruling council. Humans are not required to pay an annual fee.

5. The Consortium can revoke the membership of any full or associate member if the member violates the code, betrays other members, discloses the meeting places or identities of the ruling board, or fails to pay annual dues.

6. The Consortium agrees to house, protect, and offer compensation to humans Turned by members of the Consortium, whether or not the Turning was sanctioned.

7. Any Consortium member who murders, tortures, or perpetuates vile crimes on humankind or parakind will be sentenced by the ruling board. Such sentences can include imprisonment, banning, or death.

8. Lycans are the paid guardians of Consortium board members. Every member on the board will be assigned at least one guardian. Consortium members can also contract the services of a guardian or, if necessary, the ruling board can pay for the guardian protection of any of its full or associate members.

9. The Consortium has the right and the responsibility to protect the organization, its members—parakind and mankind—in any and all ways it sees fit. As long as the ruling board and the voting membership agree on its policies and procedures, the Consortium may employ any and all tactics necessary to preserve its mission and its members.

10. Padriag and Lorcan O'Halloran, as the founders

of the Consortium, will have permanent places on the ruling council. However, just like all Consortium members, they are bound by the code and these guidelines.

Note: The current chairman of the Consortium council is Ivan Taganov of the Family Koschei.

GLOSSARY

Ancient: Refers to one of the original seven vampires. The very first vampire was Ruadan, who is the biological father of Patrick and Lorcan. Several centuries ago, Ruadan and his sons took on the last name of O'Halloran, which means "stranger from overseas."

Banning: (see: World Between Worlds) Any vampire can be sent into limbo, but the spell must be cast by an Ancient or, in a few cases, their offspring. A vampire cannot be released from banning until he feels true remorse for his evil acts. This happens rarely, which means banning is not done lightly.

The Binding: When vampires have consummation (with any living person or creature), they're bound together for a hundred years. This was the Ancients' solution to keep vamps from sexual intercourse while blood-taking. No one has ever broken a binding.*

The Consortium: More than five hundred years ago, Patrick and Lorcan O'Halloran created the Consortium to figure out ways that parakind could make the world a better place for all beings. Many sudden leaps in human medicine and technology are because of the Consortium's work.

Convocation: Five neutral, immortal beings given the responsibility of keeping the balance between Light and Dark.

Donors: Mortals who serve as sustenance for vampires. The Consortium screens and hires humans to be food sources. Donors are paid well and given living quarters. Not all vampires follow the guidelines created by the Consortium for feeding. A mortal may have been a donor without ever realizing it.

Drone: Mortals who do the bidding of their vampire Masters. The most famous was Renfield—drone to Dracula. The Consortium's Code of Ethics forbids the use of drones, but plenty of vampires still use them.

ETAC: The Ethics and Technology Assessment Commission is the public face of this covert government agency. In its program, soldier volunteers have undergone surgical procedures to implant nanobyte technology, which enhances strength, intelligence, sensory perception, and healing. Volunteers are trained in use of technological weapons and defense mechanisms so advanced, it's rumored they come from a certain section of Area 51. Their mission is to remove, by any means necessary, targets named as domestic threats.

Family: Every vampire can be traced to one of the seven Ancients. The Ancients are divided into the Seven Sacred Sects, also known as the Families.

Gone to Ground: When vampires secure places where they can lie undisturbed for centuries, they go to ground. Usually they let someone know where they are located, but the resting locations of many vampires are unknown.

Invisi-shield: Using technology stolen from ETAC, the Consortium created a shield that not only makes the town invisible to outsiders, but also creates a force field. No one can get inside the town's borders without knowing specific access points, all of which are guarded by armed security details.

Loup de Sang: Commonly refers to Gabriel Marchand, the only known vampire-werewolf born into the world. He is also known as "the outcast." (see: Vedere Prophecy)

Lycanthropes: Also called lycans. Can shift from a human into a wolf at will. Lycans have been around a long time and originate in Germany. Their numbers are small because they don't have many females, and most children born have a fifty percent chance of living to the age of one.

Master: Most Master vampires are hundreds of years old and have had many successful Turnings. Masters show Turn-bloods how to survive as vampires. A Turn-blood has the protection of the Family (see *Family*) to which their Master belongs.

PRIS: Paranormal Research and Investigation Services. Cofounded by Theodora and Elmore Monroe. Its primary mission is to document supernatural phenomena and conduct cryptozoological studies.

Roma: The Roma are cousins to full-blooded lycanthropes. They can change only on the night of the full moon. Just as full-blooded lycanthropes are raised to protect vampires, the Roma are raised to hunt vampires.

Seven Sacred Sects: The vampire tree has seven branches. Each branch is called a Family, and each Family is directly traced to one of the seven Ancients. A vampire's powers are related to his Family.

Soul shifter: A supernatural being with the ability to absorb the souls of any mortal or immortal. The shifter has the ability to assume any of the forms she's absorbed. Only one is known to exist, the woman known as Ash, who works as a "balance keeper" for the Convocation.

Taint: The Black Plague for vampires, which makes vampires insane as their bodies deteriorate. Consortium scientists have had limited success finding a true cure.

Turn-blood: A human who's been recently Turned into a vampire. If a vampire is less than a century old, she's a Turn-blood.

Turning: Vampires perpetuate the species by Turning humans. Unfortunately, only one in about ten humans actually makes the transition.

The Vedere Prophecy: Astria Vedere predicted that in the twenty-first century a vampire queen would rule both vampires and lycans, and would also end the ruling power of the Seven Ancients.

The prophecy reads: *A vampire queen shall come forth from the place of broken hearts. The seven powers of the Ancients will be hers to command. She shall bind with the outcast, and with this union, she will save the dual-natured. With her consort, she will rule vampires and lycanthropes as one.*

World Between Worlds: The place is between this plane and the next, where there is a void. Some people can slip back and forth between this "veil."

Wraiths: Rogue vampires who banded together to dominate both vampires and humans. Since the defeat of the Ancient Koschei, they are believed to be defunct.

*Johnny D'Angelo and Nefertiti's mating was dissolved by a fairy wish. It is the only known instance of a binding being broken.

Read on for an excerpt from the next
romance from national bestselling author
Michele Bardsley.

In less than an hour dawn would taint the sky.
I stood in the backyard, looking up at the diamond twinkle of stars. Sleep tugged at me, impatient.

I resisted.

I stared at the velvet black night, playing connect the dots with the constellations. I was provoking the sunrise, rebelling against my vampire nature.

The same night I was gifted with demon powers.

October brought with it the first shiver of winter, the threat of snow. The undead didn't really feel the cold, which is why I was barefoot in the chilled grass and wearing an oversized dress shirt that brushed my knees.

His shirt.

I pulled at the collar. I remembered the scent that once clung to the fabric. The woodsy aftershave had mixed with his unique male essence. Eventually I'd given in and washed the shirt; tonight it smelled like the crisp clean of Gain.

Phoebe.

I stiffened. Lately, my mind had been playing tricks on me. I heard Mackenzie's Scottish-tinged voice in my head, in my heart. He used to say my name as if it were a prayer uttered to pagan gods. Some nights I dreamed that he was still alive. Trapped in the dark, he called and called to me, and I wandered through shadowy tunnels trying to find him.

We'd had one night together. The night we made Daniel. Then Mac had died. Stabbed during a mugging. Left to bleed in an alley in the wrong part of town.

He'd gone to meet someone about an ancient knick-knack. Nothing stirred Mackenzie's passions like artifacts. Not big things like gilded treasures from a pharaoh's tomb. Normal stuff intrigued him—staffs and feathers and beads.

I attended the funeral as his student, not his lover. I hadn't been able to look his widow in the eye. She cried real tears, suffered genuine sorrow. I realized then that Mac wasn't mine. He wouldn't have left his wife, though he might've lied to keep me. And lied to keep her, too.

When I found out I was pregnant, I left Oklahoma State University and went home to Tulsa. To hell. It was my penance for what I had done. Mom was really good at guilt, at shame, at throwing acid on wounds.

Shuddering, I pried off the poisoned claws of her memories.

Phoebe.

Mac's voice again. My undead heart skipped a phantom beat. Foreboding scrabbled in my belly; its frigid talons raked my spine.

The sky faded to Tyrian purple. I really needed to

return to the house and crawl into bed. Exhaustion weighted my limbs; my body clamored for rest.

Still . . .

My little house abutted the crescent curve of the woods. I walked down the slight hill of my yard, the dead grass crunching under my feet. I stopped at the tree line and peered into the forest. If I were still capable of breathing, it might've been the only sound to hear.

Phoebe. Go in the house. It's past your bedtime, lass.

"Mac?" I whispered. It was stupid to call for him, but I couldn't stop myself. Sheesh. My imagination was outta control.

The stinging scent of pine mixed with the sweeter redolence of honeysuckle flowers. Honeysuckle bushes bloomed all over the place. Even in winter, when the plants slept, their light scent lingered.

Had I not been a vampire, I might not have had the courage to search for the source of my angst. It helped my bravery to know that the Invisi-shield was up and running. The technology not only made our little town of Broken Heart invisible; it created a force field that no one could penetrate. For the first time since the Consortium and its vampires had arrived, we were safe.

My two-year-old son slept peacefully in the house behind me, his room magically resistant to danger. The local Wiccans had blessed our home and wove their protection spells in Danny's room. Nothing could harm him.

My undead Spidey senses tingled. Out in the dark, I sensed someone. Something.

I took a faltering step back, and then hesitated. I had nothing to fear. Too bad my body didn't get the message. It was all about being afraid, and didn't much care about my mental reassurances.

Seriously. What could hurt me, the vampire mom?

The bloodsucker brigade had strength, glamour, speed, and übersenses. In addition, each of the seven vampire Families had a particular talent. As a child of the Family Durga, I had the ability to summon and control demons. Woo. I also had the powers of demons, but accessing dark desires . . . well, sometimes I got uncomfortably close to delving into unsavory temptations.

The icy wind carried another smell. The barest hint of rotten eggs tickled my nose. I studied the trees closest to me, watching shadows play tag. The stench strengthened and I stumbled backward.

Sulfur.

Demon.

Among the thick branches of the pine trees and the black crevices shielded from the lightening sky, the shadows I thought were tricks of light wiggled into one form.

Damn it! Run, you foolish woman. Run!

Mac's voice again, urgent and chiding.

I spun around, slipping on the cold, slick grass. I went down on one knee. I popped back up and ran as fast as I could. It was too close to sunrise; my vamp speed failed me. Shit! My cell phone and Glock were in the house. So were my knives.

If I hadn't stayed out here to tempt the sun's rays, I wouldn't be so weak. Orange streaked the sky. Any minute, the fiery orb would burst through the last of the indigo night and kill me.

No! My son was in that house, sleeping like an

angel. No way would I die out here and leave Danny alone.

The porch was less than a foot way. Relief skidded through me. The door was within reach—I just had to get inside. Then neither the sun nor the demon could hurt me.

The evil bastard materialized in front of me. Reached out with sharp claws to grab my shoulders. Hauled me so close, I flattened my palms against its clammy flesh.

"Slayer," it hissed. Its breath was so fetid, I gagged. It had marbled blue skin, which made it look as though a hyper kindergartner had painted it from horn to toe. It was seven feet tall, maybe taller, and had the creepiest yellow eyes I'd ever seen.

It was also naked. Demons did not have manners, much less a compulsion to clothe their ugly hides.

Its huge aroused cock pressed against my belly.

I wanted to throw up.

Demons always got hard-ons when they committed acts of evil. Sinning was their aphrodisiac.

Stupid, Phoebe. I should've gone inside. Gone to bed. Listened to my guts. Listened to Mac's dead voice.

Too late for regrets.

I tried to cast a binding spell. My magic drifted onto the demon and melted like snowflakes.

Okay. That was bad.

The black sleep of the undead pulled me into a cloying embrace. I was falling into its dark pit. Right in the demon's arms.

Fire erupted on my backside.

I screamed.

"Burn, slayer," crowed the demon. "I will spit on your ashes."

"Gross," I muttered.

Pain slashed. Jagged, fiery, deadly.

I screamed again.

"Phoebe!" yelled a man's voice. Uncannily like Mac's, down to the Scottish burr. But not in my head. Outside. Behind me.

I tried to keep my eyes open, eyes that couldn't give in to the hot ache of tears. My vision grayed, my body went limp.

Danny. Oh my God. My baby.

"Phoebe," cried the Scotsman again.

The demon who was so hoping for my death disappeared as quickly as it had appeared. I flopped to the ground. The sunrise stretched out lethal fingers of light and heat. Blood burbled in my throat. I started to convulse. Smoke curled upward from my sizzling flesh.

"Foolish woman."

I couldn't see the owner of the voice. Couldn't see anything. He must've picked up my shaking form. Safe in his embrace, I fell into the encroaching darkness, away from the pain, away from the sun.

Then there was nothing.

I'M THE VAMPIRE, THAT'S WHY

by Michele Bardsley

Does drinking blood make me a bad mother?

I'm not just a single mother trying to make ends meet in this crazy world....I'm also a vampire. One minute I was taking out the garbage; the next I awoke sucking on the thigh of superhot vampire Patrick O'Halloran, who'd generously offered his femoral artery to save me.

But though my stretch marks have disappeared and my vision has improved, I can't rest until the thing that did this to me is caught. My kids' future is at stake—figuratively and literally. As is my sex life. Although I wouldn't mind finding myself attached to Patrick's juicy thigh again, I learned that once a vampire does the dirty deed, it hitches her to the object of her affection for at least one hundred years. I just don't know if I'm ready for that kind of commitment...

"A fabulous combination of vampire lore, parental angst, romance, and mystery."
—Jackie Kessler, author of *Hell's Belles*

Available wherever books are sold or at penguin.com

Don't Talk Back to Your Vampire
by **Michele Bardsley**

Sometimes it's hard to take your own advice—
or pulse.

Ever since a master vampire became possessed and bit a
bunch of parents, the town of Broken Heart, OK, has
catered to those of us who don't rise until sunset—even if
that means PTA meetings at midnight.

As for me, Eva LeRoy, town librarian and single
mother to a teenage daughter, I'm pretty much used to
being "vampified." You can't beat the great side effects:
no crow's-feet or cellulite! But books still make my
undead heart beat—and, strangely enough, so does Lorcán
the Loner. My mama always told me everyone deserves a
second chance. Still, it's one thing to deal with the usual
undead hassles: rival vamps, rambunctious kids adjusting
to night school, and my daughter's new boyfriend, who's a
vampire hunter, for heaven's sake. And it's quite another
to fall for the vampire who killed you....

"The paranormal romance of the year."
—MaryJanice Davidson

"Hot, hilarious, one helluva ride."
—L.A. Banks

Available wherever books are sold or at
penguin.com

Because Your Vampire Said So

by Michele Bardsley

When you're immortal, being a mom won't kill you—it will only make you stronger.

Not just anyone can visit Broken Heart, Oklahoma, especially since all the single moms—like me, Patsy Donahue—have been turned into vampires. I'm forever forty, but looking younger than my years, thanks to my new (un)lifestyle.And even though most of my customers have skipped town, I still manage to keep my hair salon up and running because of the lycanthropes prowling around. They know how important good grooming is—especially a certain rogue shape-shifter who is as sexy as he is deadly. Now, if only I could put a leash on my wild teenage son. He's up to his neck in danger. The stress would kill me if I wasn't already dead. But my maternal instincts are still alive and kicking, so no one better mess with my flesh and blood.

"Lively, sexy, out of this world—as well as in it— fun! Michele Bardsley's vampire stories rock!"
—*New York Times* bestselling author Carly Phillips

Available wherever books are sold or at penguin.com

Wait Till Your Vampire Gets Home

by Michele Bardsley

Undead fathers really do know best...

To prove her journalistic chops, Libby Monroe ends up in Broken Heart, Oklahoma, chasing down bizarre rumors of strange goings-on—and finding vampires, lycanthropes, and zombies. She never expects to fall in lust with one of them, but vampire/single dad Ralph Genessa is too irresistible. Only the town is being torn in two by a war between the undead—and Libby may be the only thing that can hold Broken Heart together.

"Has action aplenty and a free-spirited, wittily sarcastic heroine who will delight [Michele Bardsley's] fans."
—*Booklist*

Available wherever books are sold or at
penguin.com